1/21

ALL
THE COLORS
OF NIGHT

ALL
THE COLORS

BERKLEY
New York

OF NIGHT

JAYNE ANN KRENTZ

BERKLEY
An imprint of Penguin Random House LLC
penguinrandomhouse.com

Library of Congress Cataloging-in-Publication Data

Names: Krentz, Jayne Ann, author.
Title: All the colors of night / Jayne Ann Krentz.
Description: First edition. | New York : Berkley, [2021] | Series: Fogg Lake
Identifiers: LCCN 2020017787 (print) | LCCN 2020017788 (ebook) |
ISBN 9781984806819 (hardcover) | ISBN 9781984806833 (ebook)
Subjects: GSAFD: Romantic suspense fiction.
Classification: LCC PS3561.R44 A79 2021 (print) |
LCC PS3561.R44 (ebook) | DDC 813/.54—dc23
LC record available at https://lccn.loc.gov/2020017787
LC ebook record available at https://lccn.loc.gov/2020017788

Printed in the United States of America
1 2 3 4 5 6 7 8 9 10

Jacket image by Miguel Sobreira / Arcangel Images
Jacket design by Rita Frangie
Interior art: Northern Lights © Debbie Center / Shutterstock.com
Book design by Laura K. Corless

For Frank, as always, with love

Work without Hope draws nectar in a sieve,
And Hope without an object cannot live.

—Samuel Taylor Coleridge

Hope and Love

"I don't know who I am," you say,
"Or why my hands deal dust,
As though the lot of cards I hold
Have crumbled as I play."

"As if my sense of self," you claim,
"Has drifted into air,
And nothing that I try to do
Brings credit to my name."

Name and Game are not the way
To find the solid ground;
Hope and Love are better paths
For what ahead may lay.

Attend and listen deep within.
Though hard to hear the voice
Calling out to you alone
In such a world of din,

The voice is patient, and will sing
The notes that help you close the ring.

—Jared Curtis

ALL THE COLORS OF NIGHT

CHAPTER 1

W hy kill me?" Sierra Raines said. "I'm just the go-between."

"I'm sorry, Ms. Raines," Parker Keegan said. He aimed the pistol at her. The weapon shook a little in his hand. Keegan's eyes were wild with lust—not the sexual kind; a different sort of madness, but just as dangerous. "I'm afraid this is the end of our business association."

Another crazy, obsessive, paranoid collector, Sierra thought. *Should have seen this coming.* The problem was that most of her clients qualified as crazy, obsessive, or paranoid—usually some creepy combination of all three. If she avoided all the collectors and dealers in the hot artifacts trade who fit one or more of the three categories, she would be out of business in a day.

Keegan, however, was proving to be more of a problem than the majority of her clients. There was the gun, for one thing. Thankfully, very few of the collectors and dealers she did business with had gone so far as to pull out a pistol, although one or two had produced large knives, and there was the scary dude who had tried to lock her up in the trunk of a car that he intended to push off a pier on Lake Washington. Most collectors were thrilled to conclude a successful transaction and were eager to do more business with her. She was slowly but surely establishing a reputation as reliable and discreet.

It shouldn't have come as a surprise that there were a few drawbacks in her new business. There had been glitches and major disasters in all of her previous attempts to discover her calling. She was starting to think of herself as a serial career killer.

They were standing in Keegan's private gallery. Like the galleries of most collectors who were obsessed with artifacts that had an association with the paranormal, the room was a converted basement. There was no one else in the big house and the nearest neighbors were a mile down the road. If Keegan shot her, no one would hear the crack of the pistol.

"Don't misunderstand, Ms. Raines," Keegan said. "I am very grateful to you for locating the artifact and delivering it so promptly and so discreetly. The problem is that you now know far too much about my collection and my business affairs."

Keegan was not particularly dangerous looking. Thin, short and middle-aged, he had the vibe of a fussy academic. But if there was one thing Sierra had discovered in the past few months, it was that when it came to collectors and dealers, looks were invariably deceiving.

Mirrors, however, never lied, not to someone with her talent. And there happened to be one—a large, elaborately framed nineteenth-century looking glass—hanging on the wall directly behind Keegan. When she jacked up her talent she could see the reflection of his energy field. *Unstable* was the only way to describe it.

Not that she had needed a mirror to arrive at that diagnosis, she thought.

"I'm a Vault agent, Mr. Keegan," she said, keeping her tone polite but firm. "You know as well as I do that Mr. Jones is not going to be happy if one of his go-betweens gets murdered on this job."

"I have considered the problem of Mr. Jones. Don't worry, Ms. Raines, your body will never be found. I intend to tell Jones you failed to deliver the artifact. He will be convinced you stole it and disappeared with it."

"No," Sierra said. "He won't believe it. You do not want to cross Mr. Jones."

"I'm not afraid of Jones," Keegan snapped.

But he sounded as if he were trying to convince himself rather than her.

"There is no reason to kill me," she said gently. "You've got the artifact. Mr. Jones has built a reputation for confidentiality. As long as his clients don't try to cheat him, he keeps their secrets. So do his agents."

"Unfortunately, I have trust issues," Keegan said.

"No kidding. As it happens, I have a few myself." She gave him her flashiest smile and casually stripped off one of her sleek black leather gloves. "That is, of course, why I take precautions at every stage of the delivery."

Keegan frowned. "What's that supposed to mean?"

Sierra raised her ungloved hand to the small locket she wore. She flipped it open to reveal the mirror inside. It was not a standard mirror, but rather a flat circle of highly reflective crystal.

"I won't bore you with a lengthy explanation of how this works," she said. "That would involve some complicated physics. All you really need to know is that you're about to faint."

"Faint? You're crazy. Why would I faint? I'm in excellent health. I'm a vegan."

She focused quickly and channeled a little heat through the mirror crystal, reflecting the currents of Keegan's energy field straight back at him. The rebounding waves sent the equivalent of an electrical shock through his aura, effectively short-circuiting it.

Keegan stiffened. His eyes fluttered and closed. The gun fell from his hand and he sank to the floor without so much as a groan.

There was a sharp crack as the handsome nineteenth-century mirror on the wall fractured into a spiderweb of fissures.

Control was everything, Sierra reminded herself. She was pretty good when it came to channeling energy through the crystal, but when she got nervous, stuff sometimes happened. It was a pity in this case because the old mirror had definitely had a paranormal vibe. In good condition it would have been worth a lot of money on the underground market.

She had bigger problems, however. Her fingers burned. She flicked her hand several times in an instinctive but utterly futile attempt to cool the singed sensation. Hastily she pulled on the leather glove.

"Shit," she muttered. "Shit, shit, *shit*."

She took a few deep breaths and gritted her teeth until the burn began to fade. Using her talent at full throttle always gave her an unpleasant psychic jolt, but lately the experience was more painful than usual because she had not yet recovered from the severe burn she had received on the last job. Her senses tended to overreact to anything with a disturbing psychic vibe. She had never been comfortable coming into physical contact with strangers because she never knew what to expect from their energy fields, but these days the simple act of touch had become an extremely fraught experience.

Her mother had suggested the leather gloves. They had been made for her by a family friend who knew a lot about the physics of the paranormal. Leather was a reasonably good insulator. Not as good as steel or glass, of course, but definitely more fashionable. Walking around with chain-mail gloves or a pair made of glass would have drawn a lot of unwanted attention.

Sierra closed the locket and hurried across the gallery. She crouched beside Keegan, unwilling to take off a glove to touch his throat to check for a pulse. Luckily his chest was rising and falling in a normal fashion. He was alive but unconscious. There was no way to know how long he would remain in that state or what he would remember when he woke up.

It didn't matter. The deal was off as far as she was concerned. She had done her job. The buyer had failed to hold up his end of the bargain. It was bad enough that he had tried to murder her. The bastard hadn't paid his bill. Jones would not be happy about that. Keegan would not be able to purchase the services of a Vault agent in the future.

In addition, she would make sure the news that Keegan was both dangerous and a deadbeat went out on the rumor network that linked the freelance go-betweens who worked the Pacific Northwest market. Keegan would find it difficult if not impossible to hire another reliable transporter. He would be forced to deal with the raiders, who were far more dangerous than he was.

She moved to the display stand and winced when she picked up the vintage desk calendar she had just delivered. She could feel the vibe even through the leather glove. The thing was really hot. Definitely a lost lab artifact. It had absorbed some serious paranormal radiation from the office in which it had been used decades earlier. She detected a whisper of panic, too. Whoever had left the calendar behind had been terrified. It was not an uncommon kind of heat in the lost lab artifacts she transported. She had come to think of the residual emotions as a psychic signature of relics connected with the government's secret Bluestone Project.

She inserted the desk calendar back into the leather bag she had used to transport it and headed for the door.

"I'll see myself out," she said to the unconscious Keegan. "And just to be clear, you and I will not be doing any more business in the future."

She went up the basement steps to the ground floor of the big house and hurried along the darkened hall to the back door. When she had arrived she had deliberately parked behind the mansion to reduce the possibility of her car being noticed by a passerby. She had covered her license plates as an added precaution.

She had also driven a complicated, circuitous route to Keegan's house, making certain she had not been followed. Raider crews sometimes tailed go-betweens like vultures, hoping to swoop in to grab the relic before it could be delivered to a client.

Outside she hurried through the light rain to her black SUV. The vehicle looked like a gazillion other SUVs on the road in the Pacific Northwest, but she was proud of it. The car represented her biggest investment to date in her new career. She would be making payments on it for a long time. It wasn't as if she'd had a choice. A go-between couldn't operate without a sturdy, reliable vehicle. The SUV was specially equipped with a steel lockbox in the cargo compartment. Steel was an effective insulator. It blocked most paranormal energy.

She vaulted up into the driver's seat, dumped her backpack and the leather bag onto the passenger's seat, fired up the engine and drove down the long, narrow driveway to the main road.

When she was well clear of the house, she stopped long enough to toss the pistol into the lake. There was no point leaving the gun around, because it was evidence that might lead to questions about her presence in the house. Worst-case scenario was that Keegan would go to the cops and accuse her of being an intruder, although that was unlikely. Collectors avoided the authorities for the same reason others in the artifacts trade did: no one wanted that kind of attention. But you never knew for sure how an irate collector would react. They were all unpredictable.

Once the gun had vanished into the lake, she uncovered the SUV's license plates and got back on the road.

Satisfied that she did not have a tail, she motored sedately across the 520 Bridge, heading toward the bright lights of downtown Seattle. It was after midnight and there was very little traffic. Seattle was a boomtown these days thanks to the tech industry, but it was still a relatively quiet place in the wee hours of the morning. That worked out well for her because a lot of her business was conducted during those hours.

She drove straight to an alley in Pioneer Square, the old, historic section of the city. The narrow lane between two brick buildings was lit only by a weak yellow bulb over an unmarked door. It was the sort of location sensible people intuitively avoided, especially at night.

She parked directly in front of the unmarked door. A burly figure dressed in a dark jacket and a knit cap detached itself from the shadows of the vestibule and ambled around to the driver's side of the car. He opened the door.

"Valet parking, Ms. Raines?" he asked in a voice that had been dug out of a rock quarry.

"No thanks, Brick. I won't be here long tonight." Sierra grabbed her pack and the leather bag and jumped down to the pavement. "I just need to drop off a return and then I'm going home to get some sleep. It's been a long night."

She handed over her keys and a few bucks.

"No problem," Brick said. "The car can sit right here until you get back." He glanced at the black bag. "A return, huh? Mr. Jones won't be happy."

"Neither am I."

She followed Brick up the three steps to the entrance. The door was clad in wood and covered in peeling paint. Looking at it, you would never know that under the veneer was a solid steel plate. Of course, looking at Brick, you wouldn't know he was wearing a holstered gun under his jacket.

Okay, maybe you would have a hunch about the gun.

"How did the date with Deandra go?" she asked as she watched Brick open the door.

Brick lit up like an LED sign. "It went great. Did the old-fashioned thing like you suggested. Dinner and a show, and afterward we went somewhere and talked about the movie. Deandra knows a lot about films. Got another date lined up this weekend after we get off work here at the Vault."

"That's wonderful. I'm so glad things went well."

"Thanks to you pushing me to ask her out," Brick said. "It took all the nerve I had. When she said yes, I could hardly believe it."

"I had a hunch the two of you would get along together. Good luck."

"Thanks."

Brick ushered her into the shadowed hall. The two men running the security scanner were lounging in a couple of folding chairs. One was middle-aged and bald. The other was much younger and on the twitchy side. They got to their feet and grinned in welcome.

"Good evening, gentlemen," she said.

"Why do I have the feeling the delivery didn't go well?" the bald guard asked.

"You must be psychic, Clyde," Sierra said.

"Do you know how many times a night I have to listen to that joke?" Clyde snorted. Energy shifted in the atmosphere around him. He was a very high-level intuitive talent. It made him an ideal security guard. His brows rose when he saw the leather bag. "Well, well, well. Looks like the buyer is returning the purchase."

"Unsatisfied customer?" Twitch asked with a knowing look.

"More like an unsatisfied go-between," Sierra said. She put the leather bag and her backpack on the scanner belt. Next she stripped off her leather jacket, sat down on a handy stool and pulled off her leather boots.

Most go-betweens wore a lot of leather. It had become the unofficial uniform of the profession, but it wasn't a fashion statement. Go-betweens wore leather for the same reason bikers did—protection. When you worked in a business that involved a lot of paranormal artifacts, you had to be prepared for the occasional supercharged surprise. Brushing up against the most innocent-looking relic could send a staggering shock across the senses. Leather muted the jolt.

She added the jacket and the boots to the other items on the belt and then she walked through the metal detector. "Among other things, the funds were never transferred to my account here at the Vault. I didn't get paid."

"If you didn't get paid, then Mr. Jones doesn't get his commission," Clyde said. "The boss is not going to be happy."

"He is not the only unhappy individual involved in this business tonight," Sierra said.

"Don't worry, Mr. Jones will eighty-six the deadbeat," Twitch said.

"I certainly hope so." Sierra collected the leather bag, her pack, her jacket and her boots from the other end of the scanner. "I will take some satisfaction from knowing Keegan won't be doing any more business through the Vault. One thing Mr. Jones won't tolerate is a customer who doesn't pay his bills. Also, the creep pulled a gun on me."

Clyde whistled softly. "That settles it, then. Mr. Jones really doesn't like it when a client threatens an agent."

"When word gets around that Jones kicked him out of the Vault, Keegan won't be able to get any of the reliable go-between agencies to work with him," Twitch said.

Clyde grunted. "Serves him right."

Doing business in the underground trade of hot artifacts entailed a lot of risks for all parties involved. Obsessive collectors, con artists, fraudulent dealers, ruthless freelancers and raiders were all part of the dangerous ecosystem—to say nothing of the occasional psychic monster. To normal people who did not believe in the paranormal, such creatures were the stuff of legends and nightmares, but when you worked in the underworld, you took them seriously.

All of which explained the success of Ambrose Jones and his thriving delivery business. Go-betweens who worked for the Vault received several important benefits. Jones acted as a broker between buyers and sellers. He secured the hot relics in his own private vault until they were delivered. He arranged for the safe transfer of the very large sums of money involved in the deals. And if things went wrong, as they had tonight, he would punish the offender. In return for those perks, he took a hefty commission.

Worth every penny, Sierra thought.

A door opened midway down the hall. The rock music got a little louder but it was still muffled. Jones walked out of his office. Sierra noticed that the lights inside the office had been turned down low. She smiled. Mr. Jones was entertaining a lady friend this evening. She was pretty sure she knew the identity of the woman.

Jones had opened the Vault a couple of years ago. No one seemed to know much about him. He was somewhere in his early forties. His dark hair was turning silver at the temples but he kept himself in excellent condition. He looked very good in the sleek, tailored trousers, black turtleneck and slouchy black linen jacket that seemed to be his uniform. He had the face and the profile to go with the buff body—strong, and even handsome, if you liked the cold-eyed, gunfighter type.

Sierra found him intriguing, but that was as far as it went. He would probably make an interesting date but her intuition told her there would be no future with him. And since Jones never dated his own agents, even the possibility of an interesting date was out of the question.

Generally speaking, she was about ready to give up on dating altogether. It had become a depressing business. She longed to meet someone with whom a future at least looked possible, just as she wanted a career that centered her and gave her a sense of satisfaction. She was good at authenticating and transporting hot artifacts but it didn't feel like something she wanted to do for the rest of her life.

Jones looked at her. "What went wrong?"

"Keegan tried to kill me," Sierra said.

"Obviously he didn't succeed. Congratulations on that, by the way. I wonder what made him think he could get away with murdering a Vault agent?"

"He's a collector." Sierra shrugged. "They're not known for being an especially stable bunch. He's got just enough talent to think he's the smartest man in the room."

"I will terminate his membership in the club immediately." Jones examined her with a critical eye. "You look like you need a drink. On the house tonight."

"Thanks, I do need a drink, but I'd rather go home and have one there."

"I understand." Jones picked up the black bag. "I'll find another buyer for the artifact."

He went back into his office. Just before the door closed, Sierra heard a sultry, feminine voice. She smiled, recognizing it. Molly Rosser was a high-end artifacts dealer.

"Something go wrong with a delivery?" Molly asked.

"One of my best agents was nearly murdered tonight," Jones said. "As a result I have a few things to take care of. I'm afraid I'm going to have to say good night."

"I understand," Molly said.

Molly was an excellent match for Jones, Sierra thought. She handled his unusual business, his powerful talent and his dangerous edge with cool ease. But then, she was a strong talent herself.

The door to Jones's private quarters closed.

Clyde leaned toward Sierra and spoke in low tones. "Between you and me and Twitch, here, I think our Mr. Jones has got it bad for Ms. Rosser."

"I'm not surprised," Sierra said. She pulled on her boots and jacket. "They're perfect for each other."

"Nice of you to introduce them," Twitch said. He grinned. "The boss has been in a pretty good mood lately."

CHAPTER 2

A short time later Sierra drove into the underground garage of one of the gleaming apartment towers in the South Lake Union neighborhood. She shut down the SUV's big engine and sat quietly for a moment, checking the side mirrors and the extra-wide rearview mirror for indications she might not be alone. There were no auras reflected in the glass.

Satisfied, she collected her pack, got out of the car and headed for the elevator lobby at a brisk pace. The fact that she could not detect any auras in the car mirrors was no guarantee there was no one hiding in the emergency stairwell or around the corner of a concrete wall. The mirror locket worked reasonably well in a one-on-one situation at close quarters, but it had some serious limitations.

She used her key fob to access the elevators, but she did not allow herself to relax until she reached the twelfth floor and was safely inside her small one-bedroom apartment.

Cozy was the term the leasing agent had used to describe the small space. Sierra had stuck with the term because it sounded more upbeat than *cramped*. It would have made more financial sense to go with one of the tiny studios but she knew she would not have been able to handle the claustrophobia. She had grown up on a rural island in the San Juans surrounded by a heavily wooded forest and a rugged landscape. City living had required some major adjustments.

She had worked as a Vault agent for less than four months. She was still struggling to recover from the financial hit that had struck when she had lost the job at Ecclestone's Auction House in Portland. In the meantime she told herself she was okay with the small apartment. It wasn't as if she spent a lot of time in it. Like the other agents who worked for Ambrose Jones, her "office" was a booth in the underground level of the Vault nightclub.

Out of habit, she made her way through the apartment, locket in hand, checking to make sure she truly was alone. Mirrors glittered on every wall. She thought they made the place look bigger. Also, she liked mirrors.

Satisfied there were no zombies hiding under the bed and no psychic monsters in the closets, she changed into pajamas and slippers and padded into the kitchen to pour herself a large, medicinal glass of wine. It had been a very long night—also a very unprofitable night.

She sat down at the dining counter and picked up her phone. She had deliberately left it behind when she set out to deliver the artifact. Vault protocol dictated that agents carry minimal tech when operational. It was a precaution that made it more difficult to be tracked.

She hesitated before turning on the phone. Adrenaline mingled with exhaustion was still charging her senses. She should probably wait until morning to check her messages. But Mr. Jones might have decided to throw another job her way to make up for the Keegan fiasco. If she didn't jump on the opportunity, he would offer the delivery to another agent.

She swallowed some of the wine, took a deep breath and turned on the phone. There were not a lot of messages. That was directly attributable to the fact that she did not have a lot of friends at the moment. Her former colleagues at Ecclestone's had ghosted her in the wake of the scandal that had shaken the exclusive auction house to its foundations.

Someone had to take the fall for the fraudulent art and antiques that had been evaluated and authenticated by the experts in the house. The clients who had been scammed wanted blood. The firm's reputation had been on the line. When rumors surfaced that the con artist was the new associate in the American Antiques Department, the CEO had leaped on the opportunity to throw Sierra under the bus. Julian Mather, the man she had been dating, was the first to disappear. The colleagues she had considered friends had vanished shortly thereafter.

Sierra told herself she understood. No one with a viable career in the world of fine arts and antiques could afford to maintain a relationship with someone who was rumored to deal in frauds and fakes. Reputation was everything. So, sure, she understood. Nevertheless, it hurt.

It didn't help that losing the job had proven her parents right. Again. She was not cut out to live in the normal world, a world where those who claimed to have psychic talents were viewed with deep suspicion or, equally unsettling, a scary fascination. She had done her best to conceal her abilities during her tenure at Ecclestone's, but the need to hide that part of herself was stressful, and it was a huge barrier when it came to establishing personal relationships. One of the quickest ways to lose a date, it turned out, was to tell him you could make him faint by using your psychic powers on him. A lot of people in the so-called normal world were not exactly open-minded when it came to the paranormal.

There was another issue that had made passing for normal difficult. She had been raised in what sociologists called an intentional community. Quest had been founded by an eclectic group of artists, misfits, neohippies, psychics—fake and real—and others seeking an alternate path. The thing about growing up in Quest was that none of her friends and neighbors had a problem with the concept of the paranormal.

That was because a number of residents, including her parents and grandparents, had come from Fogg Lake, the rural town deep in the mountains of Washington State that had the unique distinction of being a community in which psychic phenomena were accepted as normal. There was a reason for that attitude—in Fogg Lake, the paranormal *was* normal.

Decades earlier, in the latter half of the twentieth century, Fogg Lake had been the unwitting subject of a government experiment gone very wrong. An explosion in a secret laboratory concealed in the nearby caves had shrouded the entire area in a strange fog laced with unknown paranormal radiation. The locals had slept for a couple of days, and when they woke up they discovered that things were different—*they* were different. The ability to see auras was suddenly commonplace in Fogg Lake. Many people began to experience visions. Others heard strange voices or perceived colors that had no names.

The range of paranormal talents varied widely, and it wasn't long before it became apparent that the changes had gone all the way down to the DNA level. The result was that Sierra and the other descendants of those who had been living in Fogg Lake at the time of what came to be known as the Incident were also endowed with paranormal abilities.

The first message on the phone was from her grandmother, reminding her that her grandfather's birthday was coming up in three weeks during the Moontide celebration. Sierra dutifully responded that she was looking forward to the event and reminded herself that she had yet to find the right gift. She needed to focus on the problem. It wasn't easy coming up with the ideal birthday present for a man who prided himself on a life of reflection, meditation and the study of philosophy. She would probably end up taking her usual gift—a bottle of good wine.

The second message was from Gwendolyn Swan, the proprietor of Swan Antiques in Pioneer Square. Interested in hiring you to authenticate an artifact rumored to be of unusual provenance . . .

In the underground market, *unusual provenance* was code for an object that was believed to have a paranormal vibe. Swan's shop specialized in such artifacts. When Sierra had first entered the competitive go-between business, Gwendolyn Swan had helped her establish her reputation as a true talent by asking her opinion on a couple of relics. Sierra had identified one as a fraud and the other as an item that had probably come from a Bluestone Project lab. Swan, a strong talent herself, had been pleased. That, in turn, had convinced Ambrose Jones to give Sierra a chance.

Gwendolyn Swan paid well and Sierra appreciated the additional income. The money she made as a go-between for the Vault was good, but Jones couldn't keep her busy all the time. Agents were free to take outside contracts. She could certainly use one to make up for the lost commission tonight.

The last message was from her father. She hit *Call Back*. Byron Raines answered on the first ring.

"What's wrong?" he asked.

She smiled. Her father had the voice of a poet—probably because he was one.

"How did you know?" she asked. "A delivery went bad."

"How bad?"

"The client tried to kill me. I had to use my locket to escape."

"Honey, I know you can take care of yourself. But your mother and I really don't think this go-between business is your calling."

"I know, Dad, but I'm good at it. Usually. And after what happened at Ecclestone's, I agree with you—the normal business world isn't a good fit for me, either."

There was a short silence.

"Need a poem?" Byron asked.

"Yep. I could use one."

Some kids were raised with bedtime stories. She had been brought up on bedtime songs from her mother and bedtime poems from her father.

"I think I know of one you might find helpful," Byron said.

"One of yours?"

"No, the poem I'm thinking of was written by someone else. Give me a few minutes to find it. I'll e-mail it to you."

"Thanks, Dad. Love you. Love to Mom."

"Love you, too, kiddo. See you soon when you come home for the Moontide celebration. Oh, and don't forget your grandfather's birthday."

"I won't. Looking forward to seeing everyone."

Sierra ended the call and sat quietly, drinking the wine and trying to decompress.

The poem popped into her inbox a short time later. She read the first few lines and smiled. Her father had a gift for finding or crafting a poem that went straight to the heart of the problem.

"I don't know who I am," you say,
"Or why my hands deal dust,
As though the lot of cards I hold
Have crumbled as I play."

She finished the poem and then she finished the wine.

"Message received, Dad," she said to the empty room. "I'll keep listening for my calling."

CHAPTER 3

The Fogg Club was not the most exclusive nightclub in Las Vegas—far from it. Anyone willing to pay the reasonable cover charge was welcome. However, the location, a couple of blocks off the Strip in a dimly lit alley between two massive hotel and casino parking garages, guaranteed that very few tourists stumbled into the place.

From the outside the club looked like a typical low-end Vegas venue, complete with an acid-green LED sign that spelled out the name of the establishment and the slogan *Get Lost in the Fogg*. It was something of an inside joke. The owner, Hank Sheffield, was from Fogg Lake, Washington.

North Chastain pushed open the door, nodded a greeting to the beefy bouncer and went to stand at the railing, surveying the crowd on the lower level. He tried to make it appear that he was just checking out the scene, searching for friends and acquaintances on the dance floor. But the truth was he had to give his eyes a moment to adjust to the low light and the flashing strobes. The damned glasses he was forced to wear prevented him from accessing his preternatural night vision.

The glasses had been designed to look like mirrored, wraparound sunglasses, but the lenses were unique—high-tech crystals that had come out of a Foundation lab. According to the doctors, they were all that stood between him and the hellish hallucinations. The lenses might save his sanity but they could not halt the steady deterioration of his talent. The experts had warned him that eventually, probably within a month or so, he would be psi-blind.

Until a few weeks ago he had taken his special vision for granted. For him the world at midnight had been a dazzling place, one he could navigate with the same ease he used to move around in daylight. His talent had enabled him to see the energy that was only visible after dark. Paranormal auroras flooded the skies. Currents and waves of light illuminated the world in an array of hues and shades and shadows that had no names. The colors of night were magic, the real deal.

It wasn't just the thrill he got from the experience of viewing the world after dark that he would miss for the rest of his life. His ability had made him a damn good cleaner, one of the best. He could track the psychic monsters through the darkest night. When he was in his other vision, the tracks of the bad guys seethed with violent heat.

Going psi-blind would soon cost him his job, the one thing he had been good at—hunting monsters. It had been his way of proving to everyone associated with the Foundation that the Chastains were trustworthy, honorable and loyal; his way of living down his grandfather's reputation as a traitor.

When he lost his talent completely he would not belong here at the Fogg Club. Hell, he wouldn't be any good to the Foundation. He would be looking for a new path out in the normal world.

Okay, time to stop feeling sorry for yourself.

The lenses in his glasses had adjusted to the low light level of the club. He made his way along the mezzanine to the bar. Hank Sheffield was pouring drinks. When he saw North he grabbed a bottle of whiskey off the top shelf and a glass.

"I was wondering when you'd get here," Hank said. He put the glass on the gleaming bar top and poured some of the expensive whiskey into it. "The rest of the team rolled in a couple of hours ago."

"I stopped off at Area Fifty-One to play some blackjack," North said. He picked up the whiskey and took a healthy swallow.

"Any luck?"

"Some," North said. He had pocketed a few hundred bucks. He probably could have won more but he never played for high stakes. Gambling was just a game, after all. Winning was certainly better than losing but he never got a genuine rush out of the experience.

Hank got a shrewd look. "Good crowd at Area Fifty-One?"

For the first time that evening, North felt a spark of amusement. Hank's ex-wife, Jeanie, owned the Area 51 club. It was no secret that the two were still sharing the same house and, no doubt, the same bed, but they had concluded they did not make good business partners. After the divorce, Jeanie had opened Area 51 and become Hank's chief competitor. They both catered to the same clientele— the employees, consultants, museum staff and researchers associated with the Foundation. The secretive organization devoted to all things paranormal was headquartered in Las Vegas.

"The place was busy," North said, determined to remain neutral. "Jeanie said to give you her best, by the way."

Hank snorted. "Bullshit. Jeanie has never once in her entire life told anyone to give me her best."

"Okay, what she actually said was that if you ever decide to give up running this hotdog stand she will consider hiring you to tend bar."

Hank nodded. "That sounds like my Jeanie. I talked to some of the other cleaners on your team tonight. They said the takedown went well today."

"We found the guy we were looking for," North said. "A serial killer who was using his psychic vibe to attract his victims."

No need to mention that the case was probably the last time he would go out into the field with the team. If he stayed with the Foundation, he would end up behind a desk. That wouldn't go well, not for him.

"So you took down one of the monsters. Good job." Hank folded his arms on the bar. "In that case, why aren't you out on the dance floor or buying drinks for one of the nice ladies who come in here to have a little fun?"

"Give me time," North said. "The evening is still young."

"It's one o'clock in the morning."

"I thought it was always midnight here at the Fogg."

The atmosphere inside the Fogg was mostly the same as it was at any other Vegas nightclub—a lot of intimate shadows, high energy, pulsating music and a dance floor lit with dazzling strobes. There was also some fake fog that glowed a fluorescent green. But the real vibe, the one that brought in the regulars, was created by the array of paranormal artifacts displayed in a floor-to-ceiling clear plastic vault in the center of the room.

The objects inside appeared ordinary enough. Mid-century office chairs, ashtrays, a metal filing cabinet and a couple of old-fashioned, black landline telephones were arranged on the tiered glass shelves and illuminated with the glowing green fog. All the artifacts were standard-issue vintage government surplus. But at some point in its history, each antique had been associated with one of the lost labs of the Bluestone Project. Each had absorbed some kind of paranormal radiation, enough so that someone with a degree of psychic awareness could sense the energy.

He might be losing his unique night vision but the rest of his senses were still working. The fact that he was wired from what he suspected was his last field op made him especially aware of the heat in the atmosphere. He was restless, on edge and, okay, maybe depressed. He needed something to take the edge off. Sex might offer a temporary fix, but he knew most of the people in the room tonight. They were colleagues, coworkers and friends. Sex with someone you worked with was usually a mistake, although everyone knew that particular mistake happened a lot within the Foundation. He had made it himself on more than one occasion, although he had been careful to get together with women who worked in the labs or the museum, not someone on his own cleaner team.

Sex with someone who had heard the rumors about his prognosis, however, would be a full-on disaster. It was a good bet everyone in the Fogg tonight knew what was happening to him. The last thing he wanted was a pity fuck.

And when you got right down to it, he wasn't especially interested in sex these days anyway. He was living under a sword of Damocles, waiting for the last of his night vision to disappear entirely. It didn't help that he didn't dare let himself fall into a deep sleep. He was getting by on short naps, setting alarms so that he woke up frequently to make sure the glasses hadn't fallen off.

There were other reasons why he didn't want to sleep soundly. Deep sleep brought dreams, and in his dreams he was always on the verge of falling into the absolute darkness of an abyss.

He did not dare remove the glasses for more than a few seconds at a time. He even wore them in the shower. The doctors had warned him that every minute he spent with his eyes unshielded, the greater the risk of getting lost in the ghostly hallucinations.

"About time you got here. Where have you been?"

North turned and saw Jake Martindale. They were both on the same team of cleaners. They were more than colleagues; they were friends. He trusted Jake and he was certain Jake trusted him. Jake didn't give a damn that North was the grandson of the notorious Griffin Chastain, a man believed to have betrayed his country. Sure, everyone else at the Foundation pretended the past didn't matter. The sins of the fathers were not supposed to be visited on the sons and grandsons. But North knew the reality was that there were a number of people affiliated with the Foundation who questioned the integrity of Griffin's descendants.

"Spent a little time at Area Fifty-One first," North said. "Looks like the party is just getting started."

"It is. Most of these folks will be here until dawn." Jake raised his bottle of beer in a toast. "We did good work today, pal."

"Yes, we did." North clinked his glass against Jake's beer. "So why are you drinking alone here at the bar? What's the matter? Won't anyone dance with you?"

Jake looked across the room. "I don't feel like dancing."

North lounged against the bar and followed Jake's gaze to a booth that was occupied by a man and a woman. The two sat very close together, sipping cocktails. Grant Wallbrook and Kimberly Tolland were scientists who worked in one of the Foundation labs. Wallbrook was a smart, ambitious researcher with a lot of degrees after his name. North was pretty sure Kimberly was every bit as intelligent as Wallbrook—she had a few degrees herself—but she lacked the charismatic energy of the man sitting beside her. She was an attractive woman with serious glasses and a quiet, studious air. Jake had been secretly lusting after her for months.

"Okay," North said. "Now I understand why you're drowning your sorrows here at the bar."

"Wallbrook is using her for some purpose," Jake muttered. "I know it. He doesn't care about her. He's a self-centered narcissist."

"Give it time. She's a smart woman. She'll figure it out."

"Sure. But probably not before she gets hurt. And even if she does see him for what he is, she's not going to turn to a guy like me. She'll go for someone else with a PhD after his name. I'm just a college dropout who hunts bad guys for a living."

"You really are in a mood tonight, aren't you? Have another beer."

"Good idea." Jake raised his hand to signal Hank.

"Look on the bright side," North said.

"What side would that be?"

"Got a feeling Victor Arganbright is going to put you in charge of a cleaner team one of these days. You're good, and he knows it."

Jake narrowed his eyes. "You're talking about me taking over your job, aren't you? That's not the way I want to advance my career."

"We both know it's not going to be long before Arganbright removes me from the team. I won't be any good to him once I'm totally psi-blind."

"Shit, man. I can't believe this is happening to you."

"If you had to wear these damn glasses day and night, you'd believe it."

"I think we both need another drink."

"A brilliant plan," North said.

Being pulled from the one job he was good at was going to be bad enough. He had not told anyone—not even the doctors or his parents—his deepest fear. He was terrified he was losing his sanity as well as his talent. He worried that even the special lenses in his glasses could not save him. The hallucinations were getting worse.

No one wanted to work with a talent of any kind who might be mentally and psychically unstable. That went double if the talent in question happened to be the grandson of Griffin Chastain, the man who was believed to have sold some of the secrets of the Bluestone Project to the former Soviet Union. The fact that Griffin had disappeared altogether after betraying his country had convinced everyone that he had been quietly executed by the Soviet spy who had recruited him.

Griffin Chastain had vanished not long after North's father, Chandler, was born. North knew that his dad had carried the burden of the dishonor that Griffin had brought upon the family name all of his life. North had also understood from a very young age that the weight of that dishonor had fallen on him as well.

"Some good news headed your way, at least," Jake said.

North watched a long-legged brunette in a snug red dress emerge from the crowd. She stopped in front of him and gave him an inviting smile.

"How about a dance?" she said.

Her name was Larissa Whittier. She worked in the Foundation museum. She was smart, talented and ambitious. They had dated a couple of times but it had quickly become obvious to both of them they were doomed to remain friends.

North managed a smile. "Thanks, Larissa, but I'm beat. Long day."

And an even longer night lay ahead. He knew he was seriously sleep deprived. Relying on his psychic senses to supply the energy he needed to maintain the inner balance required to keep from falling into the abyss was weakening him on several fronts. He had a hunch that when he finally went down, he would go down hard. And when he woke up, he would be psi-blind. Or insane. Or both.

"I heard you and the team took down that serial killer they called the Spider," Larissa said. "Congratulations. You cleaners are usually ready to party after a successful case."

"Hate to admit it but there is the faint possibility that I'm getting too old to party after a takedown," North said.

He kept his tone light and easy but Larissa gave him a knowing look.

"Everything okay?" she said gently.

Shit. This was not good. If the people who knew him were starting to notice a change in his mood or behavior, he was sailing into real trouble.

"Just tired, that's all," he said. "Rain check on the dance?"

"Of course." Larissa grinned and patted his arm. "Go home and get some sleep, old dude."

"I'm going to do that."

Larissa started to turn away but she paused. "I forgot to tell you my good news."

He smiled. "Let me guess. You got assigned to the Fogg Lake project."

The recent discovery of one of the lost labs in the caves near the rural town of Fogg Lake had sent a shock wave of excitement through the Foundation. Every ambitious researcher wanted in on the excavations.

"I'm so excited. I leave tomorrow with one of the museum teams. We'll be there for a couple of months. This is the biggest find in the history of the Foundation. There's so much waiting to be recovered in that old lost lab. I can't wait to get started."

"Congratulations," North said. He meant it. "You deserve to be on that team."

"Thanks." Larissa laughed. "I hear conditions at the site are a little Spartan. No nightclubs, cell phones don't work and there's only one restaurant in town. Most of the Foundation crew is being housed in trailers."

"You'll love it," North assured her. "You're going to be uncovering incredible secrets. So much history was lost when they shut down the Bluestone Project. There's no telling what's waiting for you in those caves."

"I know. I really am thrilled. Take care, and I'll see you in a couple of months when my assignment ends."

"Right."

Larissa went up on tiptoe and gave him an affectionate little kiss on the side of his jaw. Then she slipped away into the crowd.

North watched her join a group of people on the far side of the room. He knew all of them. They were friends. Colleagues. Teammates. A couple of months ago he would have been with them, sharing the rush of a successful takedown.

It occurred to him that he was seriously flirting with depression.

Maybe it hadn't been a good idea to drop in at the Fogg after all. He had hoped it would distract him but it was having the opposite effect.

"I'll see you tomorrow, Jake," he said.

"You're leaving?" Jake asked. "So soon?"

Not soon enough, North thought.

"Yeah," he said. "I'm going home."

Alone.

CHAPTER 4

He walked out into the balmy desert night. The atmosphere was warm and pleasant but the world after dark was no longer the wondrous experience he had taken for granted ever since he had come into his talent.

Unable to resist a peek at what he was going to lose, he paused in the shadows and used both hands to take off the glasses. For a couple of seconds the night came alive. Even the bright lights of the Strip could not overpower the paranormal auroras that illuminated the sky.

But in the next moment the ghostly gray figures appeared, first at the corners of his eyes. The hallucinations advanced rapidly and soon threatened to swamp his vision. The whispers began.

Hastily he put on the glasses and took a couple of deep breaths until the visions and the whispers receded.

When he was sure he was back in control he cut through one of the heavily shadowed parking garages, entered the adjoining casino via the service door and made his way across the busy gaming floor.

He went out onto the crowded sidewalks of the Strip. The flashy, glittering casino hotels that lined both sides of the street blazed in the night with their own kind of energy, but it wasn't the same.

Three-quarters of the way down the Strip he passed a set of shimmering mirrored doors. There was no sign. Most passersby probably assumed it was the private entrance to a condo tower. But behind the reflective doors were the offices, museums, libraries, storage vaults and research facilities of the Foundation.

The private quarters of the director, Victor Arganbright, and his husband, Lucas Pine, occupied the entire top floor. There was a large pool and elaborate gardens on the roof.

North walked on, turned a corner and used a ride-hailing app to summon a car to take him to the big house that sat alone out in the desert.

Half an hour later the driver stopped in front of the gated entrance.

"Thanks," North said.

The driver studied the high-walled estate through the windshield. "Isn't this the old mansion that belonged to that famous magician?" he asked. "The one who disappeared a long time ago?"

"Griffin Chastain," North said.

"Right. Heard the house is called the Abbey or something."

"The Abyss," North said. "He named it after his most spectacular trick. No magician has ever been able to duplicate it."

"They say the place is haunted. You know how it is here in Vegas. Everyone loves a good celebrity legend. According to the story I heard, Chastain's body was never found. They say he probably died in that house while trying to perfect one of his dangerous tricks and that he still haunts the place."

"I've been living here for nearly a year," North said. "I haven't seen a ghost."

He had uncovered some fascinating secrets inside the Abyss but, to date, no specters.

"Surprised the place is still standing," the driver said. "It's been sitting out here in the desert since the middle of the last century. Abandoned. They say even the squatters and the transients didn't try to go inside."

"The house can take care of itself." North opened the door and got out. "Thanks for the ride."

"Sure. Anytime."

The driver made a U-turn and sped off toward the lights of Las Vegas in the distance.

The security box looked vintage mid-twentieth century but the electronics inside were anything but standard issue for the era. Behind the panel there was a green crystal.

He opened the panel, touched the crystal and sent a little energy through the stone. At least he could still summon enough heat to open his own front gate. He remembered his advice to Jake. *Look on the bright side.*

The heavy steel gates swung inward.

He walked into the big desert garden and used the crystal on the inside wall to relock the gates.

He pushed a whisper of energy through another crystal to bring up the low lighting that illuminated the winding walk through the cactus garden. Until recently he hadn't needed the small lamps to make his way through the maze of cacti planted around the house. But with the glasses on he had no choice.

It was an interesting collection of exotic cacti, but the garden had not been designed for decorative purposes or to conserve water. The sharp thorns of the plants served as a defensive perimeter. An intruder who managed to get over the high walls at night would be faced with a dangerous obstacle course. Only someone who was a direct descendant of Griffin Chastain could activate the footpath lights.

The cactus garden would be the least of an intruder's problems. There were far more dangerous barriers waiting in the shadows, security devices only a master magician with a psychic talent could have engineered.

When North reached the grand entrance he touched another crystal lock. The big red lacquered doors swung open. Once inside he touched the crystal switch that turned on the massive chandelier that hung from the ceiling above the two-story circular foyer.

Arched doorways off the rotunda opened onto the ground-floor rooms. A grand staircase provided access to the upper floor. The house had been decorated in what his mother described as mid-century-Vegas-over-the-top. Okay, so Griffin Chastain had liked mirrors. Most magicians did.

Lily Chastain had shaken her head when he had announced that he planned to move into his grandfather's mansion. "It's too much house for anyone, especially a single man, and trust me, no woman will want to live there. It may not be haunted but it gives me the creeps."

His father, Chandler, had understood. The house was, after all, a large, ongoing crystal light engineering experiment.

People assumed the mansion had been built for the customary reasons—to show off the owner's success and to entertain on a lavish scale. But they were wrong. Griffin Chastain had been a brilliant magician whose stage tricks had become legendary but he had also been an engineering talent with a gift for manipulating light from the dark end of the paranormal spectrum. In the tradition of all great magicians, he had taken care to guard his secrets.

He had designed every room in the house as if it were a stage set. If you simply walked through the various spaces you would think they were normal, if wildly glamorous and theatrical. North knew his mother was right. The decorator had gone overboard with red velvet, gold satin and mirrored ceilings and walls, but he didn't care. What intrigued him about the mansion was the part that was hidden.

Griffin Chastain had been inspired by the designs of ancient Egyptian pyramids and the great castles of Europe. There were hidden corridors and secret rooms everywhere. It was in those spaces, behind the scenes, that the magician had set up his private research laboratory.

During the construction phase Griffin had hired a number of different contractors. Each had been assigned to build a small section of the sprawling mansion. No one contractor and none of the people who had worked on the house had been allowed to view all the floor plans. No electricians were involved, because the house was powered by crystals, each of which had been personally installed by Griffin. The result was that by the time the mansion was complete, the only person who knew the overall layout was Griffin Chastain. And he had never told anyone about the secrets he had concealed inside.

The result was a house of mysteries. The Abyss would have made a great roadside attraction except for the fact that the mansion was designed to terrify anyone who was bold enough to enter without permission.

The only downside was that Lily Chastain was probably right when she claimed that no woman would ever want to live in the house. North knew he was going to have to face that reality sooner or later unless he wanted to live alone for the rest of his life. But at the moment he had a bigger problem on his hands. He was fully occupied with the task of trying not to fall into a state of panic or utter despair.

———

The following morning the vibration of his phone pulled his attention away from his third cup of coffee. He glanced at the caller ID and got a little rush of adrenaline. Victor Arganbright, the director of the Foundation. With luck that meant another job, which, in turn, meant another distraction.

Or maybe Arganbright was about to inform him he was being removed from the team.

North braced himself and took the call. "You're up early, boss."

As far as anyone could tell, Victor worked twenty-four-seven. He was obsessed. The object of that obsession had a name: Vortex.

Vortex held the status of a legend within the Foundation. It was said to have been the most highly classified of all the labs associated with the Bluestone Project. There were those who were convinced it was a myth. Others were certain that if it had been real, it had been destroyed when Bluestone was shut down. But Victor believed not only that Vortex had existed but that something very dangerous had been discovered in the lab. He was afraid that now, after all these decades, someone or some group was intent on discovering Bluestone's greatest and most deadly secret. "Where are you?" Victor growled.

North got a little ping of premonition. Victor Arganbright growled a lot but there was something different about his tone today.

"I'm at the Abyss," North said. "Do we have a new case?"

"What we have is an as-yet-unidentified problem. Pack a bag. The Foundation jet is being readied for a flight to Seattle. You and your mother are going to be on board."

A ghostly whisper of intuition iced the back of North's neck. His father had gone to Seattle three days earlier on Foundation business.

"Is this about Dad?" he asked.

"A short time ago Chandler was found conscious but unresponsive in his hotel room."

North felt as if he had just taken a body blow. For a few beats he could not think.

"What?" he finally managed.

"Your mother got a feeling. She couldn't get ahold of him. She called me and I called the hotel. The front desk sent security up to check on Chandler. That's when they found him. An ambulance was called. He was taken to Harborview. It's a level one trauma hospital.

I'm told there is no sign of physical injury. No indication he might have suffered a stroke or a heart attack. They're throwing around terms like *pseudocoma* and *locked-in syndrome*."

"'Locked-in syndrome'?"

"Trust me, you don't want to know the details. It's as bad as it sounds. But the bottom line is that the symptoms don't meet any of the standard diagnostic criteria for a coma, which makes me suspect aura trauma. Our Seattle people were notified immediately. They're with him at the hospital. They'll make sure he's protected until we can airlift him back here to Vegas."

It took North a beat to realize that *our Seattle people* meant Lark & LeClair, a small private investigation agency that had recently agreed to accept the Foundation as a client. There was also a cleaner team stationed in Seattle. The team worked out of the Lark & LeClair office.

North tried to concentrate.

"Protected?" he said. "Are you saying you think Dad was attacked? That he's still in danger?"

"We don't know what the hell happened."

"Do you think it's wise to move Dad before we have a better idea of what's going on?" North asked.

"Pretty sure we're dealing with an unusual situation."

In Victor-speak, *unusual situation* meant an incident involving the paranormal.

"Have you told Mom?" North asked.

"Yes. She'll meet you at the airport."

"You want me to escort Dad back here?"

"No," Victor said. "Your mother and some medics from Halcyon will handle that end of things. I'm sending you to Seattle because I want you to find out what happened to Chandler."

Halcyon Manor was the private psychiatric hospital run by the Foundation. It specialized in treating diseases of the paranormal senses. North knew it all too well. He had spent a lot of time there in recent weeks getting fitted for the special crystal glasses that were supposed to keep him sane while he lost his night vision.

He steeled himself for what had to be said.

"Of course I'll go to Seattle," he said. "But under the circumstances I may not be the best investigator. You know what's going on with my talent."

"You haven't lost it entirely and my intuition tells me you are the best person for this job."

"Why?"

"Because your father's last stop before he returned to the hotel was at an antiques shop that specializes in hot artifacts. He had contacted your mother to tell her that he had a lead on a relic that might have belonged to your grandfather. Chandler said he thought it might be an object that was tuned to Griffin Chastain's psychic signature. But when Olivia LeClair from Lark & LeClair went through your father's hotel room and belongings after he was taken to the hospital, she found no sign of an artifact."

"Stolen?"

"There's a high probability that is the case," Victor said. "But if it's tuned to Griffin Chastain's signature—"

"Only another Chastain would recognize the relic. In other words, you don't have any choice but to send me out on this case, because I'm the only Chastain available."

Victor grunted. "That pretty much sums it up. Pack that bag and come in to headquarters. I'll tell you everything I know before you go to the airport, but I'll warn you up front, I don't have a lot of information."

Victor ended the connection.

North was already on the grand staircase, moving fast. He was used to packing in a hurry. It did not take long to throw the essentials into a backpack.

When he was ready he opened the gun safe, took out the holstered pistol, hoisted the pack and went back downstairs.

The steel-gray SUV was waiting inside the garage. He drove out through the front gate and headed toward the Strip. He did not bother to glance back at the Abyss. There was no need to make sure he had turned off the lights or locked the doors.

The house could take care of itself.

CHAPTER 5

Delbridge Loring stopped at the end of the long workbench, picked up the vintage radio and hurled it against the nearest wall. The artifact struck hard and fell to the floor. The plastic casing cracked. A knob fell off. The small glass screen shattered.

"You son of a bitch, Chandler Chastain, you cheated me."

Ignoring the radio, Loring resumed pacing the laboratory, trying to get a grip on the rage threatening to consume him. He had risked so much only to discover that all he had to show for his efforts was a broken radio. Sure, there was a little heat in it, but nothing special. It was not the tuning device he desperately needed.

After all the planning, all the experiments, all the waiting, things were starting to go wrong. Chandler Chastain should have been dead; instead he was in a sort of unresponsive state. With luck he would not come out of it, but who knew how things would turn out? What if he regained the ability to communicate? How much would he remember? Would he be able to identify the person who had attacked him with the night gun?

The disaster was the Puppets' fault. They had fucked up the entire operation. That was the problem with Puppets. They were, by nature, unstable and impulsive. Typical cult recruits. But it wasn't as if he'd had a lot of options when it came to hiring muscle. He'd needed men with minimal talent, just enough to activate the weapons. Men who were hungry for more power. He'd needed men who would believe him when he promised to transform them into invincible psychic warriors armed with untraceable weapons. He needed people he could manipulate. That sort didn't come equipped with the ability to think logically. There was a reason that within the paranormal community they were referred to as Puppets. So simple for a smart man to pull the strings.

Still, the four Puppets were all he had to work with. Well, there was Garraway, but he was just the money man and the window dressing needed to make the Riverview operation appear legitimate.

Loring went to the window and stood looking out at the high walls of the psychiatric hospital. Beyond lay nothing but vast stretches of forest and the cliffs above the Pacific Ocean. There was a small town a few miles away but the locals were not friendly. They had not been happy when they discovered that the old, abandoned mansion had been converted into a private asylum. They kept their distance. That was fine by Loring. He wanted nothing to do with the people in town. He was here to fulfill his destiny.

He turned away from the window and contemplated his state-of-the-art lab. It was everything he had ever wanted. He had been determined to succeed where Crocker Rancourt had failed; where the entire Bluestone Project had failed. He had a talent for crystals and he was close to discovering the secret of weaponizing paranormal energy.

All he needed was Crocker Rancourt's tuning crystal.

He forced himself to calm down. He was a scientist. He knew how to recover from disastrous experiments. It was time to go back to some of the original data. He had not looked at the logbook in months, because he had read it cover to cover and made copious notes when it first came into his hands. He had practically memorized the formulas and the math.

But maybe, just maybe, he had overlooked something that could set him on a new path.

He crossed the lab and punched a code into a security panel. The heavy metal door of the small walk-in vault swung open. A number of artifacts were arrayed on the shelves, various items that he had collected in the course of his research. None had proven helpful. Everything had led to a dead end—everything except the logbook.

If there were more secrets to be found, they were in Griffin Chastain's notes.

He went to the glass case where Chastain's logbook was stored. He opened the case and reached inside to pick up the leather-bound book.

It took him a few seconds to realize it was the wrong logbook. Another leather-bound logbook—a vintage document from the same era—had been left in its place.

It took him a moment to process what had happened. *Someone had stolen the logbook.*

One of the Puppets, perhaps, who planned to sell it on the underground market. But even as the possibility came to mind he dismissed it. They had no reason to steal it. They believed they were going to be the beneficiaries of the secrets in the logbook. More crucially, they understood he was the only one who could comprehend the complicated paranormal physics.

It was equally unlikely that Garraway had taken it. He was good with money but he couldn't possibly grasp the scientific concepts and formulas in the logbook. Besides, he was committed to the Riverview project for the same reason as the Puppets—he lusted after the promise of paranormal powers.

Loring forced himself to think about the timeline. It had been over two months since he had last had occasion to take the logbook out of the glass case. Only one disturbing event had occurred at River-view during that time.

A patient had escaped.

CHAPTER 6

ere's what we know." Victor pushed himself up out of the big
leather desk chair and crossed the paneled office to the windows
that looked down several stories to the fantasyland of the Strip.
"As I told you on the phone, late yesterday afternoon Chandler visited a shop in Seattle called Swan Antiques. Over the years the Foundation has done a fair amount of business with Gwendolyn Swan, the
owner. She's got a feel for artifacts with a paranormal vibe."

That was high praise coming from Victor Arganbright, North
thought. He and Victor were not related by blood, but the Chastains
and the Arganbrights had been close for three generations. The Arganbrights had always refused to believe that Griffin Chastain had
betrayed his country and sold the secrets of the Bluestone Project.
Like North and his father, they were convinced Griffin had been
murdered because of his research work, but no one knew exactly
what that research had involved. Left unspoken was the grim speculation that Griffin might have been working on paranormal weap-
onry. The one thing they knew for certain was that when Griffin had

been recruited into the Bluestone Project he had been assigned a re-search partner—Crocker Rancourt.

In the wake of the destruction of the Bluestone Project, the Foundation had been established. Crocker Rancourt had been the first director. After his death, control of the organization had been passed down to his son, Stenson Rancourt, who in turn had planned to hand things off to his son, Harlan.

While in charge, the Rancourt family had run the Foundation as if it were their own private money-making fiefdom. They had ruled it like a mob family. That had come to a screeching halt five years earlier when Victor Arganbright and Lucas Pine had staged an internal coup that was most charitably characterized as a hostile takeover. Stenson Rancourt had died in a mysterious explosion. His body had been found in the wreckage. His son, Harlan, was presumed to have died in the fire as well, but his body had not been found.

Victor was in his early fifties. He had the bold profile and the amber eyes that were typical of the Arganbright men. He was a driven man, a man with a self-imposed mission. He was convinced the Foundation and, quite possibly, the nation faced a grave threat from the past. He feared the secrets of the old Bluestone Project were rising from the grave. Of all the mysteries connected to Bluestone, the secret lab code-named Vortex represented the greatest danger.

The problem for Victor was that Vortex and the other lost labs had been involved in clandestine research into the paranormal, a subject that was no longer taken seriously by reputable researchers, academic institutions or governments. Politicians and career military personnel ignored the subject for fear of being laughed out of their jobs. Admitting to a belief in the paranormal was a good way to terminate a career.

With the sole exception of the tiny, woefully underfunded Agency for the Investigation of Atypical Phenomena—a one-desk (currently unstaffed) operation buried deep in the basement of a building somewhere in Washington, DC—the US government had officially abandoned paranormal research in the latter half of the previous century. For all intents and purposes, the Foundation was on its own.

"You think Dad was attacked because of whatever it was he bought at Swan Antiques," North said.

Victor hesitated. The energy in the atmosphere around him got a little more intense. "I don't have any proof, but the timing makes me suspicious. If Chandler discovered a valuable artifact in the shop, it's possible a raider followed him back to the hotel, attacked him and stole the object."

"Hard to believe a raider would take the risk of assaulting someone directly affiliated with the Foundation," North said. "They usually go out of their way to avoid getting on your psi-dar. The last thing a low-level operator wants is to become the target of a cleaner team."

Raiders worked in the shadows of the paranormal trade. Most were small-time con artists who made a living selling fraudulent artifacts to gullible collectors. The more adventurous ones engaged in burglary and theft. For the most part they were opportunists who worked alone or with a partner. There were, however, a handful of more sophisticated rings run by smart, ruthless leaders. But even the big outfits usually took care to steer clear of the Foundation.

Victor turned around and began to prowl the large room. He paused from time to time to contemplate one of the myriad paintings that covered the walls. More paintings, framed and unframed, were stacked on the floor. Some of the art that littered the space was valuable; some was not. Some was old. Some was new.

Victor didn't collect the pictures because he expected them to increase in value. He had picked them up over the years because he was obsessed with the subject matter. Each was a depiction of the Oracle of Delphi.

In most of the pictures the Oracle was shown in the traditional pose, draped in robes and seated on a three-legged stool that straddled a crack in the floor of a cavern. In that position she inhaled the vapors that wafted up through the opening, went into a trance and delivered prophecies. There had been a fee, of course, but it was up to the client to interpret the cryptic prophecies.

The Oracle had been an extremely popular attraction for the ancient city of Delphi and a source of great revenue. North figured the operation had probably worked a lot like modern-day Las Vegas. You paid your money and you took your chances.

"It's possible we're dealing with a new, unidentified raider crew," Victor mused. "But it doesn't have that feel."

North did not question the conclusion. Victor was very, very good at what he did because his intuition was extremely sharp when it came to predicting how the bad guys would act. He was not, however, infallible. When he screwed up there were usually a lot of fireworks.

"You mentioned there were no outward signs of violence," North said. "Do you think someone used drugs on Dad?"

"Maybe. We will know more once we get him back here where the specialists can examine him. In the meantime, I want you to retrace Chandler's footsteps yesterday and last night. Start at Swan Antiques."

"Will the owner be cooperative?"

"I think so. Gwendolyn Swan doesn't want any trouble with the Foundation. It's not as if we're blaming her for what happened to Chandler. We just need to find out what, exactly, she sold him and see if the information gives us a lead."

North reflected briefly. "I'm good at finding people but I'm not so great when it comes to tracking down artifacts. I'm going to need help from a specialist, preferably someone who knows the local hot artifacts market in Seattle."

"Lucas has been going through the files. He's got a name for you."

The door opened as if on cue. Lucas Pine walked into the room, a file in one hand. Silver haired, sophisticated and elegant even when casually dressed, he appeared at first glance to be Victor's exact opposite. But the energy between the two of them was unmistakable. The pair had been devoted to each other for a couple of decades. Their wedding had been a huge, splashy, Las Vegas–style party.

"The name," Lucas said in a voice that sounded like it had been trained for the stage, "is Sierra Raines."

"She knows the Seattle market?" North asked.

"Yes." Lucas glanced through the file. "Currently she's an agent for the Vault, a business that handles transport and delivery of artifacts. According to Ambrose Jones, she's good. Very good."

"Ambrose Jones?" North asked.

"Jones owns and operates the Vault," Victor said. "We've worked with him before. He has always been reliable. He told us to ignore Ms. Raines's somewhat checkered job history, specifically what happened at her previous place of employment."

North raised his brows. "What, exactly, did happen?"

"Until a few months ago she worked for one of the big auction houses, Ecclestone's," Lucas said. "She was let go amid rumors that Ecclestone's was peddling fraudulent antiques. And before you ask, no, we don't know if she was guilty. What we know is that she is now working as a go-between in the paranormal market in Seattle—specifically the deep end of that market."

"I see." North took the file. "And is Ms. Raines still selling fakes?"

Victor's jaw tightened. "Jones says we can trust her. It's not like we've got a lot of choice here."

Just as you don't have a lot of choice when it comes to investigators, North thought. *You're stuck with me. And it looks like I'm stuck with Sierra Raines.*

"You want me to team up with a shady go-between who may or may not be dealing in fraudulent artifacts?" he said.

"I think it's safe to assume she won't try to con someone from the Foundation," Victor said. "Not with Jones looking over her shoulder."

"I'll take your word for that."

North flipped open the file. There was a small glossy photo of a woman who appeared to be about thirty years old. Her whiskey-brown hair was pulled back in an elegantly stern knot at the back of her nicely shaped head. She gazed out of the photo with brown-and-gold eyes that somehow managed to project a mix of wide-eyed innocence and bone-deep watchfulness.

Sierra Raines was attractive, but not Las Vegas beautiful. Nevertheless, in a town that boasted a lot of spectacular, long-legged women, she would stand out. At least, she would stand out to him. Somehow he knew that if she walked past him on the crowded Strip he would notice her.

What she had was an edgy, intriguing quality that came through even in a photograph. He was very sure those deep eyes concealed secrets and mysteries.

He made himself focus on the two pages of data. There was a very long list of very short-term jobs, ranging from interior decorator at a firm named Psychic Designs to bookseller at a shop called Paranormal Readings. In between, Sierra Raines had done stints as a psychic therapist, dream interpreter and meditation guide.

He scanned the list and then studied the last entry. *Previous Employer: Ecclestone's Auction House. Reason for Termination of Employment: Suspected of fraud.*

He looked up. "Sierra Raines looks like a flake as well as a con artist."

Lucas smiled. "She does seem to be having some trouble settling into the right job, but as far as the fraud goes, we are convinced she was set up to take the fall at Ecclestone's."

North turned to the second page of the report.

Grandparents resided in Fogg Lake, Washington, at the time of the explosion and were affected by the paranormal radiation that was released. Parents were raised in Fogg Lake. Moved away as young adults. Eventually settled in an intentional community, Quest, in the San Juan Islands, Washington State. Father, Byron Raines, is employed as an online psychic poet. Mother, Allegra Raines, is a psychic song therapist.

North glanced up again. "Her father's a psychic poet? What the hell kind of career is that?"

Lucas shrugged. "You contact him online, tell him your problems, ask for his advice, he sends you a poem that gives you guidance. It's the customer's job to interpret the poem, of course."

Victor glanced at the nearest painting. "Rather like receiving a prophecy from the Oracle."

"Rather like a scam, if you ask me," North said. "Can I assume Mrs. Raines is running a similar con with the psychic song therapy gig?"

Victor narrowed his eyes. "Forget the parents. Focus on Sierra Raines. You need her help."

North closed the folder. "Not a lot of information here. You don't even have a current address for her."

"After she left Ecclestone's she went mostly off the grid," Lucas said. "We know she's working in the Seattle area but, no, we haven't been able to come up with a home address. That phone number is good, as far as we know, but she never answers. The only thing you can do is leave a message and hope she gets back to you. I didn't call her about this case because I didn't want to make her nervous. She might decide to bolt. I've asked Jones to set up the meeting between the two of you."

"Calls from the Foundation have a way of making people in the artifacts trade uneasy," Victor muttered. "That goes double for go-betweens. They have a tendency to disappear if they think we've taken an interest in them."

"You need to work on your people skills," North said.

Victor ignored that. "If she's as good as Jones says, she's your best shot at tracking down the artifact your father bought from Swan."

"I'd work with the Devil herself if that's what it takes to find out what happened to Dad," North said.

Victor nodded, satisfied. "Figured you'd see things that way."

CHAPTER 7

The ambulance with Chandler Chastain on board was waiting at the airport in Seattle.

A stylishly dressed woman, her auburn hair cut at a sharp angle that emphasized her striking features, came forward to greet them.

"I'm Olivia LeClair," she explained. "I am so sorry about what happened to Mr. Chastain. My partner, Catalina Lark, is out of town. She and her husband are doing some research on another possible lost lab location, but I or my assistant has been with Mr. Chastain every moment since I got the call from Victor Arganbright. I want to assure you that no one except medical personnel who were personally vetted by me have been allowed near Mr. Chastain and I authorized no procedures, just as Arganbright instructed."

"Vetted by you?" North asked.

"I'm a very good aura reader," Olivia said.

North nodded. A strong aura analyst was usually able to discern potentially dangerous energy in an individual's aura.

"Understood," he said.

"Thank you for protecting my husband until we could get here," Lily said.

"From what I can tell, Mr. Chastain's aura appears strong," Olivia continued, "but some of his energy bands are oscillating erratically. I hope the doctors at Halcyon Manor can correct the problem quickly. I understand they are doing a lot of advanced work on disorders of the paranormal senses there in Vegas."

"Yes," Lily said. "They are."

Two medics opened the back door of the ambulance and removed the gurney. The Halcyon doctors took charge, moving swiftly.

North had talked to the medics during the flight from Las Vegas. They had tried to tell him what to expect. He thought he had steeled himself for the sight of his father in an unnerving state. He was wrong. It shook him to the core.

His mother, however, appeared strong and resolute.

"We will get through this," she said quietly.

They fell into step alongside the gurney.

"Hello, darling," Lily said. She clasped Chandler's hand and continued talking as the group moved toward the plane stairs. "I'm here to take you home, where the doctors will know how to deal with this situation. Meanwhile, North will find out who did this to you."

She spoke in a calm, utterly convincing tone of voice that left North speechless. He had always known his mother was a strong woman but he had never seen her in action in such devastating circumstances. He watched his father's face while Lily continued to talk and squeeze his hand.

Chandler opened his eyes. He gave no indication that he recognized his son or his wife. Instead he gazed into the distance as if he was staring at something only he could see. But North was suddenly very sure that his father had responded to Lily's voice.

"He knows who you are, Mom," North said quietly.

"Of course he does," Lily said.

The medics halted at the foot of the stairs and prepared to carry the gurney and its passenger up into the plane.

"Wait," North said.

"Orders are to get Mr. Chastain home as fast as possible," one of the medics said.

"I just need a minute," North said. "Mom, I think Dad's responding to your energy on some level. I want to try asking him a couple of questions."

Lily paused and then she nodded once. "Go ahead."

North touched his father's shoulder and tried to think of questions that required only simple yes or no responses.

"Dad, were you attacked?" he asked.

There was no visible response but Lily stiffened. She gazed down at her husband, transfixed.

"Yes," she whispered. "I'm sure I felt something just now. A vibe. I can't explain it but it felt like a yes."

North kept his hand on Chandler's shoulder. "Dad, do you know who attacked you?"

There was a moment of fraught energy in the atmosphere. Lily frowned and then tightened her grip on Chandler's hand.

"No," she said. "He doesn't know."

"We need to get in the air," the pilot said.

North asked the only other question he could think of in that moment. "Dad, were you attacked because of the object you bought at Swan Antiques?"

Another shiver of energy. Hot and intense. This time North could have sworn his father was struggling to focus on him. But the effort cost him. Chandler closed his eyes and went limp.

"Yes," Lily said. She looked at North, her eyes very fierce. "The answer is yes."

"I can work with that," North said.

He stepped back from the gurney. The medics carried their patient up the stairs and disappeared through the door.

Lily turned to North. "Do what you have to do," she said. "But be careful. Your father and I love you."

"I know," North said. "I love you, too."

Lily gave him a brief hug and then hurried up the stairs.

North waited until the Foundation plane was in the air. When it was gone he concentrated on the task at hand. He turned to Olivia LeClair.

"I need to locate a go-between named Sierra Raines," he said.

She smiled. "Yes, Victor Arganbright said you wanted to hire her. She's waiting for you at the Vault in Pioneer Square."

"Sounds like a nightclub."

"It is."

"It's almost noon."

"The Vault is open twenty-four hours a day," Olivia said. "I'll give you a ride."

"Thanks," North said.

CHAPTER 8

"Are you all right, Mr. Chastain?" Sierra asked.

North Chastain was clearly startled by the question. It immediately became obvious he was also seriously pissed off.

"I'm fine," he said.

He was lying. She could see enough of his reflected aura in the mirror on the wall behind him to tell her that the man from the Foundation was sleep deprived. She was sure North Chastain was drawing energy from his paranormal senses not simply to stay awake but to ward off the disorienting effects that resulted from a severe lack of sleep.

It wasn't just lack of sleep that was disturbing his senses, she concluded. There was something else going on with his aura, something more complicated. The dark reflections in the mirror were difficult to interpret. She might be able to get a better read on him if she could get a look at his eyes—she was pretty good at reading eyes—but that was impossible at the moment because North was wearing wraparound mirrored sunglasses. Indoors. In the shadows of the dimly illuminated basement of the Vault nightclub.

He did not appear to be the kind of man who adopted dramatic affectations like sunglasses in a nightclub. The glasses were part of the mystery that enveloped him.

With his hard, sharp profile, he had a predatory edge that gave him an intriguing but decidedly ominous vibe. He was not a man you would want to cross. Like her, he was wearing a lot of leather—jacket and boots but no gloves. She assumed he wore it for the same reasons she did. Cleaners kicked down a lot of dangerous doors and had to be prepared to come in contact with some hot artifacts. They chased the bad guys, after all.

Beneath the jacket North wore a gray crew-neck pullover and black cargo trousers festooned with a lot of pockets. He had dropped a pack onto the floor when he sat down in the booth.

"Thanks for agreeing to meet with me," North said. He sounded cool and professional now, having evidently managed to control his short rush of irritation.

She gave him her most polished smile. "Anything for the Foundation."

North winced. "In other words you figured that if you didn't agree to see me, you might be looking at trouble from Las Vegas."

"Exactly. Also, I need the money and Mr. Jones assures me the Foundation always pays its tab. Okay, I'm here. You're here. Tell me about the case."

North drank some coffee and lowered the big mug. She was drinking coffee, too, a frothy cappuccino. North had ordered a triple-shot grande.

"Are you aware of Swan Antiques in Pioneer Square?" North asked.

"Of course," Sierra said. "Gwendolyn Swan is a player in the hot artifacts market. I've done a few jobs for her. Why?"

"Yesterday afternoon Chandler Chastain bought an artifact from her."

"I'm assuming the Chastain name is not a coincidence?"

"No," North said. "Chandler is my father. At some point after he purchased the artifact, he was attacked. He's awake but he's almost entirely unresponsive, although he does seem to be able to communicate a little through Mom when they have physical contact."

Shocked, Sierra set her cup down. "I'm so sorry. Was he shot?"

"No. There is no evidence of physical trauma, which makes me think he was attacked with something that affected his paranormal senses. He may have been drugged. That's the theory the doctors are going on at the moment. But there is another possibility."

Sierra eyed him warily. "What?"

North hesitated. "The attacker might have used a hot artifact, one infused with a lot of dangerous, unknown radiation that destabilized Dad's aura."

Sierra went still. "Are you talking about a paranormal weapon? That's the unholy grail of the underground collectors' market. If such a thing existed the Foundation would be breathing fire down the neck of any dealer or go-between or collector who tried to buy or sell it."

Too late she realized she should have kept her mouth shut.

"Have you picked up any rumors about a para-weapon coming onto the market?" North asked.

She cleared her throat and reminded herself to proceed with caution. "There are always rumors in the underground market."

"New rumors? Maybe a device from one of the lost labs?"

She folded her gloved hands on the table. "I assure you, I have no personal knowledge of any artifacts that might be weapons from the Bluestone Project."

"Talk to me, Sierra. I'm on the clock."

She spread her hands. "All I can tell you is that recently I've been approached by a couple of clients who made it clear that if anything that could be considered a functioning paranormal weapon came onto the market, they wanted to be in on the auction. Price was no object."

"That's all you know?"

"Yes," she said. She said it very firmly because it was the truth. "It occurs to me you picked the wrong go-between. You would probably do better with someone who's had more experience in the Pacific Northwest market. I'm still fairly new in this line of work. I've been doing it for only a few months."

"Victor Arganbright and Lucas Pine think you're the best one for this job. They're almost never wrong."

"Almost never?"

"When they screw up, they tend to go big."

"I think you should consider the possibility they screwed up when they sent you to me."

"Unfortunately, I don't have time to line up another go-between," North said. "Our first stop is Swan Antiques. We're going to find out exactly what my father bought and take it from there."

Grim determination charged the atmosphere. She understood. If it were her father who was trapped in a nonresponsive state she would be doing exactly what North was doing—using any means or any person necessary to get answers. Family was family.

"You do realize I'm not in business to do favors for the Foundation," she warned. "My hourly rate is high. Very high."

"Don't worry, you'll get paid. Now that I'm officially a client, let's move. We're wasting time."

She held up a forefinger. "Just one more box to check off before I accept you as a client."

North was starting to look pissed again. "What?"

"You're not a Puppet, are you?"

"What self-respecting Puppet would work for the Foundation?"

He had a point. There were a lot of loose screws rattling around at the fringes of the paranormal underworld. Some were mentally ill individuals who heard voices or experienced hallucinations and believed they were being manipulated by people with psychic talent. There were also those with a measure of genuine talent who were unable to handle their psychic side. Instead of rationally processing the input from their paranormal senses they grasped at bizarre conspiracy theories to explain what seemed otherwise inexplicable. And then there were those who preyed on such individuals, conning them or luring them into cults.

All the so-called Puppets had one thing in common, aside from their fascination with conspiracies. They were afraid of the Foundation. They were convinced Victor Arganbright and his cleaners were bent on hunting them down with the intent of silencing them. Some believed that if they were picked up by the Foundation teams they would end up as test subjects in strange paranormal experiments.

Those who ran the cults and the scam artists who took advantage of the gullible also feared the Foundation. Victor Arganbright and his cleaners had developed a reputation for taking down the cons and the frauds. Most were handed over to regular law enforcement, but the underworld whisper mill held that some of the really dangerous people disappeared into a locked ward at Halcyon Manor, the private psychiatric hospital run by the Foundation.

So, yes, it was unlikely a Puppet would want to be connected in any way to the Foundation.

"Just checking," Sierra said.

"Fine. You checked." North downed the last of his triple-shot grande and got to his feet. "Let's go."

Sierra reminded herself that she needed the work. A woman in her current financial situation could not afford to be too picky.

She got to her feet. "Swan's shop isn't far from here. We can walk to it."

CHAPTER 9

It was weird, North thought, but until he walked into the Vault and saw Sierra Raines waiting for him in a booth, he had never realized he had a thing for women in leather. Leather, after all, wasn't unusual or exotic or trendy in his world. A lot of cleaners, including the women, wore it. But on Sierra it looked different. Sexy as hell.

It wasn't just the leather that appealed. He had been right when he had studied her photo in the file that Lucas had given him. Sierra wasn't Las Vegas beautiful. No, she was compelling. Strong-willed, intelligent and gutsy. It was, of course, the perfect camouflage for a professional con artist.

But something—everything—about Sierra had revived his spirits, and not just the physical side of things. He reminded himself that she might be an experienced con artist, but his intuition was sending him other messages. Or maybe it was another part of his anatomy that was making him want to trust her.

All he knew was that her energy quickened his senses and offered him what was probably a false sense of hope. He seized on that silent promise because he was in desperate need of hope. Then again, that was the core talent of a professional con artist—the ability to make the mark believe that what he wanted most in the world was within reach. *Just trust me.*

Having agreed to work with him, she had lost no time in taking him straight to Swan Antiques. He probably would have wasted an hour or more trying to find the place on his own. The shop was located halfway down an alley in the Pioneer Square neighborhood, an old part of town distinguished by narrow lanes and unmarked doorways.

The best thing you could say about the address of Swan's shop was that it was atmospheric. But alleys were alleys the world over. He had seen enough of them to know that by their very nature they attracted those who preferred to avoid the bright lights of busier, more crowded thoroughfares. A lot of trade in hot artifacts was done in alleys.

"Of course I remember Mr. Chastain," Gwendolyn Swan said. "I sold him a vintage radio. There was definitely some heat in it but it was low-level energy, the kind that gets picked up from sitting around in a hot environment. Why are you interested in it?"

"I'm trying to trace the artifact," North said. "It's a crucial element in my investigation."

"I just told you, your father purchased it. I never saw it again after he took it out of this shop."

"Chandler Chastain was attacked a few hours after he bought that artifact from you," North said. "The relic has gone missing. That means there's a connection."

Gwendolyn bristled. "I'm sorry to hear that, but if you're implying I had something to do with the attack on Mr. Chastain—"

"No, damn it. I'm trying to get a lead."

Gwendolyn Swan was an attractive woman in her thirties, very businesslike. Her hair was pinned up in a no-nonsense twist. She watched him with undisguised wariness. He didn't take it personally.

He had learned long ago that no one in the underground market liked to start the day with a visit from someone from the Foundation.

Before entering the shop Sierra had suggested he let her handle the inquiries. He had brushed aside the offer. He was the investigator, after all. He knew what he was doing.

Swan was cooperating, but in a minimalist way. Like most dealers she was suspicious of anyone connected to the Foundation. The Rancourts had left a legacy that was proving hard to overcome. And, okay, he was probably not handling things in the most diplomatic manner. He couldn't help it. The abiding sense of urgency was riding him hard.

"I'm afraid I can't help you," Gwendolyn snapped. "I can show you the paperwork involved in the sale and I can assure you the artifact had a paranormal provenance. I picked it up at an estate auction. It was in a crate together with a lot of other low-level artifacts. Your father examined several items that came in the same shipment but the radio was the only thing he took with him."

Sierra apparently concluded there was nothing for her to do. She turned away from the counter and started to wander through the array of statues, vases and miscellaneous antiques that littered the shop floor. As far as North could tell everything looked like a reproduction or an outright fake.

Sierra had explained that everyone in the trade knew the real artifacts were downstairs in the basement of Swan's shop. That was typical of most dealers. The good stuff was always stored belowground, where the earth and sturdy construction materials, such as concrete and steel, shielded the paranormal currents and made it harder for raiders to detect the objects.

"Do you think the radio came from one of the lost labs?" North asked.

Gwendolyn shrugged. "In my professional opinion it's a possibility. But I make no guarantees when it comes to the authenticity of lost lab artifacts. Mr. Chastain understood that. The relic could have picked up some energy simply by sitting around in a collector's vault for several years."

Out of the corner of his eye North saw Sierra stop in front of a display stand that held an old twentieth-century camera. She picked it up to take a closer look.

Gwendolyn watched her with slightly narrowed eyes, as if she was afraid Sierra might try to slip it into her pack.

"Did any of your other customers show an interest in the radio?" North said.

"What?" Frowning, Gwendolyn switched her attention back to him. "No."

Her responses were growing increasingly curt. Her eyes flicked back to Sierra, who had just put the camera back on the stand.

"Interesting artifact," Sierra said, returning to the counter. She stopped next to North, almost touching him. "I'm surprised you've got it on display up here."

Gwendolyn blinked. "Why is that?"

"It's hot," Sierra said. "Feels like lost lab energy."

Gwendolyn was riveted now. "Do you think so?"

"I'm almost sure of it. If I were you I'd store it downstairs for safekeeping. You know how rumors fly in this business. The raiders wouldn't hesitate at a quick smash-and-grab operation."

Gwendolyn relaxed a little. "You're right. Thanks for the tip. I'll move it downstairs later. No sense taking chances."

North glanced at the camera and hesitated a little. Lost lab artifacts were always compelling to anyone who knew the history of the Bluestone Project. But he had a job to do.

Resolutely he turned back to Gwendolyn and opened his mouth to launch into another question. Before he could speak Sierra kicked his foot. He gave a small start of surprise and glanced at her. She ignored him.

"You mentioned you got the radio from an estate sale," she said.

Gwendolyn waved a hand. "That's right. There were several arti-facts in the collection that were far more interesting."

Once again North started to insert a question. Again Sierra abused his foot. She smiled at Gwendolyn.

"Did you ask Mr. Chastain why he wanted the artifact?" she said.

"Yes," Gwendolyn said. "I was curious because he was obviously an expert and I didn't understand why he would be so interested in it. He told me he thought it might have belonged to one of his grand-parents. I realize family heirlooms hold a sentimental appeal for those in the bloodline, but beyond that there was absolutely nothing special about that radio."

"Yet someone thought it was worth stealing from my dad," North said.

Gwendolyn sighed. "I understand your concern, Mr. Chastain. I wish I could help you but I honestly don't know anything else about the radio."

Sierra narrowed her eyes ever so slightly. "Did Mr. Chastain show interest in any of the other artifacts in your collection?"

Gwendolyn raised her brows. "Yes, he did, as a matter of fact." She shot North an icy glare and cleared her throat. "He made another purchase."

North stilled. "Why didn't you mention that?"

"Because you asked about the object he took with him when he left my shop," Gwendolyn said, a little too sweetly. "And because you were starting to annoy me."

Sierra cleared her throat. "Moving right along, please tell us about the other artifact that Mr. Chastain bought."

Gwendolyn turned back to her. "Of course. I was going to tell you anyway before you left the shop. Mr. Chastain said he intended to return to pick up the other artifact today. But he added that if he didn't come by, someone from the Foundation might show up to col-lect it."

"What happened to the other relic he bought?" North demanded.

"Your father asked me to store it in my vault until he came back for it. If you'll wait here, I'll go downstairs and get it."

North felt his pulse kick up. "We'll wait."

Gwendolyn whisked out from behind the counter and disappeared into a back room. North heard a door open and close. He knew Swan was on her way down into her basement.

Sierra looked at him. "Are you thinking the same thing I'm thinking?"

"My father knew or suspected that someone was following him," North said. "He bought two artifacts—the one he took with him was a decoy. The other one he left here at the shop until he thought it was safe to come back for it."

"Yes," Sierra said. "That sounds logical."

The door in the back room opened and closed again. Gwendolyn Swan appeared. She had a black metal rod in her hand. It was about a foot long.

"Don't ask me what this is," she said. "I suspect it was part of a machine or a tool. I asked your father why he wanted it. He said he thought you might find it interesting. Something about you having an engineer's mind."

She handed the rod to North. The instant his fingers closed around it he felt a familiar rush of recognition. He tightened his grip on it.

"Yes," he said. "I am interested in it."

Gwendolyn eyed him. "Any idea what it is?"

"You're right. It was probably part of an old lab machine. I find vintage engineering artifacts very intriguing. I collect them."

"It's all yours," Gwendolyn said.

"Is there anything else you want to tell me?" North asked.

"Nope. Now, if we're done here, I've got work to do."

Sierra smiled at Gwendolyn. "I do have one more question."

Gwendolyn tipped her head slightly. "Yes?"

"The crate of artifacts that you bought, the one that contained the radio and the metal rod, I assume it was delivered by a go-between?"

"Matt Harper," Gwendolyn said. "One of my regulars."

"Thanks," Sierra said. "By the way, I got your message. When I finish this job I will be glad to authenticate your artifact."

"Right," Gwendolyn said. "Thanks."

Sierra glanced at North. "We can go now."

He was still trying to process the information she had extracted from Swan. Now they had a name. Matt Harper.

"All right," he said.

She led the way out of the shop. North waited until they were well clear of the door before he spoke again.

"I had a few more questions," he said.

"I think Gwendolyn Swan told you the truth. She doesn't know anything else that would be useful. Our best bet now is Matt Harper."

"The go-between who transported the crate that contained the rod and the radio?"

"Right. I'll contact him. He may not know anything helpful but I think he'll talk to us—or, at least, to me."

"Why?"

"Matt owes me," Sierra said. "Among go-betweens, repaying favors is not just good karma, it's essential for staying in business. What the heck is that metal rod?"

"I have no idea," North said. "But I do know one thing for certain."

"What?"

"It belonged to my grandfather."

"Griffin Chastain?" Sierra said. "Really? You're sure of that?"

"I can feel his paranormal signature. Dad must have felt it, too. It isn't the radio that's the family heirloom. It's this relic."

"So we know it's valuable but we don't know what it is."

"No," North said. "But I'll figure it out."

"Hmm."

He looked at her. "What?"

"Griffin Chastain was a famous magician, wasn't he?"

"So?"

Sierra smiled. "It just occurred to me that the rod looks a lot like a magic wand. What do you want to do while we wait for Matt to get back to me?"

"Track down every dealer and collector here in Seattle who might have heard rumors of a recently stolen Bluestone artifact."

"That will definitely keep us busy for the rest of the day and half the night."

CHAPTER 10

Gwendolyn waited until the door closed before she came out from behind the counter and walked to the front window of the shop. She watched Chastain and Sierra leave the alley and disappear around the corner.

Satisfied her visitors were gone, she locked the door and started back toward the counter. Midway across the room she stopped to contemplate the vintage camera. She could sense the heavy energy infused into the machine. She knew it was still functional but she could not activate it.

Sierra had definitely sensed the camera's vibe but it was impossible to tell if she could figure out how to use it.

Gwendolyn went back behind her desk and picked up the old landline phone. When it came to calls to her sister, low-tech was far more secure than high-tech.

Eloisa Swan answered immediately, which indicated she was in her office at the pharmaceutical company where she was employed as a research scientist.

"Someone responded to the camera's vibe?" she asked.

If she felt free to mention the artifact it meant she was alone.

"A go-between named Sierra Raines," Gwendolyn said. "She's handled a couple of deliveries for me lately. I was going to hire her to check out the camera. She just did by accident. She's good. Smart. Honest. Reliable. I'm sure she detected the energy but I couldn't tell if she was able to resonate with it."

"What do you mean?"

"It wasn't as if I could come right out and ask her. She wasn't alone. Unfortunately she was here with a new client who happens to be from the Foundation. North Chastain."

"Shit. You've had *another* visit from someone from the Foundation? That makes, what? Three of them in the past month?"

There was a sharp note in Eloisa's voice. Gwendolyn understood. She was a little anxious, too. There had been a lot of attention from the Foundation recently. That was not good news.

A couple of weeks earlier Slater Arganbright, one of Victor Arganbright's many nephews, had arrived in Seattle on the trail of a killer. Gwendolyn had been unnerved when he had walked into her shop accompanied by Catalina Lark from the Lark & LeClair investigation agency. The pair had asked for information regarding a certain hot artifact.

She did not mind doing occasional business with the Foundation—Victor Arganbright always paid his bills—but she did not like getting entangled in a murder investigation, especially one that involved rumors of Vortex. Arganbright and Lark had closed their case without realizing how close they had come to discovering the link between Swan Antiques and Vortex, but it had been a near thing.

Now, twice within the past twenty-four hours, she had found herself dealing with two more Foundation agents, Chandler Chastain and his son, North. It was enough to make anyone with an ounce of psychic-grade intuition uneasy.

"I don't think we need to worry about the Chastains," she said.

"There is nothing to indicate they are chasing a Vortex rumor. Chandler Chastain purchased a couple of artifacts from me yesterday. He took one with him and left the other one behind. Said he'd be back for the second one. He also said that if he didn't return I was to give it to whoever came around asking questions. Evidently someone attacked Chastain last night and took the first relic. He was badly injured but not killed. North Chastain is trying to find the person responsible."

"And his first stop was your shop? That's not good."

"I did what I told his father I would do—I gave North the second artifact. Both relics are now out of my shop, and so is Chastain. Good riddance. There's no reason for me to be involved any further in the Foundation investigation."

"What kind of relics did you sell to Chandler Chastain?"

"Neither seemed important. One was a vintage radio. It may or may not have been from one of the lost labs. That's the one Chandler Chastain took with him."

"The one that was stolen?"

"Right. The second artifact was just an old metal rod. Probably a machine part. It might have come from one of the labs, but other than that there was nothing unique about it. A low-level collectible."

"You're the expert on artifacts," Eloisa said. "But if someone attacked Chandler Chastain because of that radio, I think you'd better assume it had some unique qualities."

"Maybe. But even if the radio is more interesting than it appeared to be, there's nothing to link it to the old Vortex lab or to our project. There's no reason why the Foundation should take any more interest in my shop. We need to focus on the camera."

"I agree. It's our best lead. But this princess-and-the-pea experiment of yours is not working."

"It's only been on display for a few days."

"We're wasting time, Gwen."

"It's too soon to give up the test. Sierra Raines obviously sensed the energy in the camera. If she can do that, there will be others like her."

Setting the camera out in the middle of the sales floor, where it was surrounded by fakes and reproductions, had been a tactic born of desperation. The plan was to see if one of the clients who frequented Swan Antiques responded to the device. Gwendolyn had been hopeful at first. But now she was afraid Eloisa was right. The princess-and-the-pea experiment might have to continue for a very long time before the right talent walked into the room.

Still, what choice did they have? It wasn't as if they could place an ad on one of the online sites devoted to the paranormal. *Seeking high-level talent who can figure out how to operate vintage camera. Oh, and by the way, once the artifact has been unlocked we will have to kill you.*

"I'm starting to wonder if the camera was tuned to the psychic signature of the original owner," Eloisa said, her tone very grim.

"Don't go there," Gwendolyn said. "If that's the case we've got an even bigger problem than we do now. It means the only person who can activate it is a direct descendant of the owner."

"I know," Eloisa said.

"Shit," Gwendolyn said.

There was a short silence.

"Well, on the upside, at least we know the identity of the descendant," Gwendolyn said.

"That's not exactly an upside," Eloisa said. "You're talking about taking an enormous risk."

"I agree. I'll keep the camera on the sales floor a little while longer and hope that we get lucky."

"One more thing before we hang up," Eloisa said. "Are you finished decoding the diary?"

"Almost. Just a few more pages."

"Anything new we can use?"

"I think so," Gwendolyn said. "Aurora Winston notes that she was able to overcome the last technical hurdle in tuning the weapons. Evidently the initial experiments provided proof of concept but a new problem came to light. Of the three people who were able to activate and fire the devices, two of them suffered immediate and severe blowback issues."

"What happened?"

"When you fire a conventional gun there's always a recoil," Gwendolyn said. "Apparently something similar happened when they fired the prototype Vortex weapons. But instead of a physical kickback the subjects got a shock wave of paranormal energy that disrupted their auras."

"What were the effects?"

"Both subjects were initially rendered unconscious. When they woke up they were disoriented. Hallucinating. One went insane and became paranoid. He murdered two lab techs before he could be stopped. The second one suffered a complete loss of his paranormal senses. He took his own life."

"What about the third subject?" Eloisa said. "The one who didn't suffer complications."

"Winston writes that she considered him a success for a while. She planned to conduct further research on him. But he deteriorated rapidly, slipped into a coma and died."

"Damn, damn, *damn*," Eloisa muttered. "Did Winston indicate that she considered further research useless?"

"No," Gwendolyn said. "Just the opposite. Wait until you hear how she decided to move forward."

"Talk to me, Gwen." There was renewed excitement in Eloisa's voice. The scientist in her was intrigued.

"Winston writes that the setbacks made her realize she needed an entirely different approach to the problem of weaponizing paranormal energy. She came up with a bold new theory and was starting to run some experiments when the orders came to shut down the Bluestone Project, including Vortex."

"Fortunately for us it's impossible to destroy all evidence of a government project the size and scope of Bluestone."

"Someone certainly tried," Gwendolyn said.

Most of the people associated with the old lab had died under mysterious circumstances within months after it was shut down. Aurora Winston may have been the only one who survived, and that was probably because she had managed to disappear with her young daughter, Gwendolyn and Eloisa's mother.

Aurora Winston had ended her days in an insane asylum. Gwendolyn and Eloisa had not discovered the truth about their grandmother until they found her private journal while cleaning out their mother's attic.

Gwendolyn told Eloisa about Aurora Winston's solution to the problem of weaponizing paranormal energy. When she was finished there was a lengthy silence while Eloisa processed the information.

"Brilliant," she finally whispered. She sounded genuinely awed. "Grandmother was fucking brilliant. We have to find that old lab, Gwen."

"We're getting close," Gwendolyn said. "I'm sure of it. The camera is the key."

A muffled thud reverberated through the floorboards beneath her feet. She sighed.

"Sounds like I've caught a rat in my trap," she said. "I'd better go take care of it. Talk to you soon."

"Right. Oh, and Gwen?"

"Yes?"

"Be careful."

"You, too."

Gwendolyn hung up, crossed the room and unlocked the door that led to the basement sales floor.

At the top of the stairs she paused to shut the door. The basement was illuminated in an eerie glow thanks to the large number of hot artifacts crammed together in the windowless space.

She flipped the light switch at the top of the stairs. The regular gallery lighting came up, revealing the glass and steel display cases.

She descended the stairs and made her way through the crowded space to the rattrap. Sure enough, there was a body on the floor. She did not recognize the raider.

She donned her leather apron and a pair of gloves and went through the dead man's pockets. She found a wallet. The driver's license identified the raider as one Harold Molland. The address was a town in California.

Gwendolyn looked at the four-foot-tall clockwork doll dressed in a vintage nurse's outfit, complete with perky white cap, white dress and white shoes and stockings. The doll held a syringe in one mechanical hand.

The rattrap was efficient and lethal. The nurse was stationed near the concealed tunnel. The syringe in the doll's hand was filled with a drug that stopped the heart within seconds. The trap was triggered by anyone who tried to enter the basement via the tunnel.

For the most part the local raiders avoided Swan Antiques. No one knew exactly what happened to those who attempted to steal from the shop, but it was no secret in the Pacific Northwest underworld that security on the premises was tight.

"He's not from around here," Gwendolyn said to the clockwork nurse. "That's not a good sign. It means the rumors about Vortex are spreading beyond Seattle."

The clockwork doll did not respond. Gwendolyn refilled the syringe and reset the old-fashioned spring mechanism in the platform. When it came to basic security, sometimes the old-fashioned ways were the most effective.

When she was finished she went back up the stairs, picked up the phone and dialed a familiar number. A gravelly voice answered.

"Pest Control."

"I need service as soon as possible," Gwendolyn said.

"Again? You'd think the rats would learn to avoid your place."

"I'm sure real rats would learn. But we're talking about the human variety. They aren't that smart."

CHAPTER 11

Another unstable client.

Sierra stifled a groan. *Just what I do not need.*

But a professional go-between had to overlook the minor inconveniences. She had already come to the conclusion that the vast majority of people connected to the underground market were weird in one way or another. Some were obsessive. Most were secretive and reclusive. A few were violent. And then there were the flat-out crazies. Figuring out how to handle the odd clients who came her way was a job requirement.

Still, she had never seen an aura quite like North Chastain's.

She eased the SUV to the curb and brought it to a halt. It was almost ten o'clock and the streets in the old warehouse district were mostly empty of traffic. Over the last several hours they had exhausted the rumor mill. No luck.

She pretended to adjust the big rearview mirror while she heightened her senses so that she could study the reflection of North's aura. There was plenty of power in it but there was something very disturbing going on as well. She already knew he was suffering from sleep deprivation, a factor that played havoc with even the strongest auras. But there was another, more alarming instability in the currents. It was obvious he was fighting the dissonance waves, but sooner or later he was going to lose the battle.

Not my problem, she reminded herself. *I'm just the go-between.*

She contemplated the boarded-up brick building looming in the shadows. A construction fence surrounded the three-story structure. Signs announced that the location would soon feature a new mixed-use office tower, but there was no indication the developer had begun the demolition phase.

"According to Matt's message there's an opening in the fence," she said. "He'll meet us inside the building."

North studied the darkened structure through the windshield. "Out of curiosity, how often do you do late-night meetings like this?"

"Most of my work is done at night. This isn't late. It's only just ten."

"Does it strike you that you're in a high-risk business?"

"You're a badass Foundation cleaner," she said. "Talk about high risk. Ready to do this?"

"Ready." North reached inside his jacket and took out a gun.

Startled, Sierra turned quickly in the seat. "Hey, hey, you won't be needing that. Matt is a colleague. I trust him."

"Good to know."

But North did not holster the gun. He opened his door and got out. With a small sigh, Sierra opened her own door, jumped down to the pavement and joined him on the curb.

They found the place where the wire fence had been cut and slipped cautiously into the construction site. There was enough light from the streetlamps to guide them to what had once been a service door at the side of the building.

"None of my business," Sierra said, "but don't you find those dark glasses a bit of a nuisance at night?"

"You have no idea."

The grim emotion in the words sent a chill across Sierra's senses. *Note to self: don't mention the sunglasses again.* They were clearly not a fashion statement.

Matt Harper had said that the sheet of plywood covering the old doorway opening was loose. He was right.

"I'll go first," North said.

"I'll take the lead here," Sierra said. "Matt will get nervous if he sees you with a gun."

"You told him you would have company."

"I didn't tell him the company would be armed. At least let me alert him that we're here and that you're going in first."

"All right."

North eased the plywood aside. Sierra peered around the edge of the opening and saw a faint light emanating from a doorway in the middle of a long hall. It looked like the glow of a flashlight or a camp lantern.

"Matt?" she called. "It's Sierra. I've got the man from the Foundation with me. He's got a gun but it's just a precaution. Nothing to worry about."

There was no response.

North edged her aside.

"Stay here," he ordered in a tone that indicated he expected to be obeyed.

The problem with clients was that they often got the idea that they were the ones in charge.

He moved past her into the dark hallway. She watched him glide down the corridor. He stopped just before he reached the illuminated doorway.

"Harper?" he said quietly.

Again there was no response. Sierra watched North disappear into the room.

He reappeared a moment later. "There's a man down in here.

Alive but unconscious. I assume it's Harper but you're the only one who can identify him."

"Matt." Sierra rushed forward.

North stepped aside when she arrived at the illuminated doorway. She looked around at what had once been a studio apartment and saw Matt sprawled on the floor. The flashlight he had evidently brought with him had fallen next to his outflung hand. The beam was aimed at the doorway.

She crouched beside him, stripped off her gloves, braced herself and put her fingertips to the side of his throat. She got a small jolt but she also found a reassuring beat.

"His pulse is strong," she said. "There's no sign of physical injury but he's definitely unconscious. I'll call nine-one-one."

She reached into the pocket of her jacket and took out her phone.

"Looks like whoever attacked him is long gone," North said from the doorway. He glanced back at Harper. An eerie stillness came over him. "I think he was trying to run."

Sierra was about to make the call to the emergency operator. "What?"

"Judging by the way he's lying on the floor and the position of the flashlight, it looks like he was trying to get out of here in a hurry."

"He was probably trying to get away from whoever attacked him," Sierra said.

"Yes." North left the doorway and crossed the room to pick up the flashlight. "There's some weird energy in here. Feel it?"

"Yes," she said. She looked around. "It has the vibe of an artifact. But I don't see anything."

North switched off the flashlight. With the space plunged into total darkness, Sierra became aware of a faint glow seeping out between the cracks of a cupboard door. The eerie ultraviolet radiance was clearly paranormal in nature.

"It's in there," she said quietly, and put her gloves back on.

North crossed the space and opened the cupboard door. A small, square, steel container about the size of a jewelry box sat on the top shelf. The lid was open. The strange light originated from the interior.

North reached up for the device.

"No," Sierra said. "Let me handle it. I'm the expert, remember?"

She went to the cupboard, stood on tiptoe and stretched to pick up the artifact.

The instant her gloved fingers closed around it, she knew she had made a mistake.

She leaped back and spun around. "We need to get out of here. Now."

"Yeah, I got that impression."

"We can't leave Matt," Sierra said.

"I'll handle him. Here, take the flashlight."

He tossed it to her, holstered his gun, slung Matt over his shoulders in a fireman's carry and followed her toward the doorway.

Behind them paranormal light sparked and then blazed from the box, flooding the old apartment in a senses-dazzling glare.

Halfway to the door an icy tsunami of energy swept over Sierra. The shock to her senses threatened to overwhelm her. She couldn't breathe. She could no longer move. A terrifying darkness closed in on her. She realized she was about to pass out. Frantically she struggled to rally her talent.

North was beside her now. He ripped off his sunglasses. He had Matt draped over his shoulders but he reached out with one hand to grab Sierra's arm. Another kind of shock zapped through her, a fortifying rush of heat and power.

Suddenly she could breathe again. The waves of dazzling light crashing through the small space receded. Not because of anything she was doing to hold back the tide, she realized. Some other force was at work.

North. She realized he was using his own aura to shield Matt and her from the violent energy released by whatever was inside the steel box.

"Let's go," North said.

He hauled her toward the doorway. They made it out into the hall. There was now a solid wall between them and the exploding waves of light. It absorbed a significant amount of the energy. Sierra recovered her senses.

"I'm okay," she said.

North released her arm. In the seconds it took for him to slap on his glasses she caught a glimpse of his eyes. She could not make out the color but she had no trouble perceiving the heat of paranormal energy. Whatever else he might be, North was a very strong talent.

Together they raced down the corridor and out through the service door. When they reached the jagged tear in the construction fence, Sierra pulled aside the raw wire edges so that North could get through with Matt.

She followed and then stopped and turned to survey the boarded-up building.

"I think the energy is fading," she said.

North lowered Matt to the sidewalk and looked at the apartment house.

"You're right," he said.

There was some paranormal light emanating from between the cracks in the plywood-covered windows but the glow was rapidly weakening. Within a minute or two it was no longer visible.

"What in the world just happened?" Sierra whispered.

"I think we encountered the first working example of a paranormal weapon," North said. "Some sort of grenade that exploded with currents of dark light."

"Energy from the dark end of the spectrum? But you were able to control it, at least long enough for us to get clear of the explosion zone."

"I used to have a talent for manipulating that kind of energy." North rubbed his temples. "Luckily I still have a little left."

"A little? Looked like a lot to me."

"Not for long. Never mind. There's another reason I was able to handle that light grenade."

"What?"

"I recognized the paranormal signature," North said. "Pretty sure my grandfather built it."

"Your *grandfather*?"

"Long story. No time for it now. Stay here with Harper. Call nine-one-one."

"Where are you going?"

"Back inside that building. I need to get that light grenade."

"Are you crazy?" Sierra said. "You just said you think it's some kind of explosive device."

"It is but it's no longer active, at least not right now. If I'm right, it will have to be recharged before it can be activated again."

"What makes you think that?"

"The light in that box was coming from the dark end of the spectrum," North said. "I told you, that's my area of expertise."

"Yes, but you can't be an expert on paranormal weapons. You just said that box is the first working version of one that you've come across."

"The weapon is unique," North admitted. "But I was able to resonate with it. I can handle it. Look, I know you've got a lot of questions. I can answer some of them, but now is not a good time. We need that box."

Sierra groaned. Unstable clients. Hazard of the business.

"Fine," she muttered. "Go get the box."

CHAPTER 12

It was clear Sierra had made an executive decision to trust him, at least for now. Probably because she didn't have much choice, North thought. That was not a particularly inspiring realization, but it was nothing if not logical.

"If I don't come out with the box in five minutes, call Victor Arganbright immediately," North said. "He's got a couple of agents on the ground here in Seattle. They'll take charge."

"Go for it," she said. "You've got five minutes."

"On my way."

"And, North? Be careful."

"My middle name."

"Liar."

He ignored the observation, took out his flashlight and went back through the fence. He loped to the entrance of the building, eased aside the sheet of plywood and went along the corridor. The paranormal light from the box was no longer detectable with his crystal-clouded vision.

Once again he took the chance of removing his glasses for a quick glance. The hot currents of exploding energy were definitely gone.

A ghostly image coalesced at the edges of his vision. Hastily he put on the glasses.

He went to the doorway of the little studio and stopped. There was a lot of residual heat in the room—paranormal energy hung around for a long time—but it was weak and diffuse, nothing he couldn't handle.

The metal box was still on the cupboard shelf, its lid open, but there was no perceptible energy coming from inside. North studied the container for a moment. It was just a metal box. No buttons or switches. No wires. No timer.

He reached up with both hands and took down the artifact. There was a murky, colorless crystal inside. It was about the size of his fist. It was uncut and unpolished. Nothing special to look at. But there was energy locked inside—a lot of it.

It sang to his senses.

What the hell did you build, Griffin Chastain?

He lowered the lid and latched it. Now the energy was almost undetectable. Only someone with a lot of talent would sense it.

He did a quick circuit of the apartment, checking to see if he had overlooked anything that might tell him who had set the light grenade. There was nothing to find. Maybe Matt Harper would be able to provide some useful information.

North went back down the hall and slipped through the rip in the chain-link fence.

Harper was on his feet, leaning against the fender of Sierra's SUV. He looked exhausted and dazed.

"Did he wake up on his own?" North asked.

"Yes," Sierra said. "As far as I can tell he wasn't injured, but something rendered him unconscious for a while. He can't remember exactly what happened, though."

"I'll be fine," Matt growled. He glanced at the box North was holding. "Bad burn from that artifact, I guess."

"You touched it?" North asked.

"I—" Matt stopped, looking confused. He shook his head. "I don't remember touching it. But I'm sure I saw it."

"What happened here tonight?" North said.

"Beats me." Matt scrubbed his face with one hand. "I remember parking the car around the corner and going through the fence. I went inside to wait for you two. Everything after that is just—gone. It's like I went to sleep or something. The next thing I knew I was waking up out here."

"You don't remember seeing anyone after you left your car?" North asked.

"No," Matt said. He frowned. "At least I don't think so."

North said, "Where were you before you got into your car to drive here?"

Matt brightened a little, evidently relieved to be able to pull up some clear memories. "I had a couple of beers and a hamburger at a club in Pioneer Square. It's a place where some of the other go-betweens hang out."

"The Vault," Sierra said.

Matt nodded. "Right. I talked to a guy there for a while but that's it."

"Most of the customers are regulars," Sierra said. "Did you chat with someone you know?"

Matt hesitated and then shook his head. "No, I didn't know him."

"Someone in our business?" Sierra asked.

"Not a go-between like us," Matt said. "Figured him for a new dealer or a collector at first but then I wondered if he was just a Puppet. You know how it is. Occasionally some of them find their way to the Vault."

"Did you tell him you were meeting us tonight?" North asked.

Matt was deeply offended. "Hell, no. I knew you wanted to keep a low profile. I would never discuss business with a stranger, especially one who was a possible Puppet. But—"

"What?" Sierra asked gently.

Matt's face twisted in concentration. "Shit. I can't remember exactly what I said."

Sierra took a breath. "I might be able to help you recover your memories."

"Yeah?" Matt looked dubious but a little hopeful. "Like with hypnosis or something?"

"Just the opposite," Sierra said. "I think someone hypnotized you. I want to try to pull you out of the trance so that you can get access to all of your memories. You'll be fully aware of what I'm doing. You can stop me at any point if you're uncomfortable with the process."

North looked at Sierra but he did not ask any questions. They needed answers and she seemed to think she could get some. That was all that mattered.

"Okay, I guess," Matt said.

Sierra stripped off one leather glove, reached inside her jacket and pulled out a small black locket. When she flipped it open the streetlamp glinted on a reflective surface. A mirror, North thought, or a crystal polished to mirror-brightness. He was intrigued. The paranormal physics of mirrors and crystals that worked like mirrors were still very much a mystery as far as the experts were concerned.

Sierra cupped the locket in one hand and aimed it at Matt. North felt energy shiver in the atmosphere. He knew she had just heightened her talent.

"Matt, you talked to someone at the Vault tonight who was not a regular," she said calmly. "Do you know his name?"

Matt blinked a couple of times. Then his expression cleared. "No.

Never saw him before. Like I said, I figured him for a collector or a Puppet. Real intense."

"What did he say to you?" Sierra continued.

"He told me he'd heard I had handled the Pitchford auction delivery. He asked me if anyone had contacted me about it. I didn't let on I'd heard from you, of course. At least, I didn't intend to tell him. But I think . . . I think I said something about our meeting tonight. Damn it. I don't know why I talked about it. You know me, I'm careful when it comes to that kind of thing. Hell, I'm sorry, Sierra. I must have been drunk."

"No," Sierra said, her tone calm and reassuring. "Your aura shows some indications that you were drugged. Can you describe the man you talked to?"

"I didn't get a close look at him. You know how dark it is inside the Vault. I'd put him in his midthirties. He was wearing a dark jacket. And a baseball cap. Dark glasses."

"Dark glasses?" Sierra repeated. "Like those that Mr. Chastain is wearing?"

"Nah. Not the fancy kind. Just regular dark glasses. I think he was trying to hide his eyes so I couldn't get a good look at him. He had a weird vibe, I can tell you that. It's one of the reasons I figured him for a collector or a Puppet. They're all obsessed and paranoid as hell."

"What about his hair?" Sierra said. "Do you remember the color?"

Matt shrugged. "Light brown, I think. Couldn't see much of it because of the baseball cap. Sorry, that's about it."

"You don't remember anything else unusual about him?" Sierra prompted. "His shoes?"

"Didn't notice his shoes. He put me in mind of a professor or a scientist. A doctor, maybe." Matt stiffened abruptly. "The bastard followed me here. He wasn't alone."

"Are you certain?" Sierra asked.

"Positive," Matt said, growing angrier by the second. "I remember going through the fence and into the apartment house. I heard a noise out in the hall. The next thing I knew, the professor guy was standing in the doorway. He was carrying a briefcase. There were a couple of big men with him. Tattoos-and-steroid types."

"Muscle?" North asked.

Matt grunted. "Definitely."

"Can you describe them?" Sierra asked.

"Aside from their size and the tats, not really. It wasn't like I had a chance to take a photo. One of them had this strange flashlight-shaped artifact. I remember it was transparent. Must have been made of crystal. He aimed it at me and switched it on. There was a beam of light, but it wasn't normal light. It was like looking into a prism, or maybe a kaleidoscope. Lots of colors. I couldn't look away. I could feel it closing down my senses but I couldn't do anything about it."

"Light from the paranormal spectrum," North said.

"Yeah," Matt said. He shuddered. "Never seen anything like it. I went down to my knees."

"What happened next?" Sierra asked.

"The guy in charge, the one who looked like a doctor or a scientist, yelled at the man with the flashlight gun. Told him to shut it off because it wasn't reliable. Then he took out a syringe and injected something into my arm. Told me I was going to go to sleep and probably wouldn't wake up. But if something went wrong and I did survive, I wouldn't remember anything about him or his men or what had happened."

North held up the steel container so that Matt could see it. "Do you remember this?"

Matt peered at the container. "The doctor handed the briefcase to one of the muscle guys and told him to take that thing out of the case and put it in the cupboard. Then he told the guy to open the lid. Warned him to be careful because it was now set and would explode the next time someone with a lot of talent touched it. You should be careful with that thing. There's some energy in it. I can sense it. It's hot enough to be a lab artifact."

"Yes, it is," North said.

Matt turned back to Sierra. "That's it. I don't remember anything else after that until I woke up out here."

CHAPTER 13

Sierra opened the door of the SUV and jumped up behind the wheel. North got in on the passenger's side. They buckled their seat belts while they watched Matt drive away from the construction site.

Time was running out, Sierra thought. They had to keep moving. But North was about to collapse from exhaustion. She did not mention that fact, however. She was pretty sure he would deny it.

"What's next?" she said instead.

"I'll call Victor." North pulled out a cell phone. "Bring him up to date. Then we need to go back to the Vault and see if we can get a lead on the man who met with Harper tonight."

"Okay. The security people at the Vault should be able to tell us a few things." Sierra glanced at the metal box that North was holding in both hands. "Do you think that artifact is still dangerous?"

"No, not in its current state. There's a crystal inside. I don't know what kind. There's still plenty of energy in it, but it's not focused or channeled. It feels like a battery that needs to be recharged or an engine that requires fuel."

She caught her breath. "Do you know how to recharge it?"

"Maybe. I've got a crystal back home that I might be able to use to get this device up and running. But now isn't the time for experiments. We need to keep moving here in Seattle. Let's head for the Vault."

"Right."

Sierra put the SUV in gear and pulled away from the curb. She drove to the alley entrance of the Vault and handed the keys to Brick.

"We won't be staying long," she said. "Just need to ask security about one of the customers who came here tonight."

"Take your time," Brick said.

He opened the rear door of the club. Sierra led the way inside. North followed.

Fifteen minutes later they were back in the SUV.

"That was a waste of time," she said, firing up the engine.

"Not entirely," North said. "We learned a few things about the guy with the briefcase."

"Just that he claimed to be a collector who was trying to arrange for a delivery," Sierra said.

"We also learned that he's new in town, or at least new at the Vault," North pointed out. "And we got a name and an address. Raymond Waddell from Portland, Oregon."

"Twenty bucks says the name and the address are fake."

"I'm sure you're right, but it's something to give to Victor and Lucas. Guys who go to the trouble of paying for fake IDs usually use them more than once. Lucas will run Waddell through the Foundation database. We may get lucky."

"All right."

"You and I need to keep moving," North said.

Sierra decided she'd had enough.

"What you need," she said evenly, "is sleep."

He rubbed his eyes. "Maybe a twenty-minute nap."

"A nap isn't going to cut it. You're suffering from severe sleep deprivation, North. The only reason you haven't collapsed is because you're pulling on your paranormal senses. You're strong, so you've been getting away with that strategy. But your psychic vibe won't keep you going much longer."

"It's my problem. I know what I'm doing. I've been getting by with the naps for a few weeks."

"You burned a lot of energy tonight protecting us from the light grenade. If you don't get the rest you need, you'll drop. That might come at a really awkward moment for both of us."

"Define 'awkward.'"

"Say we encounter another light grenade or that flashlight gun that Matt described," Sierra said. "If anything like that happens again, you won't have the energy left to protect us."

North did not respond. He just sat quietly, staring through the windshield. At least he was listening. She decided to keep talking.

"Maybe the lack of sleep was your problem before you became a client," she said. "But I'm working with you now. That means your problems are now mine. Trust me, if you keep drawing on your senses you're going to crash."

"You don't understand," North said. "I'm not refusing to sleep. I'm trying to tell you that I can't sleep. Not for more than a few minutes at a time. I'm not wearing these damned glasses because they are a fashion statement."

"I see." She gripped the steering wheel and took a deep breath. "What happened to you?"

"We're in this together, so you deserve to know the facts. I'm going psi-blind. Losing my talent."

"Oh, shit. I'm so sorry."

"I don't have time for the sympathy."

"I understand. Was there an accident of some kind?"

"No. I started having problems with my talent a few weeks ago. The situation has been deteriorating. The doctors don't know what's going on. The assumption is that I may have encountered some unknown radiation on one of my jobs that affected my night vision talent. Whatever the case, the medics are not hopeful."

"I see. And the glasses?"

North smiled a cold smile. "The glasses are supposed to keep me sane."

"What are you talking about?"

"If I take them off for more than a minute or two I start hallucinating. The lab techs came up with these glasses. They've got special crystal lenses that keep me from seeing things that aren't there. They work, but when I'm wearing them I can't access what's left of my vision talent. Soon, that won't matter, because it's fading anyway."

"Will you still have your basic senses? Intuition? Your ability to detect paranormal energy?"

"Maybe. If I'm lucky. Nobody knows. Right now, it doesn't matter. I've got a job to do."

"*We've* got a job to do." She pulled away from the curb. "And you're not going to be of much use until you get some sleep."

"Where the hell do you think you're going?"

"Back to my place so you can sleep."

"I can nap in the car."

"What's the point? It's not like we've got any more clues to follow up on at the moment. Phone Las Vegas. Give them the information we just got about the guy with the briefcase, Waddell. Let Arganbright and Lucas Pine do their thing while you sleep."

For a moment she thought he was going to argue. Instead North took out his phone and called Las Vegas. By the time he was finished she was pulling into the garage of her apartment tower.

She shut down the engine and unclipped her seat belt. Automatically she checked the SUV's oversized mirrors. No auras flashed in the glass. She started to open her door but a thought made her pause.

"It occurs to me that everything about this situation involves paranormal light, specifically the kind that you can handle," she said.

"I've got my grandfather's talent," North said. "My dad has it, too, but he got a slightly different version."

"No two talents are exactly identical."

"No, but psychic signatures tend to be passed down through the bloodline."

"That's what your father sensed when he picked up that metal rod."

"Yes. And what I sensed in this light grenade."

"Hmm."

North looked at her. The cold garage lights glittered on his mirrored glasses.

"What?" he said.

"Call me a conspiracy theorist, but it occurs to me that the fact that you started losing your talent a few weeks ago, not long before your father picked up that artifact that carries your grandfather's signature, is one heck of a coincidence. And now, tonight, we nearly got burned by a light grenade that also carries your grandfather's psychic DNA."

North sat silently for a time.

"I'm open to conspiracy theories," he said finally. "Got one?"

"No. Just looking at what appear to be a couple of themes."

"Paranormal light," North said, "and Griffin Chastain's psychic signature."

"Right."

"There's something you probably don't know about my grandfather. He worked on the Bluestone Project. He was assigned to the Fogg Lake lab. He disappeared shortly after my father was born. There were rumors at the time that he betrayed his country. That he sold secrets to the old Soviet Union. The general assumption was that he either disappeared behind the Iron Curtain or was murdered by the spy who recruited him."

"What does your family think?"

"We think he was murdered, but not by a Cold War spy. Our theory is his research partner killed him."

"Why?"

"Because the partner wanted to steal the devices he and Griffin Chastain had developed," North said. "Devices like this light grenade. And maybe that crystal gun Matt Harper described. I wonder if that was what was used on Dad."

"Are you telling me your grandfather and his partner were working on paranormal weapons?"

North looked down at the light grenade he cradled in his hands. "Apparently."

"And now, after all these years, some of those weapons are starting to surface. Who was Griffin Chastain's research partner?"

"Crocker Rancourt."

Sierra gripped the steering wheel, startled. "You're kidding."

"No."

"Crocker Rancourt established the Foundation. His son, Stenson Rancourt, took over after Crocker died. My parents told me that Stenson's son, Harlan, was set to inherit the operation. The Rancourts were like a mob family."

"Victor Arganbright and Lucas Pine changed all that," North said mildly.

"So they claim," Sierra said. She paused. "How long was Crocker in charge?"

"Only a few years," North said. "He died relatively young. Heart attack. Stenson Rancourt took over after that. He ran it for decades. It was no secret he was grooming Harlan to take his place eventually."

"Five years ago Stenson and Harlan Rancourt died in an explosion at the old headquarters of the Foundation, right? So there are no Rancourts left."

North was silent for a long, thoughtful moment. He seemed to be contemplating the concrete wall in front of the SUV.

"What?" Sierra asked.

"There is a rather significant detail about the explosion that killed Stenson and Harlan," North said. "Only one body was found in the wreckage. Stenson's."

"They didn't find Harlan's body?" Sierra asked, shocked. "I never heard that."

"Victor Arganbright and Lucas Pine thought it best to keep the information quiet. They did not want to launch any new conspiracy theories. The Foundation has enough of those circulating at any given moment. Besides, the reality is that for the past five years there has been no evidence that Harlan Rancourt made it out of the blast zone."

"This is getting creepier by the minute," Sierra said.

"Want out?"

"That's not an option."

"Why not?"

"Because someone tried to murder my friend Matt Harper tonight. Matt was in harm's way because of me. The would-be killer tried to murder me as well, and one of my clients."

"Me."

"Yes," she said. "I need my clients. They are paying for this car and my apartment."

"Always nice to know one has a purpose in life."

She ignored that. "The three of us were intended to die in a blast of paranormal energy that would have left no traces of foul play, no clues that might make the Seattle police launch a homicide investigation."

"True," North said.

"Well, I take that sort of thing personally. I've got a reputation to protect. For a go-between, reputation is everything. That means we're in this together. But first you need sleep."

"A nap."

"I think I can make sure you get more than a nap."

"The same way you made Harper remember the man he met at the Vault?"

"Sort of like that, yes."

"*Sort of* like that?"

"Well, obviously you would go to sleep, assuming I do my job right. Matt, on the other hand, was wide-awake during the whole process. But with a couple of tweaks I could have made him sleep."

North was silent for a moment. When he finally spoke he sounded thoughtful. Intrigued, maybe. Curious.

"Are you a psychic hypnotist?"

"No. I can use my locket to make someone go to sleep or faint, but that's about it. In the grand scheme of things it's a pretty minor talent. I can't even see auras unless I've got a mirror or some other reflective surface handy."

"You see just the *reflections* of auras?"

"Yeah. The only real talent I've got is the ability to pick up the psychic energy laid down in an object or an artifact. That's why I thought I might be able to make it in the auction house world. I could tell the real antiques from the fakes and the reproductions. But that job didn't go well."

"I read something about it in your file."

"I'll bet you did. I'm amazed you came looking for me."

"Ambrose Jones assured Victor Arganbright that you were the best when it came to tracking artifacts."

"And that's what you needed," Sierra said. "A tracker."

He glanced at her. "I need your skills and your knowledge of the artifacts market here in the Pacific Northwest."

"That's what you're paying for, and that's what you're getting."

She opened the door and got out of the SUV.

CHAPTER 14

North walked into the apartment and stopped cold at the sight of the Zen-like decor. In spite of the harrowing events of the evening and his uncertainty about the wisdom of letting Sierra experiment with his aura, he almost smiled.

"Let me take a wild guess," he said. "You're into the minimalist style."

The small sofa, reading chair and coffee table were simple and utilitarian. The floors were some sort of high-tech gray laminate that looked like real wood. Everything else was white or gray. It all added up to a look that was about as opposite from the Abyss as it was possible to get. The only items that struck a familiar chord were the mirrors on the walls. There were a lot of them.

"Not really." Sierra took off her jacket and hung it up in the small coat closet. "But it turns out minimalism happens naturally when you're on a tight budget."

"Not necessarily." He set his pack on the floor and shrugged out of his jacket. "If I had to furnish a place, budget or no budget, I'd end up with a mishmash of stuff."

"Did someone else decorate your apartment or condo?"

"It's a house. A big one. My grandfather built it decades ago. Before he got recruited into the Bluestone Project, Griffin Chastain was a professional magician in Vegas. I sort of inherited his mansion because no one else wanted it and no real estate agent could sell it. My mother calls the decor mid-century-Vegas-over-the-top."

"What's the house like?"

"Hard to describe. Half of it is hidden behind secret doors and walls. Griffin called the place the Abyss. It was named after his most impressive stage trick. But he had a serious hobby on the side. He was obsessed with trying to harness paranormal energy. The Abyss is part laboratory, part workshop and part ongoing crystal light experiment."

"I assume it was his engineering hobby that brought him to the attention of the Bluestone recruiters?"

"Right. They needed people who had an intuitive grasp of paranormal light energy and the ability to work with it."

"Why didn't the Abyss ever sell?" Sierra asked. "Sounds like a property that would have a lot of appeal in a place like Las Vegas."

"The problem is that my father and I are the only ones who can operate any part of the Abyss. All the technology was tuned to Griffin's psychic signature."

"Which you and your dad inherited."

"Dad can manipulate the crystal tech inside the house but he's not particularly interested in it. As far as he's concerned it's all linked to the past and the rumors that Griffin sold secrets to the enemy. Dad would prefer to bury the family history."

"Understandable," Sierra said. "But now your family history is resonating down into the present."

"Looks like it."

"We can worry about that later." Sierra sat down on a small bench, took off her boots and put on a pair of house slippers. She glanced at a nearby mirror. "Time for you to get some real sleep. I'm not kidding, North. You are on the verge of crashing."

He realized she had just viewed his aura in the mirror. A strange tension gripped him.

"What did you see just now?" he asked.

She did not pretend she didn't know what he was talking about.

"You're strong but unstable, possibly from severe sleep deprivation."

He looked at himself in the mirror. "Are you sure the instability is from lack of sleep?"

"Some of it is."

She did not elaborate. That told him all he needed to know. She could see the bad vibe in his aura.

He realized he was probably expected to remove his shoes. He sat down and took off the low desert boots. He didn't travel with house slippers. That meant he was left in his socks.

"Do you mind if I have something to eat before you run your sleep experiment on me?" he said. "I'm really hungry."

"I'm not surprised, considering how much energy you've been burning lately." She gestured toward the dining counter that framed half of the small kitchen. "Have a seat."

He sat down on a stool. To his surprise the first thing she did was take a bottle of red wine out of the refrigerator. She poured a glass and set it in front of him.

"Sorry, it's cold," she said. "We don't have time to let it get properly warmed up, but it will do the job."

"I'm not feeling particular at the moment." He drank some of the wine. He was no expert but it tasted good.

In a series of smooth, almost choreographed moves Sierra opened the refrigerator and took out some butter and a covered bowl that appeared to be filled with soup or stew. She set the bowl in the microwave and hit the start button. In the next fluid motion she pulled a bread knife from a drawer and put a baguette on a cutting board.

It dawned on him that he couldn't take his eyes off her. Well, no, not exactly. He could take his eyes off her; he just didn't want to look away. He liked watching her move around the kitchen. She just sort of flowed, every motion deceptively smooth and controlled.

"Were you by any chance a professional dancer?" he asked.

She paused in the act of opening a cupboard door and gave him a surprised look. "No. Why do you ask?"

"Just something about the way you move," he said. He drank some more of the wine. "Martial arts?"

"Tai chi. My parents use it as a form of moving meditation. I've been practicing it since I was a kid."

He understood. "To help control your talent."

She buttered the bread. "You?"

"A form of karate. Same reason."

"Control."

"Uh-huh."

She studied him for a long moment. A whisper of energy—her energy—feathered his senses. It was the equivalent of feeling her fingertips on the back of his neck. It sent an exciting little thrill through him but it also made him realize how exhausted he was. Even if she was interested in having sex with him, he doubted that he could last more than five minutes in bed.

The last thing he should be thinking about at the moment was sex. Luckily Sierra appeared oblivious.

"Do you really believe that if you don't wear those glasses you might go insane?" she asked.

She sounded doubtful.

"My talent is apparently decaying rapidly. When I take off my glasses for even a minute or two I start hallucinating. What the Halcyon doctors told me is that every time I remove the damned glasses I run the risk of getting trapped in a dreamworld filled with hallucinations."

"Will you have to wear those glasses for the rest of your life?"

"The doctors aren't sure but they think that once my night vision talent has deteriorated to nothing I may be able to get by without the glasses." He paused. "They also told me it probably won't be too much longer before I get to test that theory."

"Because your talent is disappearing so quickly?"

"Right. Once it's gone, it's gone. I shouldn't have to worry about the ghosts."

"What ghosts?" Sierra asked.

"When I do take off my glasses these days I see fog and vague images that look like they walked out of a dreamscape. I think of them as dream ghosts."

"Huh."

"What?"

She glanced at a nearby mirror again. "Your aura still looks strong. Powerful."

"I'm not *dying*," he said, irritated. "I'm losing my vision talent."

"Why are you afraid to sleep?"

"Two reasons," he said. "Every time I try to sleep I walk right into the same dreamscape. I see an abyss—a real one, not Griffin's mansion. I'm afraid that if I fall into it I won't be able to wake up from the dream."

"And the second reason?"

He reached up to touch the mirrored glasses. "I'm afraid these will somehow fall off. If they do, I'll probably wake up totally psi-blind. Maybe worse."

She nodded. "You're afraid you'll wake up trapped in a nightmare of hallucinations."

"Something like that, yeah."

"Tell you what," Sierra said. "I'll check on you every half hour tonight. If your aura shows any indications that you are in a nightmare I'll wake you up immediately. Same goes for your glasses. If they come off for some reason I'll put them back on."

"If you do that you won't get much sleep yourself."

"I'll get by on naps, same as you've been doing. I can handle one night of bad sleep."

He realized he wanted desperately to believe her. He did need some decent sleep.

The microwave beeped. Sierra opened the door and took out the bowl. The fragrance acted like a tonic on his senses.

"What is it?" he asked

"Artichoke and mushroom soup. I made it yesterday. You're eating leftovers, I'm afraid."

She pulled out a small grater, took some Parmesan out of the refrigerator and proceeded to grate a thick pile of the cheese on top of the soup. She set the bowl in front of him and handed him a plate with the buttered bread on it.

He looked at the meal. "I don't think I've ever had artichoke soup."

"First time for everything. Eat."

After the first bite, he concluded the soup, the bread and the glass of wine constituted the best meal he had eaten in a very long time. When it was finished he helped her clean up the kitchen. He knew he was getting in her way more than actually assisting, but it was the principle of the thing. His mother would have been horrified if he hadn't at least tried to help.

A short time later she hung the dish towel on a rack and looked at him.

"Ready to get some real sleep?" she asked.

He propped one shoulder against the refrigerator door and crossed his arms. "You're sure you can guarantee that I won't wake up in a nightmare?"

"There are no guarantees in life. But hey, you're a badass cleaner from Las Vegas. You thrive on risk."

"Not so much these days."

"Take a chance on me, partner."

He shook his head. "Sierra, I don't think this is a good idea. A nap, maybe."

"Listen up, Chastain. It's not like we have a choice."

She was right. He could sense the shadows tugging at him. Dealing with the light grenade had pushed him too close to the edge. His intuition told him that it would be better to go down while he still had some control.

"All right," he said. He uncrossed his arms and pushed himself away from the refrigerator. "I'll try sleeping on the sofa."

"No, it's too small. Take my bed."

"I can't—"

"My bed, North. Please. We do not have time to argue about this."

She turned and led the way out of the kitchen and down the hall to the bedroom. She did not turn on the light.

He followed because he couldn't think of anything else to do. Now that he had made the decision, he could no longer muster the energy required to push back the need to sleep.

He stopped in the doorway. In the shadows he could see that the down comforter, the quilt and the pillowcases were white. The walls were white. The lampshade was white. The wood-grain flooring was bare. The pristine room looked like a cross between the cell of a cloistered nun and a meditation chamber. He felt too big and way too grimy to sleep in such a room.

"I need a shower," he said.

"Later."

"I'll get your quilt dirty."

"Is that what's bothering you?"

"Well, yeah."

"Fine." She opened a closet and took out a folded white sheet. She flipped it open and spread it across the bed so that it covered the quilt and the pillows. "There. I can wash the sheet later."

He gave up and sat down on the edge of the bed. So tired. He tried again to fend off the long shadows of the abyss, but somewhere along the line he had lost the will to fight.

Because you trust her? Yes.

"Look at me, North," Sierra said.

He glanced up and saw that she had opened the locket she wore around her neck. The mirrored crystal inside glinted in the low light. Energy whispered in the atmosphere. The crystal brightened with an eerie paranormal radiance. He did not want to look away.

He sank back onto the pillows.

"You're going to sleep now," she said.

The darkness took him before he could decide if he should be worried.

CHAPTER 15

The word on the street was that the rogue doctor in charge of the experimental lab at Riverview was in town and he was looking for her.

Marge was frightened, so terrified that she had not dared to spend the night in one of the shelters. Instead she had hidden in the stairwell of a parking garage. It had been cold but at least she had been out of the rain.

She hadn't slept. She had stayed awake not just to keep watch for Delbridge Loring but to protect herself from the assholes who prowled the streets at night looking to rob and assault people like her. She had remained awake and alert for another reason, too. She needed to think; she needed a plan. Somewhere during the night she had made her decision.

At five o'clock last night she had huddled in a doorway and watched the line form outside the All Are Welcome shelter. The folks who worked there were very nice but they didn't know about Riverview. Dr. Loring was real slick. If he came around asking about her they would probably tell him she was a regular. They'd think they were doing her a favor.

During the afternoon she had picked up the rumor that someone was searching for her. A man who claimed to be a doctor was going around to the places that provided services to street people. He told the staff he was looking for his long-lost aunt; said he had heard she was living on the streets of Seattle. He claimed he wanted to find her and take her home where she could be properly cared for. He said she was delusional because she believed she could see human auras.

Most of it was a lie, of course. She had no family. But one bit was true—she could see the energy that radiated around people.

That evening she had wanted to join the line of people waiting for the doors to open. She was hungry and it was tuna fish casserole day. The All Are Welcome staff did the best tuna fish casserole in the city.

She had almost convinced herself she could take the risk of entering the shelter when the fancy silver-gray car pulled up to the curb and stopped.

Loring had climbed out from behind the wheel. He was wearing a jacket, dark glasses and a baseball cap, not his white lab coat, but she would have recognized him and his powerful aura anywhere.

Terrified that he might notice her in the doorway, she had pressed herself against the wall and looked down at her feet so that he would not catch her eye. Even regular people who lacked the second sight could sense when they were being watched. Loring was not a regular person. He was one of the monsters.

When he had disappeared inside the shelter she had known she was in serious danger. Someone would tell him that a street lady named Marge who matched her description always showed up on tuna fish casserole day.

She had grabbed the handle of the wheeled suitcase that held all her worldly possessions and lurched out of the doorway. She had managed to slip into the garage behind a car that had disobeyed the big sign instructing drivers to wait until the security gate had closed. Once inside it had been a simple matter to hide in the stairwell.

A couple of weeks back a man from the Foundation, Slater Arganbright, had given her a card. He'd told her that if she ever felt threatened by someone from Riverview she was supposed to call the number on the card.

She had escaped from Riverview a couple of months ago and she had been doing okay on the streets of Seattle ever since. Her ability to see auras made it possible for her to avoid the real crazies and the monsters. But she lived in fear that Delbridge Loring and the clones who worked for him would track her down, kidnap her and take her back to the locked ward at Riverview. If that happened they would shoot her full of drugs again. She didn't think she could survive any more of their damned experiments.

At dawn, one thing had become crystal clear. It was time to call Las Vegas.

She waited until one of the day shelters opened at six thirty. It was a nice place that offered coffee and doughnuts. It also provided a telephone.

She called the number on the card. A man with a deep, reassuring voice answered on the first ring.

"This is Lucas Pine," he said.

Marge gripped the phone very tightly. "My name is Marge. From Seattle. A man named Arganbright gave me this number a while back. He said I was supposed to call you if the damned doctor or his clones from Riverview came looking for me. Well, the monster is here so I'm calling."

"Hang on, Marge. I think you should talk to Victor Arganbright."

A couple of beats later another man came on the line. He didn't sound as warm and polite as the one called Pine. Victor Arganbright was gruff but not mean. His voice was that of a man with a lot on his mind.

"This is Arganbright."

"My name is Marge—"

"I know who you are, Marge. My nephew Slater told me about you. You gave him and Catalina Lark a lot of help a couple of weeks ago. The Foundation is very grateful to you. First things first. Are you in immediate danger?"

"I'm okay for now. I'm in a shelter but I can't stay here long. Someone from Riverview is looking for me. His name is Delbridge Loring." Marge lowered her voice. "He's one of the monsters."

"Tell me about him," Victor said.

"He runs the experiments at Riverview. He sends the clones to find people like me, people living on the street. Folks who can see things, understand?"

"People who can see auras, yes, I understand. He targets those who won't be noticed if they just disappear."

"Exactly." A wave of relief swept over Marge. Victor Arganbright got it. "Always figured Loring might try to find me. He knows I could spill the beans about what he's up to there at Riverview. But here's the strange part—he didn't send the clones after me. He's here in town himself. What does that tell you?"

"It tells me that you may know more than you realize," Victor said. "The first step is to make sure you're safe. If it's okay with you, I'm going to send some people I trust to pick you up and take you to Fogg Lake. At the moment it's the most secure place I can think of. Do you know it?"

"Sure. I know some real nice folks who grew up there."

"Catalina Lark and Olivia LeClair?"

"Yep."

"There's a team of cleaners protecting Fogg Lake while the Foundation experts chart what's left of the old government lab there. No one gets into town unless they have been cleared by the Foundation or one of the locals. In Fogg Lake everybody knows everybody else. Strangers stand out."

"Those people in Fogg Lake," Marge said. "Are they okay with people like me?"

Victor snorted softly. "Trust me, in Fogg Lake, everyone is comfortable with people who see auras. Tell me where you are. I'll have Olivia LeClair and a couple of cleaners there within fifteen minutes."

"Okay. Thanks. I figure the Foundation is the only outfit that can handle Loring and Garraway and those damned clones. Tough bunch there at Riverview."

"I understand," Victor said. "Fifteen minutes. If Olivia is not with the people who come to pick you up, stay inside. Don't leave the shelter. Call me back immediately."

"Got it," Marge said.

CHAPTER 16

Victor ended the call to Marge and phoned Olivia LeClair. She was eating breakfast in her apartment.

"Someone from Riverview is trying to grab Marge?" Olivia said. "She'll be terrified. Getting sent back to the hospital is her worst nightmare. I know where that shelter is located. I'm on my way."

"I'll have the team that's stationed in Seattle meet you at the shelter. They will drive Marge to Fogg Lake."

"I'll be in touch as soon I know Marge is safe and on her way to Fogg Lake with the cleaners." Olivia paused. "You're worried about this doctor from Riverview, aren't you?"

"Got a bad feeling about him. Why would a doctor personally take the time and effort to search the shelters for a harmless woman like Marge?"

"Good question," Olivia said. "I'm with you. It doesn't sound right."

Victor ended the call and looked at Lucas. "Did you get all that?"

Lucas had two mugs of coffee in his hands. He set one of the mugs down on the table in front of Victor.

"Sounded like Marge, the street lady who helped Slater and Catalina track down those kidnappers a while back, believes she's in danger."

"According to Catalina, Marge was held involuntarily at the River-view Psychiatric Hospital for several months. The hospital is over on the coast. Marge escaped. Last night she picked up rumors that some-one was looking for her. She says she spotted him yesterday. His name is Loring. Evidently he was the doctor in charge of her case while she was at Riverview. Marge is terrified of him. Says he used her as a research subject for his experiments."

"I did a routine check on Riverview after Slater told us about Marge. The place appears to be a legitimate private psychiatric insti-tution. Given her aura talent, it's not surprising the staff at Riverview would have concluded she was delusional. Most doctors would have come to the same diagnosis."

Victor grunted. "Technically speaking, she is delusional. She's concocted a conspiracy theory that explains her time at Riverview. She thinks the hospital staff kidnap people like her off the streets, lock them up in Riverview and do experiments on them. Says the whole operation is run by extraterrestrials who are planning to in-vade Earth."

Lucas drank some coffee while he considered that. "The staff was probably using drugs to try to cure what they considered her delu-sions. But she's hardly a risk to herself or others. And she went missing a couple of months ago. Why would someone go looking for her now?"

"Shortly after Chandler Chastain is attacked because of an arti-fact," Victor said. "It's a coincidence, and you know how I feel about those. Take another look at Riverview, particularly a doctor who works there named Delbridge Loring."

"Do you have a theory?"

Victor contemplated one of the Oracle paintings. All the pictures he had collected over the years had an eerie, ominous quality, suited to the subject. But this one never failed to raise the hair on the back of his neck. He had picked it up for just a few dollars at an auction. It wasn't what anyone would call high art, but he was sure it was the most important painting in his collection.

Unlike many of the images on the walls of his office, it was a relatively modern work—mid-twentieth century. The Oracle was dressed in the traditional flowing white robes, a hood pulled up over her hair, obscuring her features. She was surrounded by a group of anxious onlookers, who appeared to realize that she was about to deliver a terrifying prophecy. But that was as far as the similarities with the classical pictures went.

The setting of the painting was not a cavern. It was a vintage twentieth-century laboratory. The uniforms, lab coats and eyeglasses worn by those gathered around the Oracle were clearly in the style of the late 1950s or early 1960s. But the most arresting aspect of the picture was the wealth of detail the artist had inserted into the scene.

Just as the Old Masters had used classical iconography to make certain the viewer understood the story the artist was depicting, whoever had painted the mid-twentieth-century Oracle scene had added symbolic elements that made it obvious the setting was one of the lost labs.

Victor recognized that much of the equipment and many of the instruments were standard-issue, clunky-looking mid-twentieth-century technology, but much of it had been radically modified. A chart on the wall was labeled *Paranormal Light Spectrum.* The logbook on a workbench was titled *Determining Resonance of Waves Produced by Crystals with Paranormal Properties.*

The most disturbing element in the scene, however, was a pyramid-shaped structure composed of glowing crystals. The pyramid was large enough to accommodate one individual. There was a door. In the picture the door stood open, revealing an interior that was lit with ominous energy. It was obvious that something very dangerous was about to emerge.

Victor was convinced the picture was an artist's rendering of one of the lost labs—the only such image he had ever found. The details in it made him certain it had been done from a sketch or a photograph, or quite possibly from memory. The Oracle's prophecy was written in elaborate calligraphy across the bottom of the picture: *Here there be monsters.*

There was no signature, at least not a traditional one. But the painting resonated with a paranormal vibe. He was certain the artist had been a strong talent who had infused the picture with a psychic signature.

When the labs were closed down the order had been given to destroy all the official photographs, drawings and related records. But an unknown artist who had evidently had access to a lab had succeeded in capturing and preserving a small bit of truth.

Victor was convinced the scene was the Vortex lab.

He turned away from the painting. "You know me, Lucas. I've always got a theory."

"You're thinking maybe Vortex wasn't the only lab that may or may not have succeeded in weaponizing paranormal energy. You're wondering if Griffin Chastain and Crocker Rancourt also managed to produce some weapons."

Victor rose and walked to the window. He gazed down at the hotels and casinos that lined the Strip. It was early morning. The town was never closed, never completely silent or dark. But this was the quietest time of the day. It was the one time when a man could appreciate the vastness of the surrounding desert. It had a way of putting things into perspective.

"Tell me the truth," he said after a while. "Think I've finally gone down the rabbit hole? That I'm a full-blown conspiracy theorist? That I'm ready to sign up for one of the Puppet cults?"

"No," Lucas said. He got to his feet and joined Victor at the window. "I don't have your computer brain but I've got damned good intuition. Given what happened in Fogg Lake a couple of weeks ago, and now this situation with the Chastains, I agree with you. We've got good reason to worry."

"We've always believed that if the weapons development project was successful it was in the Vortex lab, not in Fogg Lake or elsewhere. But say Chastain and Rancourt were able to produce some lethal machines that operated on paranormal principles. That would have provided Crocker Rancourt with a motive for murder."

"He killed Griffin Chastain in order to control the weapons?" Lucas nodded. "I'll buy that. But if Rancourt made it out of Fogg Lake with paranormal weapons, where have they been all these years? You can't just keep artifacts like that a secret, not for decades."

"You could if they were well hidden."

Lucas shook his head. "If the Rancourts had possessed serious paranormal weapons they would have used them to maintain control of the Foundation. Hell, they would have used them against us when we went after them."

"You're right. But what if Chastain was the one who hid them?"

"And took his secret to the grave?" Lucas considered that for a long moment. "Okay, that is an interesting theory. Either way, it looks like someone has found the artifacts."

"We've got to get on top of this situation, Lucas. We're running out of time. Right now we need to focus on Delbridge Loring and the Riverview Psychiatric Hospital."

Lucas reached for Victor's hand. Their gold wedding rings glinted in the early morning light. They stood quietly for a time, drawing strength from each other as they always did in a time of crisis.

"Give me ten minutes," Lucas said.

He squeezed Victor's hand and then he crossed the room to a desk and fired up a computer.

CHAPTER 17

North's phone rang while Sierra was slicing avocados. She glanced at the device. It was lying on the end of the dining counter. She was pretty sure she knew what was coming next, so she took the precaution of slicing a lime in half and squeezing the juice over the avocados so that they wouldn't turn brown.

North's phone stopped ringing. A couple of beats later the bells that she used for a ring tone chimed. She wiped her hands on a towel, picked up the phone, glanced at the area code and took the call.

"North can't come to the phone right now," she said. "He's in the shower."

"What the hell? This is Victor Arganbright."

"Believe it or not, it didn't require any psychic powers to figure out you would try my phone after you got dumped into voice mail on North's. I'll tell him you called."

"I want to speak to him immediately. This is critical."

He sounded sincere. Worried.

"All right," she said. "Hang on."

She traipsed down the hall and cracked open the door of the bathroom. Steam poured out.

"Las Vegas is calling," she yelled over the roar of the shower.

"Hang on. I'll be right there."

The shower abruptly fell silent. Sierra held the phone through the narrow opening. North's damp fingers closed around it. She caught patchy glimpses of his reflection in the steamed-up mirror. His aura looked much more stable. The rest of him looked interesting. Extremely interesting.

He angled his head around the door and smiled faintly. Light glinted on his mirrored glasses. She was stunned to realize that he even wore them in the shower.

"Seen enough?" he asked a little too smoothly.

She felt the heat rise in her cheeks. Hastily she turned away and hurried back toward the kitchen.

North arrived in the kitchen a short time later. He didn't appear to be a *new* man, but he was certainly in much better shape than he had been yesterday. It helped that he'd shaved and showered, of course, but the real change was in his overall vitality. She knew he was no longer drawing on his psychic senses to keep himself awake and alert.

He wore a fresh pair of dark cargo trousers and a black crew-neck T-shirt that emphasized his sleek, strong shoulders and flat belly. He sat down on the other side of the counter. She poured a mug of coffee and pushed it toward him. He put her phone down on the counter and wrapped both hands around the mug.

"That was Victor," he said.

"I know." She sprinkled coarse salt across the avocados and arranged them on large slices of toasted sourdough bread. "Was it about your father?"

"In part." North's jaw tensed. "The doctors think that Dad's condition is deteriorating."

"Oh, no. I am so sorry, North."

"He's still able to communicate a little through my mother but he doesn't seem to know any more about what happened to him than he did when I saw him at the airport. Mom says she thinks he's afraid of losing his mind. He feels trapped."

"He *is* trapped," Sierra said gently. "He's probably terrified and trying not to show it to your mother. His anxiety levels must be through the roof."

"The doctors are afraid to medicate him until they know what's wrong. Dad is strong but time is running out. No one knows what will happen. He might die or remain in a coma forever. The Halcyon experts are convinced the only hope of reversing the damage is to find the artifact that caused it in the first place. They need to know how the damage was inflicted. They have been able to establish that he was not drugged."

Sierra gave that some thought while she used a spatula to lift the four fried eggs out of the hot pan. She placed one egg on each avocado toast.

"Call Victor back and tell him he needs to get my mother to Las Vegas as soon as possible," she said.

North lowered his coffee mug, startled. "Why?"

"My mother's talent is the energy of singing. She does a lot of music therapy. She might be able to help stabilize your father's aura and buy us some time to find the artifact."

"You're serious, aren't you?"

"Yes." Sierra poured cream over a bowl of raspberries. "My mother has a gift for helping people who have problems with their paranormal senses. She's done a lot of research. There's enormous power in music, and she knows how to use it. Call Las Vegas."

North picked up his phone. "What the hell. It's not like we've got anything to lose."

He called a number. "Lucas, it's North. Sierra Raines is with me. She is convinced her mother might be able to stabilize Dad's aura and maybe buy us some time. Mrs. Raines lives on an island in the San Juans. You can arrange to have her flown to Vegas within a few hours, right?"

"Let me talk to him," Sierra said.

He handed the phone to her.

"Hello," Sierra said, wary now. It was one thing to hand out advice to the man who had spent the night in her bed. It was another to find herself dealing with the husband of the powerful director of the Foundation.

"You believe Mrs. Raines might be of some help in this situation?" Lucas said.

"Yes," Sierra said. "At the very least it's worth asking her to consult."

"I agree," Lucas said. "If you'll give me her number—"

"I'll call her and ask her to contact you," Sierra said.

"Is that your way of telling me your mother won't be thrilled with the idea of talking to someone from Foundation headquarters?"

"I'm sure you're aware the Foundation has some serious work to do when it comes to public relations."

"It's been five years since we kicked out the Rancourts," Lucas said. He sounded frustrated. "How long will it take the paranormal community to trust the new management?"

"I have no idea," Sierra said. "Do you want me to ask my mother to call you or not?"

"Yes, please," Lucas said. "I would be extremely grateful."

"I'll get in touch with her right now," Sierra said. She realized she almost felt sorry for Lucas Pine. "Don't worry, I'm sure she'll speak to you."

"Thanks," Lucas said. "By the way, between you and me, how is North holding up?"

Sierra watched North wolf down one of the avocado toasts. "He's doing fine now that he's had a good night's sleep."

"A good night's sleep?" Lucas sounded baffled.

"He was sleep deprived," Sierra said. "If you'll excuse me, I'll call my mom and ask her to contact you."

"Wait, what do you mean when you say North was sleep deprived? We didn't know he wasn't sleeping."

"Goodbye, Mr. Pine."

She ended the call and handed the phone back to North. She managed to eat a couple of bites of her own breakfast while she placed the call to her mother.

Allegra Raines answered after about three rings. "Sierra? Is something wrong? You don't usually call at this hour."

"I'm working a new contract, Mom. Don't faint. It's with the Foundation. Here's the problem: My client's father has suffered some kind of trauma. He's awake but almost unresponsive. They've got him at Halcyon Manor. The doctors there in Las Vegas have concluded that his aura has been destabilized, but aside from that they are baffled. They haven't seen anything quite like it. I suggested they ask you to consult."

"Victor Arganbright wants my help?" Allegra asked. She sounded astonished. "I thought he believed that your father and I are a couple of lightweight con artists."

"Well, specifically, Lucas Pine requested the help. They've run out of options. Would you be willing to call Foundation headquarters and discuss the problem with Pine or Arganbright?"

"Yes, of course. I can't promise that I'll be able to help your client's father, though. I haven't even examined the patient."

"I'm sure Pine will be delighted to fly you to Las Vegas for a consultation," Sierra said.

"Give me the number. I'll make the call and we'll see how things go. But no guarantees. Oh, and dear, we're all looking forward to seeing you at the Moontide celebration."

"Looking forward to seeing you, too, Mom. Got to run."

On the other side of the counter North poured himself a second cup of coffee. It was a small sound, an insignificant little noise, really. Just the splash of coffee into a cup. Sierra figured she could easily explain it, but North chose that moment to take another healthy bite out of the avocado toast. The crunching was audible.

There was a short, thunderous pause on the other end of the connection.

"Are you having breakfast with someone, Sierra?" Allegra asked.

Sierra stifled a sigh. "Early-morning meeting with my client. Kind of in a hurry here. Lucas Pine is waiting to hear from you."

"Is your new client a man?"

"How did you guess?"

"Something about the crunching in the background. Sounds like a man enjoying his food."

"His name is North Chastain. We're looking for the artifact that damaged his father's aura. We wanted to get an early start today."

"He spent the night at your place?"

"He was exhausted."

"You never let your dates spend the night."

"He's not a date, Mom. He's a client. And he's very worried about his father."

"I'll call Las Vegas right away," Allegra said.

"Bye, Mom. Love you. Love to Dad and Grandma and Grandpa."

"Be careful, dear."

"Don't worry, I can take care of myself."

Sierra ended the call and took a couple of deep breaths. "Mom is going to call Lucas Pine right now."

"Thank you," North said. He drank some coffee and munched the second avocado toast. "I appreciate it."

Sierra concentrated on finishing her breakfast.

"Your mom thought I was your date?" North said after a while.

"She heard you pouring coffee. She was just surprised I wasn't alone, that's all."

"Why?"

Sierra put down her fork. "I don't do sleepovers for two reasons. The first is that the odds are excellent the relationship won't last long, so why bother? It's easier not to have to ask someone to pack his bag and leave."

"You're right. That does sound rude. What's the second reason?"

She shrugged. "The usual problem for people like us."

"People with some talent?" He winced. "I get it."

"If I tell a normal date that I've got a weird ability to detect paranormal artifacts he'll conclude I'm either delusional or a fraud, so I have to keep quiet about it."

"Unless he concludes you're channeling some ancient sorcerer, of course."

"Or that. Either way, things never go well. On the other hand, dating within the paranormal community is tricky because it's a small world with a really big gossip network."

"Tell me about it. If you think your options here in Seattle are limited, you should try dating within the Foundation community at headquarters. It's a minefield. There are no secrets. Everyone knows who's sleeping with whom and everyone knows when there's a breakup. And everyone talks."

"Well, I might be able to give you an assist in that department," Sierra said.

North raised his brows. She couldn't see his eyes but she had a feeling they were a little hot. He was definitely intrigued.

"Exactly what kind of help are you offering?" he said, his voice very neutral.

"When this is over and you go back to your normal life, feel free to run your dates past me."

He looked flummoxed. Whatever he had been expecting her to say, that wasn't it.

"Aside from the logistical problems involved—Seattle and Vegas being about a thousand miles apart—why would I do that?" he asked.

"Because I will probably be able to tell you if your aura and that of your date's are a good match."

"You can do that?"

"With about a ninety percent accuracy rate, assuming I see the two of you reflected in a mirror." She waved a hand. "Mom and Dad said it's probably a side effect of my ability to pick up strong emotions infused into artifacts."

North frowned. "But you can't tell when your own aura is a good match with someone else's?"

"Nope. You know how it is with auras. You can't perceive your own. Enough of that subject. We've got bigger problems. Do we have a plan for today?"

"Yes." North got to his feet. "But before I tell you about it, we should talk about last night."

"Never in the history of the world has a conversation that starts out with 'we should talk about last night' ended well."

"Believe me, I'm keenly aware of that," North said. "But this is different. I just wanted to say thanks. I . . . slept. I really slept. I can't tell you that I feel normal this morning. I don't think I'll ever feel normal again. But I've got my act together now. I'm not going to crash on you."

"Good." She set her empty cup in the sink. "Now, about our plan."

"Right. You and I are going to pay a visit to the Riverview Psychiatric Hospital. It's over on the coast."

"Long drive, then. Why are we going there?"

"We need to find out everything we can about a Dr. Delbridge Loring, specifically why he is trying to locate a street woman named Marge." North carried his dishes around the dining counter. "I'll tell you all about it when we're on the road."

"Okay."

North looked at his empty plate. "Those were a couple of avocado toasts, weren't they?"

"With eggs. Figured you needed the protein."

"Don't get me wrong. They were very tasty. It's just that I'm not sure a badass cleaner from the Foundation is supposed to eat stuff like avocado toast."

"Afraid if the word gets out that you ate an avocado toast, your reputation as a badass might be damaged? Don't worry. I won't tell a soul. What happens in Seattle stays in Seattle."

CHAPTER 18

I hope this isn't a wild-goose chase," Sierra said. "If Riverview turns out to be a dead end, we've wasted a lot of time."

"Trust me, that has crossed my mind," North said.

He drove into the tiny parking lot in front of the Riverview Psychiatric Hospital and shut down the SUV. He was still mildly astonished that Sierra had allowed him to drive her shiny new vehicle. Maybe she understood that he needed something to focus on besides the unnerving sense of urgency simmering inside him. The three-hour trip from Seattle had brought them to the rugged, remote coast of the state. Narrow two-lane roads, an unreliable GPS and the steady rain had required his full attention.

He rested his hands on the steering wheel and studied the big wrought iron gates and the high stone walls that enclosed the grounds around the three-story brick building. It had evidently been a private home at one time, a retreat for some nineteenth-century lumber baron. It was probably filled with rooms that had originally been designed for entertaining guests at large house parties.

He forced himself to concentrate on the problem at hand. It was easier to think clearly this morning, thanks to a good night's sleep. As he had explained to Sierra, he didn't feel normal—whatever that meant—and the knowledge of what he was missing by not being able to access his talent whenever he desired was frustrating and depressing as hell. But he was no longer standing right on the edge of the abyss. He had recovered some sense of inner balance and taken a few steps back. He could do his job, pursue the investigation, and at the moment that was all that mattered.

The hospital was tucked away in a remote, heavily wooded property. The nearest community was a small town a few miles away that boasted a grocery store, one gas station and a couple of rustic inns.

"I told you, Victor says he has a feeling about Delbridge Loring," he said. "Ninety-nine percent of the time Victor's gut is right on target."

"And the other one percent?"

"Things usually go south in a hurry." North opened the door and climbed out from behind the wheel. "In this case I'm inclined to agree with him, and more importantly, Lucas Pine does, too. Evidently, since escaping from this place a couple of months ago, Marge has been living quietly on the streets of Seattle. Then, within twenty-four hours of the attack on my father, her worst nightmare shows up trying to find her. It's a hell of a coincidence."

"The coincidences are piling up in this case, aren't they?" Sierra opened her door and jumped down to the pavement. "But what possible connection could there be between Marge and your father and the missing artifact?"

"That's what we're going to try to find out. But Lucas did uncover some interesting information about Delbridge Loring."

"What's that?"

"There is almost nothing about him online, just a short, thin bio that Lucas says looks fraudulent. When he tried to confirm a few basic facts, like date of birth, he was unable to do so. He says that, for all intents and purposes, Delbridge Loring magically appeared about a year ago, just as the Riverview Psychiatric Hospital opened."

"Interesting."

There was a call box at the side of the massive gates. North pressed the button. A man answered.

"Who are you and what do you want?"

It was not the warmest of welcomes, North thought. The tone was impatient. Maybe suspicious. Definitely uninviting.

"We're here to speak to Dr. Delbridge Loring," North said.

"Dr. Loring isn't here."

"Can you tell me how to get in touch with him?"

"No. That's confidential. Wouldn't do you any good to give you his address anyway. He was called away on a personal matter. Did you have an appointment?"

"This is a matter of some urgency," North said, sidestepping the appointment question. "It involves a former patient, a woman who left here a couple of months ago without medical approval."

There was a short, startled pause.

"What's your name?" the man demanded.

"I'm North Chastain. My associate is Sierra Raines."

"Hold on while I check with Dr. Garraway," the voice said. "He's the director."

There was another, lengthier pause before the voice came back through the call box speaker.

"Dr. Garraway says he'll be happy to meet with you in his office. I'll unlock the gates. Follow the path to the front door. I'll meet you there."

North heard a sharp electrical snick. One side of the gates swung slowly open. He glanced up and noted the cameras.

"The place looks old but the security is good," he said. "Not state of the art, but decent."

Sierra raised her brows. "You can tell the difference at a glance?"

"Being able to assess security is part of the job description for a Foundation cleaner."

"Because once in a while you find yourself having to engage in a little light burglary or B and E work?" Sierra asked.

"You have a low opinion of my career path."

"Can you blame me? Rumors about the Foundation have been circulating for decades."

"Those rumors started when the Rancourts were in charge. Things are different now."

"Uh-huh." Sierra glanced around at the thick woods. "As for the security here, it makes sense. The hospital is in a very remote location and they are housing a vulnerable population."

"But is the security here designed to keep the patients locked up or to protect them?"

"Both, I assume," Sierra said.

"You're probably right. That's how it works at Halcyon Manor."

Sierra looked around at the barren gardens. "I wonder why Marge was locked up here. From what you say, everyone seems to think she's harmless."

"She believes she was kidnapped and used as a test subject here. But it's possible a doctor or court decided she really is delusional and managed to get her legally committed. It happens."

The front door of the mansion opened just as North reached out to press the bell. A burly man with a shaved head stood in the hall. He was dressed in green scrubs. His bulging arms were covered in tattoos. An orderly, North concluded. His name tag read *Ralph*. He narrowed his eyes.

"Follow me," Ralph grunted. "I'll take you to Dr. Garraway's office. Most of the patients are in art therapy or watching television at this hour, but if you happen to see any of them, don't make eye contact and don't speak to them. Understand?"

"Got it," North said.

Sierra did not acknowledge the instructions but Ralph did not seem to notice. He led the way across a small lobby furnished in bland, neutral shades. At the far end of the room he turned down a paneled hallway and stopped in front of a door.

He knocked twice.

"Come in," a man called in a polished, authoritative voice.

Ralph opened the door.

"Ms. Raines and Mr. Chastain, sir," he said.

Sierra entered first. North followed. The man behind the impressive desk rose to greet them. Garraway looked to be in his late forties. The lack of lines around his eyes and his tight jawline indicated he'd had a little work done. He was dressed like a lawyer or a CEO, in a jacket and tie. The outfit suited the richly appointed room, with its wood paneling, thick carpeting and cushioned leather chairs, but the jacket looked as if it had been pulled on in a hurry, and the knot of the tie was sloppy. Garraway had obviously put on both items of apparel in haste when he heard he had visitors.

"Please sit down," he said.

"Thank you for seeing us, Dr. Garraway," Sierra said, taking one of the leather chairs.

"Of course." Garraway gave her a warm, professional smile and sat down behind his desk. "We don't get a lot of visitors, as you can probably tell. Nor do we encourage them. Our patients require a tranquil atmosphere. They are easily stressed. What's this about a former resident who walked off the grounds a couple of months ago?"

"Her first name is Marge," North said. "We don't know her last name, but she was under the care of Dr. Loring. We're trying to find him because we want to ask him a few questions."

"I don't understand," Garraway said. He frowned in polite concern. "Why do you wish to speak with Dr. Loring?"

"That's the wrong question," North said. "Your first question should have been something along the lines of 'Is Marge all right?'"

Garraway's eyes hardened. "I don't have any idea who you're

talking about. Even if this Marge is a former patient, I would certainly not discuss her case with anyone except members of the family."

"That's especially convenient in this case, isn't it?" Sierra said. "Because Marge doesn't have a family. But we don't want to talk about her. We're here to find Loring."

"Dr. Loring was called away on a family emergency. I have no idea where he is or how to get in touch with him." Garraway stood. "Now, if that is all, I must ask you to leave. I am a busy man."

"We think Loring was running some experiments on Marge and possibly on some of your other patients," North said.

Garraway flushed and abruptly sat down. "Are you with the government? Because I assure you, we are in strict compliance with all the rules and regulations pertaining to our facility. I will also stress that this is a *private* institution, not a public hospital."

"This is a personal matter," North said. "You could say that Marge is a client."

"You're working for a woman whose last name you don't know?" Garraway was incredulous. "That's ridiculous. You can't possibly expect me to believe that. And even if it's true, it changes nothing. Loring isn't here. I have no idea where he is and I have absolutely no intention of telling you anything about a member of my staff."

North got to his feet and took a card out of the pocket of his leather jacket. "In that case, we'll be on our way. If you think of anything that might be helpful, let us know."

"That is not going to happen," Garraway said, jaw clenched. He got up, circled the desk and opened the door. "Ralph will see you out."

Ralph, as it happened, was conveniently standing in the hall. He looked startled when the door opened abruptly. North was pretty sure he had been eavesdropping.

"This way," Ralph said.

The screaming started when they reached the lobby.

"No, no, don't let them get me. They're monsters."

North looked at the stairs on the far side of the room and saw a man in his early twenties who was obviously a patient. He was dressed in a gray robe and slippers. He stared at North and Sierra with a wild-eyed, panicky expression. An orderly gripped the patient's arm and spoke to him in low, soothing tones.

"It's all right, Carl," the orderly said. "They're leaving. They won't hurt you. You're safe here."

"You don't understand," Carl wailed. "I can *see* them. They're strong, just like Dr. Loring, except that the colors are different. Don't let them put me in the light room. I'll be good. I promise. I'm cured."

"Remember the rule," Ralph said quietly to North and Sierra. "Don't make eye contact."

But it was too late. North was looking straight at Carl. He knew that Sierra was, too. Carl stared back, stricken.

"It's all right, Carl," the orderly said. "They're just visitors. They aren't here to give you any treatments."

He steered Carl away from the top of the stairs and guided him down a hallway.

"Are you sure?" Carl asked. "Because I really, really hate the lights."

"There won't be any more light therapy today, Carl," the orderly said. "Dr. Loring is the only one who gives you the treatments. He's not here."

"I don't like Dr. Loring. He's one of the monsters, too."

The pair vanished down the corridor.

"Don't mind Carl," Ralph said. "The poor guy is delusional. He was self-medicating with street drugs when he was brought to us."

Sierra looked at Ralph. "Carl is one of Dr. Loring's patients, I take it?"

"Yeah." Ralph crossed the lobby and opened the door. "Loring's got some theories about using light along with drugs as therapy."

North slipped him a card. "We've got a lot of questions about Loring. If you feel like answering a few, call the number on this card.

I'll meet you anywhere you choose. My client is willing to pay for information."

"You mean the woman named Marge?" Ralph snorted. "I know who she is. She doesn't have a dime to her name. She was living on the streets of Seattle when she was picked up and brought here."

"Marge just came into a large inheritance," North said. "Trust me, money is not an object."

Ralph scowled. "What's this about Marge getting an inheritance? And what's that got to do with Dr. Loring?"

"Sorry," North said. "Can't discuss the details. Client confidentiality. I'm sure you understand. But if you want to chat about Delbridge Loring, be sure to get in touch. We'll be staying in town tonight."

He followed Sierra outside. The door closed behind them. The sound of heavy bolts sliding into place could be heard. Neither of them spoke until they were on the other side of the big gates.

"Ralph knows who Marge is," Sierra observed.

"Garraway knows, too. But he's not concerned with Marge's welfare. Loring is the one he's worried about."

They got back into the SUV. North fired up the engine and drove out of the parking lot.

"Are we really going to spend the night in town instead of driving back to Seattle?" Sierra asked.

"Yes," North said.

"Because you expect Ralph to call?"

"That would definitely be a plus," North said. "But the main reason we're staying overnight is so that I can get a look inside Loring's house."

"Putting aside the pesky legalities of breaking and entering, I would like to point out that we have no idea where Loring lives."

"It's a small town, Sierra. Everyone in the area will know where Loring lives. What's more, he's not from around here. He's an outsider working at the psychiatric hospital a few miles up the road."

"So?"

"The locals won't feel any obligation to protect him. Someone will be happy to tell us where he lives."

Sierra sat quietly for a while, watching the narrow road that wound through the trees.

"That patient, Carl, could see our auras," she said at last.

"Yes."

"He said our energy fields looked like Loring's. Different colors but equally strong."

"Which tells us something very interesting about Loring," North said. "He's got some high-end talent."

Sierra folded her arms very tightly beneath her breasts. She did not take her eyes off the road.

"Carl thinks we're all monsters," she said.

"Only a real monster would run experiments on a helpless street person like Marge. I'll call Victor and give him an update."

CHAPTER 19

Victor Arganbright entered the Halcyon Manor hospital room first, making introductions with lightning speed.

"Lily, Chandler, this is Allegra Raines and her husband, Byron Raines. They are the parents of Sierra Raines, who is currently helping North locate the artifact that we need to try to reverse the damage to your aura, Chandler."

Lily was sitting by the bed, holding Chandler's hand while she read the newspaper to him in an effort to maintain some sense of normality. She put the paper aside and got to her feet.

"Thank you for coming all this way," she said to Allegra. "We appreciate your kindness."

Allegra smiled a wistful, understanding smile. "But you don't think there's much I can do to help. You may be right, but we won't know until I try."

Lily did not know quite what she had been expecting—a couple of aging neohippies who played at living a back-to-the-land, meditation-and-yoga lifestyle in an intentional community, perhaps.

At first glance, Allegra and Byron Raines fit the image she'd had in mind. Allegra wore her graying, shoulder-length hair in a casual twist at the back of her head. No makeup. Her dress was loose and flowy and definitely homemade. Clunky sandals and a small backpack completed the outfit.

Byron's hair was a little too long and a little too shaggy. He wore easy-fitting denim trousers, a plaid flannel shirt and low, scuffed boots. A pair of old-fashioned round spectacles was perched on his forceful nose. He looked like a cross between an eccentric academic and a farmer.

"The doctors are afraid the damage to my husband's aura is continuing," Lily said. She squeezed Chandler's hand. "We are willing to try anything."

"Let me see what I can do," Allegra said.

Lily felt energy rise in the atmosphere. Allegra moved to the other side of the bed and placed her fingertips on Chandler's forehead.

She was silent for a long time. Lily knew she was viewing Chandler's aura. She would no doubt sense the rising tide of panic that Chandler was working so hard to control.

And then Allegra began to sing. Softly at first and then with increasing power. Lily had anticipated a guitar and folk music. Maybe a soothing lullaby. Possibly a meditation chant or a religious hymn.

What she got was a full-throated coloratura soprano. The music resonated through the small space, filling it with power. The paranormal vibe shivered through the waves of energy, raising the hair on the back of Lily's neck and thrilling her senses.

Lily realized she was receiving only the backwash of the song. Allegra's focus was on Chandler. She kept her physical connection with him as she launched into a fierce aria that sent shock waves through the room.

There was movement at the observation window. Lily turned her head and saw that a small crowd of medical personnel had gathered there. The power of the music had reached out into the hallway.

133

Allegra sang as if she were creating a thunderstorm with the energy of her talent. When she finally stopped she was drenched in sweat. Her eyes were hot. It was clear that the effort had pushed her close to exhaustion.

Byron moved forward and put a supportive arm around her. She sagged against him.

There was a stunned silence in the space. The crowd at the window stared, openmouthed.

Victor was the first one to speak.

"I'm not a great aura reader," he said. "But Chandler looks a little stronger."

Lily tightened her grip on Chandler's hand and opened her senses. Hope bloomed deep inside her.

"A lot stronger," she whispered.

One of the doctors walked through the doorway.

"I'm a damned good aura reader," he announced. "I can tell you that Mr. Chastain's aura has stabilized, at least for now. The damaged bands are still in bad shape, but the deterioration has halted." He looked at Allegra. "Any idea how long the effects will last?"

Allegra raised her head from Byron's shoulder. "No, I'm sorry," she said. "I've never dealt with a case like this one." She looked at Lily. "Byron and I will stay here in Vegas until your son and our daughter arrive with the artifact. In the meantime I'm going to get something to eat and some rest."

"Yes, of course," Lily said. "I don't know how to thank you."

Allegra smiled. "It's what I do. If your husband's situation starts to deteriorate again, call me immediately. I will try more therapy."

The doctor looked at Allegra. "When you've had some rest, would you be willing to examine a couple of other patients here at Halcyon Manor?"

"Yes," Allegra said. "I just need time to recover."

"I understand," the doctor said. "Thank you."

Lily watched Byron guide Allegra out of the room. When the door closed behind the pair she turned to Chandler.

"It's going to be all right," she said. "North will be here soon, and he'll have the artifact."

She felt a whisper of energy and knew that Chandler understood. She also sensed that his panic had receded. He was calm now. It was as if he was in a more peaceful, meditative state. That alone was a very great gift.

"Thank you, Allegra," Lily whispered.

CHAPTER 20

"ooks like Loring left town in a hurry," Sierra said. "There are still a lot of clothes in his closet and there are dirty dishes in the sink."

It was after midnight and it was raining again. Another wave of storms had moved in off the Pacific. She and North were standing in the second bedroom of the rustic cabin that Loring had rented from the owner of the town's small grocery store. It was obvious the doctor had used the room as a home office. There was a desk near the window. A couple of file cabinets stood against one wall.

North had been right about one thing, she reflected. The locals were only too happy to talk about the creepy doctor who worked at the insane asylum a couple of miles out of town. The owner of the inn had been especially informative.

It turned out that everyone in the area had been shocked and alarmed when the Riverview Psychiatric Hospital had opened a year earlier. But there was nothing the town could do to prevent the trust that owned the mansion from selling it to the shadowy medical corporation headed by Dr. Garraway. When the first patients arrived, everyone in town had purchased new locks for their doors. Those who didn't already own guns bought them and kept them handy.

The innkeeper admitted that there had been no problems from the patients at Riverview, although there had been rumors that a few had escaped. *It's the orderlies who make people nervous around here. Tough-looking bunch. Keep to themselves for the most part, though. They sleep at the hospital.*

"You start on the file cabinets," North said. "I'll take the desk."

Sierra glanced at him. His mood had undergone a distinct change after the phone call from Victor Arganbright informing him that Allegra Raines had stabilized Chandler Chastain's aura. In doing so she had bought everyone involved some time. North was still focused, intense and determined to move as quickly as possible, but she sensed he was able to think more coolly and logically now that he knew his father was no longer deteriorating.

She crossed the room to the nearest file drawer. "It's locked. Needs a key."

"Yeah?"

North took three strides to the file cabinet, grabbed the metal handle and yanked. Hard. Sierra heard something metallic snap. The drawer popped open.

"Okay, that works," she said.

North went back to the desk.

She started flipping through folders.

"What have you got there?" North asked. "Patient records, by any chance?"

"Yes, but the names on the folders appear to be coded," she said. "The sex and age of the individual are on each label, though. I'll concentrate on the files for female subjects. What are you finding?"

"A lot of charts and graphs." North whistled softly. "Loring was conducting experiments involving crystal-generated paranormal light."

"Light is everywhere in this case."

"Yes. Judging by these scientific logs, Loring knows a lot about the subject."

"We are seeing a pattern, aren't we?" Sierra said.

"Yeah."

"You know this is illegal as hell."

"So is conducting experiments on people like Marge."

"True. On another topic, do you think it's weird that Loring kept so many files in paper form instead of on a computer?"

"No. People who are conducting unauthorized paranormal research are usually paranoid about keeping their records in digital form," North said. "Sooner or later they end up online."

"And the Foundation is always watching?"

"Yes, but it's not just the Foundation that makes them nervous. They're afraid of the Puppets, too. Those conspiracy crazies are always combing the Internet looking for hints of secret paranormal research."

"Those of us in the go-between business try to be careful not to leave footprints online, too," she said. "Lot of weirdos out there."

North looked up, frowning. "You're in a dangerous line of work."

"You're a cleaner. You have no room to talk."

"I've had training. I've got the Foundation behind me. That's a lot of backup. Go-betweens operate alone. All it takes is one bad client and you find yourself in real trouble."

"I can take care of myself."

"Famous last words," North said. "Are you planning to work as a go-between for the rest of your life?"

"You want to know my five-year plan?"

"Got one?"

"No, unfortunately. Still trying to hear my calling."

"I'll be looking for a new career soon, too." There was a grim edge to the words.

"Think you'll stay with the Foundation?" she asked.

"Victor and Lucas will find a place for me if I want it. Maybe training cleaners in the basics of investigation techniques. But I won't feel comfortable there after I lose my talent. You want to know the truth? I don't know what the hell I'm going to do next and I don't like to think about it."

"Believe me, I understand. You're talking to someone who has screwed up every job she's ever had."

"Yeah, there was a note about the auction house scandal in your file."

"Don't believe everything you read in a Foundation file," Sierra said.

"I don't. And for the record, you haven't screwed up your current job. According to Victor you're one of the Vault's best agents."

"That's nice to hear, but I don't get a lot of satisfaction out of delivering hot objects to obsessive collectors. It's just a job. I'll admit it gets exciting once in a while. The night before I met you, a client pulled a gun on me."

"Shit." North looked up, mirrored glasses glinting in the shadows. "Are you serious?"

She flipped through the file she had removed from the drawer. "I don't make jokes when it comes to guns. Here's the conclusion I have recently arrived at: I am willing to risk my neck for a really good cause, but damned if I want to do it just to deliver hot artifacts to collectors."

"Sounds like a sensible career decision." North paused. "I can't help but remember that last night someone tried to blast our senses with some kind of light grenade. You could have been seriously injured or killed."

"But for a good cause. We're trying to save your dad's life here."

"You don't even know him."

"So what?"

"Sierra—"

"Hmm?"

"Thank you."

"Don't worry, you'll get my bill." She scanned the handwritten notes in the file she was examining. Excitement shot through her. "I think I may have something here. Listen to this. 'Female patient. Homeless. No known family. Strong aura reader. She is clearly delusional. Convinced she is the subject of experiments conducted by extraterrestrials. Refuses to cooperate in the experiments. I am convinced she has enough talent to operate the devices, but she pretends she can't sense the energy. Will try the new hypnotic drug.'"

"Think that's Marge's file?" North asked.

"There's no photo and no name but the age and gender are right. Also the nature of her delusions." Sierra flipped to the final page of notes. "Yes, this must be Marge's file. Here's the final note. 'Subject escaped her cell during the night. A search of the grounds was conducted but no trace of her was found. Garraway is convinced that she hiked out through the woods and either fell off the cliffs or caught a ride from a passing car. Regardless, she doesn't know enough to do any damage. No one will believe her story.'"

"Could be Marge, all right," North said. "I found an interesting file, too. Bring those records over here and spread them out on the desk. I'm going to take photos of everything and send them to Victor and Lucas."

Sierra crossed the room and arranged the papers from Marge's file on the desk. North put several printouts down, too. She glanced at them.

"Newspaper articles?" she said. "Why are they important? Oh, wow." She read the first paragraph of one of the pieces. "'Stenson Rancourt, director of a private foundation headquartered in the Los Angeles area, and his son, Harlan, were killed in an explosion early this morning. The cause of the blast is under investigation, but authorities suspect a gas leak.'"

The rest of the printouts were obituary notices and business articles detailing the abrupt closure of the Los Angeles–based headquarters of a vaguely described charitable foundation. The date was five years earlier.

North took out his phone and began snapping photos of the printouts. "Dr. Loring was not only conducting paranormal experiments on unwilling subjects but also appears to be at least slightly obsessed with the Rancourts."

Sierra caught her breath. "The family that ran the Foundation before Victor Arganbright took over."

"Victor and Lucas are going to be very interested in this."

"Why would Loring keep information about the Rancourts in his desk drawer?"

North tucked his phone into the pocket of his jacket. "Victor took control of the Foundation in what a lot of people politely refer to as a hostile takeover."

"Got news for you—that's common knowledge among those of us in the paranormal community. My parents told me the Rancourts made millions while they were in charge of the Foundation. People who got in their way had a habit of turning up dead or disappearing. Stenson Rancourt and his son would not have stepped down willingly."

"No," North said.

Sierra cleared her throat. "You know, there have always been rumors that the takeover engineered by Victor Arganbright and Lucas Pine was a lot more hostile than the average corporate takeover."

"Uh-huh."

"In fact," Sierra said, injecting some emphasis into the words, "there are those in the community who are convinced the explosion that killed Stenson Rancourt and his son was not an accident."

"Yeah, I've heard those rumors."

Sierra took a deep breath. "Do you think Arganbright and Pine were behind the explosion?"

"Most people at headquarters are careful not to voice that theory aloud," North said. "But the assumption is that there was some sort of violent confrontation between Victor and Lucas and the Rancourts. Victor and Lucas survived. The Rancourts did not. No one seems to think that was a bad outcome."

"Okay, I get that. But why would Loring care about the Rancourts?"

"Good question." North looked at her. "Remember that one small, interesting detail about the explosion that I mentioned?"

"Only one body was recovered—Stenson Rancourt's. Harlan's body was never found."

"If Harlan were alive he would be about Loring's age. Let's get out of here. We've got another stop to make tonight."

"Where is that?"

"The Riverview Psychiatric Hospital."

Sierra followed him to the door. "We're going to break into the hospital? That sounds awfully risky."

"Shouldn't be too much of a problem. I told you, the security there is decent but not exactly state of the art. It's not like there are a lot of armed guards around the place."

"Just some really big orderlies."

"Who will probably be asleep."

They moved outside and paused under the eaves. The storm was at full throttle. It charged the night with energy that spanned the spectrum from normal to paranormal. The wind-driven rain caused the limbs of the trees to creak and moan.

"We'll stick to the center of the driveway," North said. "We don't want to risk getting struck by a falling branch. I'll go first. Stay close."

Sierra pulled up the hood of her parka. She had to hold it in place with one hand because the stiff wind threatened to blow it off. The rain lashed her face. North settled a baseball cap on his head and went down the steps. He headed off into the wet darkness, using the narrow beam of a penlight to navigate.

At least they didn't have far to go, Sierra reflected. The SUV was parked in the trees a short distance down the road. North had chosen the location because the vehicle wouldn't be seen by a passing motorist—not that there were many of those out at this hour.

The violent energy of the storm excited all of her senses but it also distracted them. She did not pick up the vibe of the man who leaped out from the cover of the side of the house until he wrapped an arm around her throat. He hauled her back against his big body.

"I got her," he shouted.

Sierra fought a wave of nausea. The heavy jacket her captor wore offered a lot of protection but she could feel his unwholesome vibe all the way through the fabric.

"I really do not like to be touched by strangers," she said.

"Tough, bitch," the man growled.

She felt something sharp at her throat and realized he had a knife in one hand.

The beam of a flashlight suddenly speared the night.

"That's far enough, Chastain," Ralph said. "One more move and Joe will slit her throat."

CHAPTER 21

take it you're not here to sell me some information about Loring," North said.

He spoke to Ralph but Sierra realized he was watching her very intently. She knew he was trying to determine if she was going to panic. She raised one hand slightly and unobtrusively slipped off a leather glove. Her captor paid no attention. Joe's attention was fixed on North.

"We'll ask the questions," Ralph said. "What were you looking for inside Loring's place?"

"I told you earlier today we're trying to locate him," North said. "That was the truth. We were hoping to find something inside the house that would tell us where he's headed."

"What did you find?" Ralph demanded.

"Not much," North said. "Do you know where he is?"

"None of your business."

"Why do you two care if Ms. Raines and I want to find Loring?" North said.

"Isn't it obvious?" Sierra said. "They're working for him."

"She's right," Joe said. "We're his private security team. It's our job to protect him."

Fierce pride rang in his words.

"Well, damn," Sierra said. "Looks like we've got ourselves a couple of Puppets."

"In hindsight, I guess we should have seen this coming," North said.

"I suppose so," Sierra said. "By the way, don't worry about me. I've got this one."

"You're sure?"

"Yep. Joe here is not my first Puppet."

"Shut up," Joe yelled.

"What the fuck are you two talking about?" Ralph demanded.

"You obviously think Loring has some serious psychic talent," North said. "And maybe he does. But if he told you that he could give you paranormal powers, he was lying. That's what guys like Loring always tell their Puppets. Doesn't work like that."

"You don't know what you're talking about," Ralph snarled. "Dr. Loring is fucking brilliant."

"Puppets," North said. "They'll believe anything."

"Are we done here?" Sierra asked.

"Yes," North said. "You go first."

"Stop talking," Ralph shouted.

Sierra gripped her locket, got it open and sent a wave of destabilizing energy into Joe's aura.

Joe went abruptly limp. His arm fell away from her throat. He dropped to the ground. The knife landed in the mud.

Alarmed, Ralph swung the beam of the flashlight toward his partner. The glow played across the unconscious man.

"*Joe,*" Ralph said. "What the fuck?" He aimed the light at Sierra's face. "What did you do to him?"

"I told him I don't like to be touched by strangers," she said.

"You heard the lady," North said.

Ralph appeared to remember he had another problem. He started to turn back toward North, but it was too late.

North was already spinning into him with a high-flying karate kick that sent Ralph to the ground.

North glanced at Joe.

"How long will he be out?"

"I don't know," Sierra admitted. She picked up the flashlight and aimed it at Joe. "I haven't done this sort of thing often enough to collect a lot of data. It's not exactly the kind of trick you can practice whenever you have some free time. Hard to find volunteers."

Ralph groaned and started to pull himself up out of the mud. North gave him a swift chop that sent him onto his back. This time Ralph did not move.

North crouched beside him and quickly went through the downed man's pockets. He confiscated Ralph's wallet and keys, rose and crossed to Joe, where he repeated the pat-down and retrieved another wallet and more keys.

Joe groaned. North straightened. "Let's go."

"Are we just going to leave them here?" Sierra asked.

"Were you thinking of hauling them inside and making them a cup of hot cocoa?"

"Ah, no," Sierra said. "No, I wasn't thinking that."

"Don't worry, they're not going to drown. We need to get on the road."

"Shouldn't we call the local police?"

"We don't have time. It would take too long to explain this situation to a local cop."

"You're still planning to hit Riverview?"

"Yes."

"What do you expect to find there?"

North held up the key ring that he had taken from Ralph. "I

would really like to get a look at Loring's lab. I want to know what instruments and drugs he was using in his experiments."

They reached the SUV. North climbed in behind the wheel. Sierra opened the passenger-side door and jumped up onto the seat.

"If you're going in, I'm going with you," she said.

North cranked up the engine. "Bad idea."

"Maybe, but there is no other idea handy. We're in this together. We're a team now."

North concentrated on navigating the driveway. When they reached the main road he evidently came to a decision.

"Yes," he said. "A team."

CHAPTER 22

Riverview Psychiatric Hospital appeared even more ominous and disquieting at night than it did by day. Dim lights illuminated some of the rooms, but most of the windows were dark. There were a couple of streetlamps at the front gate, one over the main entrance door and one at the loading dock behind the mansion. The parking lot in front was empty.

North led the way through the woods to the rear of the mansion, aware of Sierra following close behind. He knew they were both still wired from the violent confrontation at Loring's house, and there was a risk that Ralph and Joe might figure out they were headed to Riverview. A couple of sensible criminals would cut their losses and run.

But it was clear that Ralph and Joe were Puppets. They had bought whatever wild promises Loring had made to them. The lure of serious paranormal power was enough to cause even smart bad guys to make poor choices, and there was no indication that Ralph and Joe had ever been particularly intelligent to start with.

The worst of the storm had passed but the ground was soggy and, in places, treacherous. A couple of vehicles were parked outside the rear gate.

"The night staff," North said. "With luck, just the other two orderlies. According to the people we talked to in town, there are only four and they all sleep here. Victor said Marge told him the lab was on the top floor at the end of the hall. The night she escaped she went down what she called the *other* stairs, the ones the clones used—not the main staircase."

"An old set of service stairs?" Sierra suggested.

"Probably. We'll try for those."

Sierra studied the rear of the mansion through the bars of the gate. "There's a door beside the loading dock," she said.

"Ralph's key fob will probably work on the gate and the door. Ready?"

"Sure. We're about to break into an insane asylum. What could possibly go wrong?"

"Keep that positive attitude," North said.

He left the cover of the trees. Sierra followed, moving in the light, nearly silent way that fascinated him.

The second fob on Ralph's ring opened the gate. North eased inside, waited for Sierra and then closed the gate.

They made their way past a couple of industrial-sized trash bins and what looked like a gardening shed.

One of Ralph's other fobs opened the service entrance door. North moved into a large, unlit room. Sierra followed. He closed the door behind her and waited a beat.

There were no warning pings from the security box on the wall. No red lights flashed. They were in.

It would have been convenient to call on his talent to help navigate the pitch-black space. There was a time when he had prowled the dark as effortlessly as any night predator. But those days were, if not quite gone, fading fast. Using his talent would just hasten the blindness that was setting in. And then there was the risk of getting trapped in the ghost world.

He switched on the penlight instead and did a quick scan of the room. It was cluttered with a jumble of large cardboard boxes containing supplies and canned goods. Various items of cleaning equipment were stored in a corner.

The storage room was unlit, but a bulb glowed dimly over the entrance to a narrow staircase.

They climbed the steps, trying to make as little noise as possible. The muffled chatter of late-night television could be heard from the first floor. North hoped that meant the night staff was occupied and would not notice any small unusual sounds that emanated from inside the stairwell.

The door at the top of the stairs on the third floor was locked. North looked through the narrow, wired window. He saw twin rows of closed doors on either side of the hall. Each door was set with a small window. Midway down the corridor there was a nurses' station, but no one was around.

If Marge's description of the layout was accurate, the door to Loring's laboratory was at the far end of the hallway.

North looked at Sierra. "The patients could be a problem. If we disturb them there will probably be a lot of noise. It might attract the attention of the night staff."

Sierra opened her locket. "If one of them becomes agitated I might be able to keep him calm."

"All right, but be careful. I know you're good at doing whatever it is you do with that mirror, but we don't know anything about these patients. Some of the auras up here might be pretty badly damaged."

"I understand. I'll be careful. Meanwhile, don't make eye contact with any of the patients. I think they would find that alarming, especially if they can see our auras."

"Understood."

"Whatever else comes out of this, we have to find a way to rescue these people."

"Don't worry, now that we know this place is not a legitimate hospital, Victor and Lucas will take care of things here."

North opened the door with Ralph's fob. Sierra followed him into the hallway. A couple of faces appeared at the windows in the doors. North avoided looking at the people inside the locked cells. He wondered if all of them had been grabbed off the streets or if some were actual patients.

He and Sierra made it past the unstaffed nurses' station without creating a disturbance. And then they were at the end of the hall. This time Ralph's fob did not work.

"Well, damn," North said quietly.

Sierra looked at him. "What?"

"Old-fashioned security. This lock takes a key. What do you want to bet that the only person who has it is Loring?"

"Are you saying we can't get inside?"

"No." North took a high-tech lockpick out of one of the pockets of his black cargo trousers. "But it's going to take me a minute."

In the end it took about fifteen seconds, not a minute. The lock was good but nothing extraordinary. It had been installed by a skilled locksmith, which meant that it could be broken by a skilled burglar or a reasonably proficient cleaner equipped with the proper tools.

He got the door open and they moved into an unlit room.

He closed the door and switched on his penlight. The light played over a couple of stainless steel workbenches laden with a variety of instruments and electronic gear. Much of the equipment looked new, but one device standing alone on a separate table appeared to be of an old-fashioned design.

Sierra headed straight toward it, stripped off a glove and touched it cautiously. She winced.

"Hot," she said. She pulled on her glove. "Lab heat."

North felt his pulse kick up. A thrill of excitement flashed through him. He moved across the room to get a closer look at the artifact.

The square black metal box measured about a foot on all sides. It was rusty in places. The cloudy display screen was dark. Instead of a computer keyboard, several rows of knobs and dials studded the front of the machine. Wires were attached to the top.

"Looks like it came from one of the lost labs, all right," he said.

"I can tell you right now that, whatever it is, it's worth a fortune on the underground market," Sierra said. "I'm surprised Loring would leave it here."

"It looks heavy," North said. "Also, it's awkward. Probably takes two hands just to carry it. Why not stash it here? Who's going to look for a valuable artifact from the Bluestone Project in a locked lab inside an asylum?"

"Gee, I don't know. How about you and me?"

"Right." North felt a visceral tug on his senses. Experimentally he reached out to touch the metal box. Familiar energy whispered through him. He smiled. "I think I know why Loring left this behind."

"Why?"

"It's infused with Griffin Chastain's psychic signature. Got a hunch Loring couldn't make it function correctly, assuming he got it to work at all. If he did try to activate it, he would have run the risk of damaging his own aura in the process."

"I assume we're taking that thing with us when we leave?"

"Oh, yeah. But first we need to see what else we can find here."

Sierra walked across the room and stopped near a wall. "How about a vintage radio?"

She stripped off a leather glove again and bent down to gingerly pick up an object from the floor. She winced a little and transferred the artifact to her gloved hand.

"Well?" North asked.

"It's a radio that looks like it dates from the era of the lost labs," she said. "There's definitely some heat in it, but nothing spectacular."

"The radio Dad bought from Gwendolyn Swan?" North asked.

"I wouldn't be surprised." Sierra took a closer look. "The plastic is cracked and one of the knobs fell off. There's some hot rage infused in it. Got a feeling Loring or someone hurled it against the wall in a fit of anger."

"Because it wasn't the artifact that he had been expecting," North concluded. "Dad fooled him."

"Do you want to take it with us?"

"No, it's useless." North got a familiar frisson of energy across the back of his neck. His intuition was warning him that it was time to leave. "Let's go. I need both hands to carry Griffin Chastain's machine. You'll have to handle security until we get out of the building."

"Right," she said. "I'll go first."

She paused at the door long enough to check the view of the hallway through the small window. Then she cradled her locket in her ungloved hand.

"All clear," she announced softly.

She opened the door and moved out into the hall. North followed with the machine. The ward was still relatively quiet but now there were more faces at the windows of the cells.

They made it past the nurses' station before disaster struck. The door at the end of the ward slammed open. A massive figure loomed in the doorway. He was dressed in scrubs and, like Ralph's and Joe's, his arms were sheathed in tattoos.

He aimed a pistol at Sierra.

"Stop," he roared.

The screaming started then. One patient howled. Within seconds the rest joined in. Some of the cries morphed into panicky shrieks. A terrible keening echoed from one room.

The chorus of the doomed grew to a thunderous roar.

"Sierra?" North said.

"I've got this," Sierra said.

North felt energy charge the atmosphere. Sierra's locket glowed like a white-hot mirror. The tattooed man staggered as though he had been struck with a blunt object, pitched forward and went down. There was a reverberating thud when his unconscious frame hit the floor.

"The gun," North said.

She swooped down and picked up the pistol.

Together they ran toward the doors. Tattooed Man had not bothered to lock them.

Sierra plunged down the stairwell. North followed with the artifact, listening for the sound of footsteps from below. It was unlikely the tattooed orderly was the only person on duty.

Sierra was on the first-floor landing when the hall door slammed open.

Another big man in scrubs appeared.

"Walt? Is that you? Everything okay up there?"

Then he noticed Sierra. She showed him the pistol.

"Shit," he yelped.

He retreated at full speed and slammed the door shut.

"Keep going," North ordered.

Sierra didn't pause. She switched on a penlight to guide them across the storage room and then they were through the rear gate. No one followed them.

They made it to the SUV. North dumped the metal box on the floor behind the front seat and leaped behind the wheel. Sierra scrambled up into the passenger's seat and slammed the door closed.

North drove out of the trees and onto the narrow, winding road.

"Watch our tail," he said.

Sierra twisted around in her seat to peer out the rear window.

"No one is following us," she said.

"We had the element of surprise on our side this time. They were watching for us at Loring's house but they didn't expect us to go into the asylum. It will take them a while to figure out what happened and where we might be headed."

"I assume we're going back to Seattle?"

"Not until we have a chat with Garraway."

"The director of the asylum?" she said. "When do you plan to do that?"

"The sooner the better. Now would be good."

"I'm not sure that confronting Garraway tonight is a good idea," she said. "We both burned a lot of energy in the past few hours, physical and paranormal. We need time to recover."

"We'll get some rest right after we talk to Garraway."

Sierra did not argue. She understood, he thought. They were running out of time.

Earlier that evening he had obtained the directions to Garraway's house from the same helpful local who had told them how to find Loring's place. At the time Loring had been the priority, but now North's intuition was raging at him, telling him he had to confront Garraway immediately. Too much was happening too fast. The situation was starting to spin out of control.

The house Garraway was renting was located at the end of a short drive about half a mile outside of town. The windows were dark. No lights burned over the front porch. A Porsche was parked at the foot of the steps.

North pulled up to the front of the house and brought the SUV to a halt. Sierra studied the dark windows.

"Does it strike you as strange that a guy like Garraway, a man who wears expensive jackets and ties and drives a Porsche, would accept a position as the director of a small private asylum located in a remote corner of the state?" she asked.

"Yes." North opened the door of the SUV and got out. "A guy like Garraway should be working at a prestigious institution or a hospital located in a major city."

"Maybe he went to Riverview because he felt a true calling."

"I think it's a hell of a lot more likely he took the job because someone convinced him that he stood to make a lot of money."

"Loring?"

"Maybe."

Sierra got out and joined him. Together they went up the steps. North tried the bell first. When there was no response he rapped sharply on the front door.

No one answered. Sierra watched him reach into a pocket of his cargo pants and pull out the lockpick.

"You know, if you keep this up we're probably going to get arrested," she said.

"No, we won't," he said. "I've got some solid government ID that will cover us if the local cops try to pull us in."

"Government ID? Is it real?"

"I know this will come as a shock, but yes. It's issued by the Agency for the Investigation of Atypical Phenomena."

"Never heard of it."

"The agency likes to keep a low profile."

"No kidding."

He was about to insert the pick into the lock but he paused long enough to try the doorknob.

It turned easily.

"Huh," he said. He slipped his gun out of the shoulder holster. "Stand on the other side of the door."

Sierra obediently moved out of what might become the line of fire. North flattened himself against the wall, opened the door and shoved it inward.

"Government agents," he said in a loud, authoritative tone. "Come out with your hands up."

Silence reverberated from deep inside the house. So did a sense of wrongness. You don't have to be psychic to sense death, especially the violent kind. Humans have acute instincts for it.

"This is going to be bad," North said quietly. "You'd better wait out here."

He reached around the edge of the doorframe and flipped a light switch. Sierra pushed herself away from the wall of the house and looked through the doorway.

The hall light illuminated two suitcases.

Garraway's body was sprawled on the floor. He had been shot twice, once in the chest and once in the head.

North went through the ritual of checking for a pulse, but he didn't expect to find one and he was proven right. After a moment he got to his feet and contemplated the suitcases.

"Garraway was trying to run," he said. "He shouldn't have stopped to pack."

North crouched and opened one of the suitcases. Sierra watched him flip through some clothing. At the bottom of the case there was an envelope. He opened it. A flash drive and a sheaf of computer printouts fell out.

North flipped through the printouts. "Spreadsheets. Financial stuff. Looks like Garraway was the money guy."

Sierra took off one glove and gingerly touched the doorknob. A shock of fury zapped across her senses. She jerked her fingers off the metal and shook her hand in a futile attempt to ease the burn.

North stood, envelope in hand. "Are you okay?"

"Hurts like hell but I'll be all right. If it helps, I can tell you a few things about the killer."

"Talk."

"Whoever it was is unstable."

"How unstable?"

"Without being able to see a reflection of the person's aura in a mirror, I can't give you a lot of details. All I know for sure is that the shooter's aura is pretty messed up."

CHAPTER 23

"To be honest, I didn't think Sheriff Kincaid was going to buy that government-issued identification you showed him," Sierra said. "But he seemed thrilled with it."

She and North were finally warm and dry and ensconced in front of a fire in room 210 of a local inn. She had not protested when North had decreed that they would share a room. It was a pragmatic decision. They now knew for certain they were chasing a killer. They needed sleep and they needed to watch each other's backs. The most effective way to do both was to remain in close proximity.

She and North had stayed at the scene of the Garraway murder until the sheriff and his team had assessed the situation and taken their statements. It had soon become apparent that all four orderlies had vanished, leaving no one to manage Riverview. That presented a host of additional problems.

North had contacted Victor and Lucas to give them a rundown on the rapidly evolving situation. Victor had dispatched a forensics team from Las Vegas to take charge of the investigation and some members of the Halcyon Manor staff to assume control of Riverview. They were expected to arrive midmorning. In the meantime the sheriff had called in a retired doctor and a couple of former military medics who lived in the area. They had agreed to keep the situation at the asylum under control until the medical team from Las Vegas could get there.

It was clear the local authorities could not wait to hand all the problems connected to Riverview to the agents of the Foundation.

"Sheriff Kincaid didn't question my ID for two reasons," North said. "The first is that it's legit. The Foundation is a genuine government contractor."

"What's the second reason?"

"Kincaid is smart enough to know there's no upside for him if he gets involved in the investigation. Think about it—Garraway and the orderlies are from out of town and are widely disliked by the locals. The Riverview hospital makes everyone around here nervous. And now a card-carrying agent of a government contractor says his employer will be arriving to make all his problems go away. No one is going to be happier than Kincaid when the Foundation teams get here."

"I see what you mean. But our problems are just beginning."

"No," North said. He contemplated the machine he had taken from Loring's lab. It was currently sitting on the coffee table in front of the couch. "We have a lot more information than we had at this time yesterday."

Sierra followed his gaze. "Yes, but it's not getting us anywhere. That machine seems to be important, but we don't even know what it's supposed to do."

North drank some wine. He did not take his attention off the machine.

"We have an eyewitness who may be able to answer some of our questions," he said.

Sierra started to ask who he was talking about but the answer dawned on her in the next breath.

"Marge, the street lady?" she said.

"According to Victor she spent a lot of time in Loring's lab."

"Marge is now in Fogg Lake," Sierra said. "I assume that's our next stop?"

"I think so. It feels like the right move."

"Long drive to the mountains from here. We need some sleep. A couple of hours, at least."

North did not respond at first. Then he turned his head to look at her. The firelight glinted on his mirrored glasses. His jaw was tense.

"You could have been killed tonight," he said.

"We both could have been killed."

"I never intended for you to be put in the line of fire."

"I know." She wrinkled her nose. "I'm just the hired go-between. You thought you could use me to track down an artifact and then, when you got what you wanted, you could kick me to the curb."

He winced. "That's a little harsh considering the fact that I am paying you a hell of a lot of money."

"It's the truth. Don't bother denying it. You're still thinking you can dump me. But you're afraid to cut me loose and send me back to Seattle because I might be in danger. I know too much for my own good now, don't I?"

"Probably. Until this thing is over it would be best—"

"If you shipped me off to Las Vegas."

"I've got a solid lead on Loring now," North said evenly. "I may be losing my talent but I'm still a decent investigator. I'm good at finding people."

"Forget it. You still need me, because I'm the one with the feel for artifacts."

"Damn it, Sierra—"

"Give me a minute." She stripped off one glove, sat forward, reached out and touched the black box machine. She winced and quickly removed her fingers.

"You said you could sense your grandfather's signature in that device. I can tell you that the last person to handle it was really, really pissed off. But there's a layer of much older rage and frustration infused in it, too."

North's expression sharpened. "How old?"

"Lost lab–era old."

"But some of the anger is fresh?"

Sierra sat back against the cushions. "Definitely."

North considered briefly. "The more recent prints most likely came from Loring."

"Who may or may not be Harlan, Crocker Rancourt's grandson." Sierra paused, processing what she had experienced when she touched the machine. "There might have been more than one set of new prints. Maybe one of the Puppets touched it."

"They're definitely hot-tempered."

Sierra eyed the black box. "Think it's another weapon?"

North sat forward on the sofa, his forearms resting on his thighs, and studied the machine. "I can sense the heat in it and Griffin Chastain's vibe, but there's only one way to get a real feel for it."

"You're talking about using your talent?"

"What's left of my talent," North said.

"You'd have to remove your glasses to do that, wouldn't you?"

"Yes. It's a risk, but I don't have a lot of choice. I need information."

He took a deep breath and reached up with both hands to remove the mirrored glasses. He set them down on the coffee table.

For the second time since they had met, Sierra saw his eyes. The first time had been in the abandoned building when they had encountered the light grenade. She had not been able to get a close look on that occasion. But tonight she could see them clearly. North's eyes were a mysterious shade of green and gold. They burned with energy. For a few seconds she could not look away.

North was the one who broke the moment of connection between them. He blinked several times as if trying to clear his vision. Then he turned back to the machine and reached out to put both hands on it.

"Hot as hell," he said. "Light energy."

"That makes sense if it has your grandfather's vibe," Sierra said. She started to say something else but a tingle of heat snagged her attention.

The vibe was not coming from the machine. North's mirrored glasses were the source.

Slowly she removed her glove. "Can I touch your glasses?"

"What?" North was concentrating on the machine. "Sure. Help yourself."

She picked up the glasses and opened her senses. *"Shit."*

A shock of chilling awareness rattled her so badly she almost dropped the glasses.

North turned his head to look at her. "What is it?"

She took a breath, tightened her grip on the glasses and concentrated.

"Rage," she said. "And frustration. Some instability."

North froze. "Heat laid down by me? Are you picking up my frustration and the deterioration of my talent?"

"No." She took another breath. "This feels like some of the new stuff I sensed on that machine."

"The same sensation you got off the doorknob at Garraway's house?"

Sierra hesitated and then shook her head. "No, I don't think so." She raised her eyes to meet his. "You told me you got these glasses from a lab at Halcyon Manor."

"Yes."

"I think whoever handled these lenses before you started wearing them hates you, North. I think the radiation infused in the crystals is poisoning you slowly but surely. Someone is deliberately trying to destroy your talent and drive you mad."

CHAPTER 24

For a few seconds North stopped breathing. He was so stunned that he neglected to put on the glasses until the visions at the edge of his awareness began to seethe and roil.

"Damn," he whispered.

He grabbed the glasses and put them on. The hallucinations faded. Sierra watched him, not speaking, silently challenging him.

He took a determined breath, braced himself for the hallucinations and removed the glasses. Deliberately he opened his senses. For a few seconds everything seemed normal. He could access his talent, whatever was left of it.

But in the next moment the apparitions began to coalesce at the edges of his vision. The ghosts whispered to him of the madness that awaited. His nightmares rose up in waves.

He could not afford to be running dangerous experiments on himself, he thought. He had to stay focused on saving his father. With a groan that was part disgust and part despair he started to put on the glasses.

"Wait," Sierra said. "Please. What do you see?"

"What I always see when I take off the glasses for more than a minute or two. Nightmares. Ghosts."

"Tell me about the ghosts."

"They are vague, foggy images for the most part, but I can hear them. They are telling me the glasses are the only way to save my sanity."

"Hypnotic suggestion," Sierra said. "Not the first time we've run into it in this case. The man Matt Harper met at the Vault, the one we assume is Delbridge Loring, gave Matt a hypnotic suggestion meant to keep him from remembering any details of what happened that night."

"You don't understand," North said. He looked at the glasses. "I was having visions and hallucinations before I got the glasses. They started soon after my team closed a case. That night I went to a club to celebrate with the others, went home to bed—and woke up the next morning to the nightmares and hallucinations. I thought I had gone insane overnight. Eventually the doctors concluded that I was going psi-blind. They gave me the glasses."

"I don't know how the first dose of poison was delivered, but I'm sure the crystals in those glasses are continuing to administer a low-level dose," Sierra said quietly.

He stared at the mirrored glasses in his hands.

"Even if you're right, there's nothing I can do about it now. I've got a job to finish, and I can't work with these hallucinations constantly clouding my vision. Hell, I can't even drive this way, let alone try to control my talent. At least the glasses allow me to function."

"Here's the thing, North. There's no way to know how much of that hypnotic radiation you can absorb before it destroys your talent and maybe does make you go insane. The more you wear those lenses, the worse things are going to get. I'll do the driving from now on."

"While I have visions and nightmares? I'll be useless, maybe even dangerous."

"You've been receiving a very low dose of the radiation through those glasses. Whoever infused the energy into the crystals was probably afraid to use too much heat, because it would have been detectable to a lot of people with talent. Sooner or later someone would have noticed and started asking questions."

"So?"

"So the good news is that it is a low dose. It might not take long for the worst of the effects to wear off. In the meantime, you can practice trying to control the visions."

"How do you control a vision?" North demanded.

"You know when you're hallucinating, right? You're aware that what you're seeing and hearing is not real."

"Yes, but that doesn't make them any less disturbing. The voices . . . whisper."

"Tell me about the hallucinations you're having right now," Sierra said. "What do you see?"

He concentrated on a foggy figure. Gradually it coalesced into a recognizable image.

"This one is different," he said. "It's Garraway, the director of Riverview."

"Why is this vision different?"

North shrugged. "He's not whispering."

"Focus on him," Sierra said.

"Why?"

"If my father were here, I think he would say that your intuition is trying to tell you something. Describe Garraway to me. Is he lying dead on the floor the way we found him?"

"No. He materialized out of the abyss. He's sitting behind his desk. Just sort of floating there."

"The abyss is probably a manifestation of your anxiety about the possibility of losing control of your talent," Sierra said.

"No shit. I'm not a doctor, but even I could figure that out."

"Sorry. Let's keep going here. Why did Garraway appear?"

"How should I know? He's a hallucination."

"Think of him as a manifestation of your intuition," Sierra said patiently. "We spent some time with him in his office. You found those financial papers in his cabin. We were in a hurry but you must have collected a lot of impressions at the scene of the murder. Maybe we missed something important? Try asking Garraway why you're seeing him."

North studied the dead man and tried to ignore the ghostly whispers telling him that he was risking his sanity by talking to a vision.

"Why am I seeing you?" he asked half under his breath.

Isn't it obvious? I was just the money guy.

North stilled.

"What is it?" Sierra asked. "Did you get an answer?"

"He was the money guy. He financed Riverview. That was clear from the records we found in his house. But I figured that out already, so why would he repeat the information?"

"Keep going with questions," Sierra said.

North made himself concentrate on the vision. "Why did the Puppets murder you?"

I knew too much about what went on in Loring's lab. Things were coming apart because you showed up. Couldn't take the risk that I'd talk.

"Now you're dead, so you can't talk," North said, feeling his way through the crazy conversation.

True, but I'm the money guy, and money always talks.

"Damn, you're right," North said.

Garraway vanished back into the abyss.

North realized that Sierra was still watching him.

"Well?" she said.

North tried to blink away a few more ghostly images while he concentrated on what had just happened. "If we're right about Garraway, he provided the financial backing for the whole Riverview setup, including Loring's lab."

"So?"

"So the ghost of Garraway reminded me of one of the most basic rules of crime solving. Follow the money."

"Okay, that sounds like a great idea."

"Victor is probably already tearing into the Riverview finances. He's got a whole team of forensic accountants. But I'll call him just to make sure he's pushing in that direction. We need to know how and why Loring got involved with Garraway."

"You and I should get a couple of hours' sleep before we head for Fogg Lake."

North scrubbed his face with the heels of his hands. "You get some sleep. I won't be able to sleep, not unless I put on the glasses."

"I honestly don't think that would be a good idea. You need to let the poison wear off."

"Assuming you're right, that could take days."

"No, I don't think so. I think we're talking hours, not days, for this stuff to wear off. We know you still have your talent, because you used it to douse that light grenade. You can try accessing it. Maybe that will help suppress the hallucinations."

"It's going to be a long night," North said.

With no guarantee that, come morning, he would still be sane. But Sierra's certainty gave him the first real shot of hope he'd had since the hallucinations had set in. If she turned out to be right, he would deal with the implications later.

"Forget sleep." Sierra got to her feet. "I'll make some coffee."

"You're going to stay awake with me?"

"I might be able to use my locket to help you concentrate on suppressing some of the effects of the poison, especially the whispers. I think they are the real problem."

"You're going to use your talent the way you did to help me sleep last night and the way you used it to help Matt Harper recover his memories?"

"I'm pretty strong." She paused, tilted her head slightly and gave him an unreadable look. "Some people would say that my talent makes me one of the monsters, the kind the Foundation cleaners hunt."

"No," he said. "I've met monsters. You're not one of them. What you are is amazing."

CHAPTER 25

North sat quietly while Sierra got the small coffeemaker going. He watched the whispering images come and go at the edges of his vision, first attempting to suppress the panic they inspired and then trying to banish them through sheer force of will. He discovered he could suppress them temporarily, but as soon as he stopped concentrating on one, it popped up again.

Sierra hit the switch to turn on the coffeemaker. Then she folded her arms and leaned against the counter.

"Any idea who might want you psi-blind?" she asked.

"No," he said. "Probably the same bastard who tried to murder my father—Loring. This all seems to have roots in the past. But I'll figure it out later. Right now we need to stay focused on finding the artifact that partially destabilized Dad's aura."

"It strikes me that any way you look at this thing we're dealing with paranormal weapons," Sierra said. "I thought that, technically speaking, it was impossible to construct such a device. Something to do with tuning problems."

He got to his feet and went to stand in front of the fire. "The Foundation experts say the problem with weaponizing paranormal energy is that to be effective, each individual gun or pistol would have to be tuned to the aura of the user. In addition, only someone with a very powerful aura could operate such a device. The risk of blowback would be extremely high."

"Blowback?"

"Similar to the recoil you get when you fire a conventional weapon. Except that in the case of a paranormal device, the energy recoil will tend to destabilize the aura of the user over time—unless the shooter is strong enough to handle the shock. It was a technical problem that supposedly was never solved while the Bluestone Project was in operation. But there have always been rumors that toward the end of the project, one lab might have made a breakthrough."

"Vortex?"

He looked up suddenly. "What do you know about Vortex?"

"Very little. But it's a legend in the underground market. There's no limit on the price of any artifact that has a Vortex provenance. But to my knowledge, none has ever come on the market."

North glanced at the machine sitting on the table. "Given what happened to my father and the fact that someone tried to kill us with that light grenade, we have to assume that there is some truth to the legends about paranormal weapons. But maybe they didn't all come from Vortex."

"You're sure Griffin Chastain and Crocker Rancourt didn't work in the Vortex lab?"

"There's no record of their being connected to that lab. According to the Foundation files, they were doing research at the Fogg Lake facility. But who knows? Maybe that was just a cover. Everything about Vortex was top secret. The thing is—"

He broke off as a tidal wave of nightmares screamed silently out of the darkness. *You must wear the glasses. You will go mad without them.*

It took everything he had to suppress them.

He became aware of a frisson of gentle energy. Out of the corner of his eye he saw the mirrored crystal in Sierra's locket spark.

The nightmares receded. He took a deep breath.

"I feel like a junkie trying to get through withdrawal," he said.

"No, you're recovering from a sickness induced by poison. What were you about to say?"

"What?" He had to concentrate to remember where he had been going with the conversation. "Right. Vortex. Everything connected to it was highly classified, so it's not impossible that Griffin Chastain and Crocker Rancourt were involved with it. But I've been studying my grandfather's private logbooks and the various experiments he performed in his lab at the Abyss—"

"His Vegas mansion?"

"Right. I moved in almost a year ago. I've had a chance to see what he was working on there. What I was about to tell you is that there is no indication that he was ever interested in creating paranormal weapons. His work was all aimed at gaining a greater understanding of the energy of light from the dark end of the spectrum."

"I can tell you for certain that if someone has found a cache of paranormal weapons, the artifacts will be worth a fortune on the underground market."

"That's true," North said. He blinked away a few more ghosts. "But using such a weapon would be extremely problematic."

"The tuning issue?" Sierra said.

"Yes."

Sierra poured coffee into two cups. "You said firing a weapon that was not properly tuned would destabilize the shooter's aura."

"That's the theory," North said.

A terrible restlessness was coming over him. He began to pace the small space. Sierra handed him one of the cups. The warmth felt good, because he was starting to shiver.

"We are definitely running into indications of aura instability in this case," Sierra said. "Would the end result be insanity or death?"

"Probably. Assuming the experts are right."

"If Delbridge Loring is Crocker Rancourt's direct descendant, he would probably know the risks involved," Sierra mused. "He would most likely be very cautious about firing any weapons he found."

North tried to focus on that. "Yes, he would. He would be very careful."

Sierra's locket sparked again. North felt another whisper of calming energy. He stopped shivering and managed to drink some of the coffee.

"That might explain the Puppets," he said.

"The orderlies?"

"Yes. Hell, it could explain the existence of Riverview. If Loring has found some paranormal weapons and if he is descended from Crocker Rancourt, he would know better than to take the risk of trying to fire the devices himself. But the promise of a psychic gun would be a lure that could be used to attract some useful test subjects."

"Puppets who would then become his dedicated bodyguards because they believed he would endow them with the perfect weapons—guns that leave no trace."

"Right."

Another wave of hallucinations danced at the edges of his vision. He stopped talking and concentrated on suppressing the ghosts.

It was going to be a very long night.

CHAPTER 26

Ralph sat behind the wheel of the SUV. Joe was next to him in the passenger's seat. Seth and Walt were in the rear seat. They all watched the windows on the second floor of the inn. The blinds were pulled shut, but firelight flickered on the shades.

Chastain and Raines were inside, but Ralph had concluded there was no way to get at them without setting off the inn's security alarms. There was also the problem of the psychic gadget the woman had used on Joe earlier that evening. Ralph knew enough about paranormal weapons now to be wary of someone who seemed to be able to use one.

But the real issue was that he and the others could not hang around long enough to try to take out Chastain and Raines. They were now suspects in the murder of Garraway. They all had to keep moving. The project was in serious jeopardy.

"We'll get another shot at them tomorrow when they leave town," Seth muttered.

Ralph gripped the steering wheel with both hands, fighting a toxic mix of frustration and fury. "What went wrong at the hospital?"

"I dunno." Walt massaged his temples. "I told you. The woman did something to me with her necklace."

"Loring is going to be pissed when he finds out that Chastain has the machine," Joe observed.

Ralph scowled. "Dr. Loring said there was a second machine, remember? That's what we're after."

"Let's get out of here." Walt slumped against the door. "I'm beat. That bitch really did a number on me. I need to sleep."

"I'm not feeling so good, either," Joe muttered.

Seth banged one fist against the back of the seat. "Fuck. It was all going so well. Now the whole plan is falling apart."

Back at the start Loring had made it sound so simple, Ralph reflected. The night gun was the perfect weapon. It left no forensic evidence. All that was required was proper tuning. He and the others had fired the gun on several occasions. They were adjusting to the powerful psychic recoil, growing stronger. And once they had mastered the gun, Loring promised there were plenty more from the cache of paranormal weapons.

Ralph was the one who had used it on Chandler Chastain. Loring had been sure the authorities would assume Chastain had suffered a stroke and died.

Ralph had felt weird afterward but Loring had explained that the crystal that powered the gun sent out some major psychic shock waves. It took time to adjust to the device. It was a little more complicated than the explosive they had set in the abandoned apartment building.

But Chandler Chastain had not died and the Foundation had not bought the stroke story. Within hours North Chastain had arrived on the scene. Then Loring had disappeared and he had taken the night gun with him. Now North Chastain had the special machine. Loring was not going to be happy about that.

Ralph watched the upstairs windows of the inn for a couple more minutes and then he fired up the SUV's heavy engine.

"If Chastain found the right artifact we'll know soon enough," he said.

"How?" Joe asked.

"He'll head straight for Fogg Lake."

CHAPTER 27

The whispering hallucinations finally began to retreat shortly after dawn.

"They're becoming faint," North said. "Just shadows now. I can't believe it. All these weeks I've been convinced I would go mad if I took off the damned glasses."

Sierra opened her senses and studied his aura in the mirror that hung over the fireplace. "The unstable vibe I noticed in your aura has diminished considerably. Got a feeling you'll still see a few hallucinations once in a while until the last of the effects of the poison are gone, but you are definitely recovering. If I were you I would destroy those glasses."

He looked at the mirrored sunglasses sitting on the coffee table next to the machine. "I'd like nothing better, but at the moment they are evidence. I should be able to use them to find out who poisoned the crystals."

"Good point." She glanced at the glasses. "Best keep them in lead or steel. You don't want any of that radiation leaking out. I've got a lockbox in the back of my vehicle that I use for transporting small artifacts. The glasses will be secure in there."

"Right."

He looked at her, his eyes heating. She knew that look. Gratitude. It was not what she wanted from him.

She jumped to her feet. "We should get on the road. Long drive ahead of us. Neither of us got any sleep last night, but you're the one who went through hell detoxing your senses, so I'll take the wheel."

He crossed the room in two strides. His hands closed over her shoulders. She wasn't wearing her leather jacket, just a long-sleeved pullover. It wasn't the first time he had touched her, but on the previous occasion in the abandoned building there had been a lot of energy flying around.

This time the situation was much more intimate. There should have been a jolt of some kind. And there was. But it was a very pleasant jolt, a thrilling spark of awareness. An unfamiliar excitement lit up her senses.

"Sierra—" He stopped, shock narrowing his eyes. He yanked his hands off her. "I'm so damn sorry. I forgot you don't like to be touched."

"No, it's okay," she said, a little breathless because it really was okay. Another wave of euphoria zinged through her. "It all depends on who is touching me."

"You don't mind my touch?"

"No."

Gently, tentatively, he put his hands back on her shoulders.

"You're sure?" he said.

"Positive." She smiled. "I'm not really Ms. Untouchable. It's just that I need to be . . . comfortable with the person who touches me."

"You're comfortable with me?"

"Obviously. But I guess that's not a surprise, given what we've been through together."

He tightened his grip a little and drew her closer. "You just saved my sanity. My talent. Maybe my life. I don't know how to thank you."

"No need. Really."

His mouth came down on hers in a crushing, energy-charged kiss that took her to an entirely new level of sensation.

Should have seen this coming, she thought.

She felt light-headed, weightless. If North had not had her clamped against his chest she would have lost her balance. Sexual attraction had never before struck her with such overwhelming force.

In the past she'd always approached that side of things with great care because of her issues with physical touch. Even when all went well, the best she could say about the experience was that it had been pleasant. Words like *exciting* and *thrilling* were not applicable. Mostly sex fell into the category of okay-but-I'd-rather-be-reading-a-good-book.

She had never been swept away by passion. In the past her relationships had always fizzled. But everything was different with North.

"Sierra?" North said against her mouth.

Her name brought her back to reality with a thud. She knew what she felt for him, and it was depressing to realize that what he felt for her was probably—mostly—driven by a profound sense of gratitude.

"We really need to get on the road," she said.

"Yes," he said.

She stepped back. He let her go.

But his eyes still burned with all the colors of night.

CHAPTER 28

Sierra was at the wheel, because although North had napped for the past two hours he was still getting flashes of hallucinations. His senses were recovering rapidly but he did not trust himself to handle the narrow, rural road that was taking them deep into the Cascades.

A while back they had stopped to do some basic emergency rations shopping at a grocery store. They were expecting to arrive in Fogg Lake before sunset, but Olivia LeClair had warned them that it was never wise to drive the isolated road without enough food and water to last for a day or two. "If you get caught in the fog you'll be stuck by the side of the road overnight," she had explained. "Whatever you do, don't try to drive in that stuff. And don't leave your car. It's not normal fog. It's extremely disorienting."

After the grocery shopping expedition, North had opened the cargo door of the SUV and taken out the machine he had found in Loring's lab. The device was now sitting on the floor between his feet. He undid the flap of one of the pockets of his cargo pants and took out a compact screwdriver.

"Do you always travel with a full set of tools, a lockpick, penlights and a gun tucked away in your clothes?" Sierra asked.

"Yeah, just the basics," he said. "I'd rather have a decent tool chest but it's hard to haul one around when you're trying to move quickly."

"I'd hate to be the person behind you in an airport security line."

"I rarely fly commercial. By the time my team gets called in to handle a problem the situation has usually deteriorated to the point where there isn't time to go through the standard airport routine. We end up on the Foundation jet or in some very good, very fast cars."

"You live an exciting life."

"I guess."

He examined the screws that held the box together. It was obvious they had been recently removed and replaced. He went to work on the metal box.

"Are you sure it's safe to fool around with that thing?" Sierra asked.

"I am not fooling around with it. I am examining it."

"Okay, okay, you don't have to act as if I just insulted you. But what if it's another paranormal weapon?"

"It's not," he said, very sure of himself now. "I can sense the vibe in it. I don't know what it was designed to do but I am certain of two things: it was built by Griffin Chastain and it is not a weapon."

He was sure of something else as well. He had screwed up that morning when he kissed Sierra. She had said she was okay with him touching her and he thought she got the same red-hot charge out of the kiss that he got. But he must have been wrong, because just when things were getting interesting she had gone cold and pulled back. Okay, maybe not *ice*-cold, but there had definitely been a chill in the atmosphere. His fault, probably. He'd moved too fast. They hadn't even had a real date. Nearly getting murdered by a light grenade and attacked by some tattooed Puppets did not constitute the start of a relationship.

"How can you tell that box isn't a weapon?" she asked. She sounded genuinely curious.

"I've been living inside my grandfather's personal lab for nearly a year," he said. "I know intuitively how to work his devices. He made his living as a magician in Vegas before he was recruited into the Bluestone Project, but he was an engineer by training."

"An engineer with a sixth sense for manipulating light from the dark end of the spectrum?"

"Right."

"Probably not a lot of job opportunities for him in the normal world," Sierra said. "No wonder he wound up with a magic act in Vegas."

"Until the Bluestone recruiters found him."

North slipped the screwdriver back into his small tool kit and gently lifted the black metal plate off the machine. He set the plate on the floor and gazed into the box. There was a compartment inside. It was made of steel. He undid the lock that secured it and found himself gazing at a chunk of colorless gray crystal.

A thrill of anticipation crackled through him. He was on the brink of discovering something very important, something that would answer a few questions.

Gently he lifted the crystal out of the inner compartment and jacked up his senses.

"Looks like a gray rock," Sierra said.

"It's a crystal." North sat back in the seat and studied the artifact. "Not a natural one. It must have been created in a lab. There's a lot of energy inside it, but it's unfocused. Shattered. Probably because whoever has been using it couldn't handle the vibe. If you don't control it, the vibe controls you."

"Any idea what that machine is supposed to do?" she asked.

"I'm not absolutely positive, but judging by the energy and what

I know of my grandfather's engineering style and interests, I've got a feeling this is some sort of tuning device. I've got a crystal on my mantel back home in Vegas that looks a lot like this one. I always knew it was important but I couldn't figure out why."

"So that crystal is not a weapon, but it may be a mechanism for tuning one to a human aura?"

North turned the crystal in his hand. "But not just any aura. It would only function properly if it was used by someone with an aura that carried Griffin Chastain's unique vibe."

"One of his descendants?"

"Right. But regardless of the original intent, it's useless now."

"I'll bet Loring was using it to try to tune the Puppets to some paranormal weapons, like the light grenade and the flashlight gun Matt described."

"Probably. If that's true, those four orderlies are in bad shape by now. This crystal was very powerful."

Sierra tightened her grip on the steering wheel. "Delbridge Loring was trying to tune paranormal weapons in his lab at Riverview."

"Looks like it. He managed to find a few people with enough talent to activate the weapons—the orderlies—but he would have needed subjects for his experiments."

"Marge and the other inmates at the hospital?"

"Yes."

"But where did he get the weapons?" Sierra asked. "I still think that if Loring had found the old Vortex lab the news would be all over the underground market."

"I agree. But this tuning device and those weapons could have come from the lab that Griffin Chastain and Crocker Rancourt controlled inside the Fogg Lake complex. That facility was huge. It covered miles inside those tunnels. There must have been hundreds of rooms, labs and offices. The Foundation has barely begun to excavate the site. Trust me, if the Chastain-Rancourt lab had been discovered I would have heard about it."

"Then where have those artifacts been all these years?" Sierra asked.

"Maybe our witness, Marge, will be able to fill in some of the missing pieces of the puzzle." North looked at the semi-dismantled tuning machine. A frisson of certainty snapped across his senses. "It all began in Fogg Lake," he said. "The answers must be there, too."

CHAPTER 29

think I just saw a wisp of fog," North said.

"Too early," Sierra said. "We've got another couple of hours before sunset."

"Olivia warned us that the fog was becoming more unpredictable lately," North said.

"Yes, I know, but—" Sierra caught a glimpse of gray mist gathering in the heavy woods on either side of the road. A chill zapped across her senses. "Damn. You're right."

They were deep into the mountains now. She was still at the wheel. They had passed the last tiny town with its lone gas station an hour ago.

Olivia had explained that, in addition to the natural hazards of the narrow, winding highway, the fog that always made driving in the area impossible after sundown had begun rolling in off the lake earlier in the evening and was lingering longer after sunrise. Ever since the explosion in the old Fogg Lake lab, the strange mist had been infused with paranormal energy. But in recent weeks the radiation was stronger and more disorienting.

Some of the Foundation scientists engaged in exploring and mapping the recently discovered ruins of the Fogg Lake lab attributed the phenomenon to global warming. But according to Olivia, the people who lived in the small community were convinced the new problems with the nightly mist were caused by the researchers and technicians who were disturbing the powerful forces that had been sealed inside the lab tunnels for decades.

"Night comes early in the mountains," North said. "And paranormal energy is always enhanced by darkness, regardless of the technical time of sunrise and sunset."

"So long as we don't make any wrong turns we should be okay," Sierra said.

They were using Olivia's carefully written directions because the closer they got to Fogg Lake, the less they could rely on the vehicle's navigation system. Sure enough, GPS had gone down an hour ago. The cell phones had stopped working shortly afterward.

"According to Olivia's directions we're only about ten miles away from the town of Fogg Lake," Sierra said.

"If the fog gets any worse it might as well be a thousand miles," North said. "It's not normal fog."

The mist that Sierra could see drifting through the trees had an eerie green glow. There were things moving in it. Hallucinations.

No, there would be no way to drive through that stuff once it covered the road.

"We may have another problem," North said.

Sierra glanced at him and saw that he had turned to view something through the back window.

"What?" she said.

"There's a vehicle on the road behind us."

Sierra glanced at the rearview mirror. She caught a glimpse of another SUV just before it disappeared into a turn.

"You're thinking it's not a coincidence that we're not alone out here on the road to Fogg Lake, aren't you?" she said.

"You must be psychic."

"Let's not jump straight into another conspiracy theory."

"We're already ass-deep in conspiracy theories," North said. "What's one more?"

"The vehicle behind us could belong to a Foundation team."

"We talked to Victor and Olivia before we set out from Riverview," North reminded her. "Neither of them said anything about a scheduled trip today. The Foundation is enforcing tight security on the town. All arrivals and departures associated with headquarters are registered with Lark and LeClair."

"Could be one of the locals returning from a shopping trip," Sierra said. "I doubt if the people who actually live in Fogg Lake feel the need to check in with the Foundation authorities or Lark and LeClair."

"Okay, I'll allow that as a possibility," North said.

"Look at it this way—worst-case scenario is that the Puppets are following us, right?"

"Right."

"They must realize they can't overtake us, not on this road," Sierra said. "And once we get to Fogg Lake there will be a small battalion of Foundation agents waiting for us. Whoever is in that car behind us will be stopped and searched."

"Maybe we're not expected to make it all the way into town," North said.

"What?"

"Pull over to the side and stop," he said.

"What?"

"Now."

She wanted to ask questions and demand answers but there was no arguing with the steel in the command. The badass cleaner from the Foundation was taking charge. She eased the SUV onto the very narrow edge of the pavement, unclipped her seat belt, popped open the door and jumped down to the ground.

"Get your jacket and pack," North ordered.

She yanked open the rear door and hauled out her things. North grabbed his jacket, his pack and the tuning machine.

"Where are we going?" she asked.

"Into the trees," he said. "We need to get as far away from the car as possible. Whatever you do, stay close to me. We can't risk getting separated, not in this terrain."

He plunged into the woods. She slung her pack over her shoulder and followed. He might be overreacting to the perceived threat of the approaching vehicle, but he was right about one thing—it would be all too easy to get lost in the woods.

They stood deep in the trees and watched the vehicle that had followed them slam to a halt behind the SUV. Car doors banged open. Four figures got out.

"Chastain probably has a gun," Ralph said. His voice carried clearly in the eerie stillness of the mountains. "We take him out first. All we need is whatever he's got on him or in the car."

"What about the woman?" Joe demanded. "She's dangerous."

"Get rid of her, too," Ralph said. "She's just a go-between."

The four men approached the SUV, pistols in hand.

"Out of the car," Ralph shouted. "Now."

When nothing happened Ralph fired straight into the rear window of the SUV, shattering the glass.

"They're gone," he announced in disgust. "Fuck it. Well, it doesn't matter. They probably won't make it out of the woods, not in this fog. Check the car. We're looking for anything that has a paranormal vibe. Anything at all."

They yanked open the SUV doors and quickly went through the vehicle. Ralph used his gun to blow open the lockbox.

"Nothing in here but those weird glasses Chastain was wearing," he announced.

"Nothing up front," Joe said. He slammed the driver's-side door closed. "Not a damn thing. If they've got the device, they took it with them."

One of the men looked around. "That damned fog is getting heavier. We can't hang around here much longer."

"That fucking Chastain," Ralph said. His voice rose in fury and frustration. "What the hell is going on?"

The three other Puppets were already moving swiftly back toward their own SUV. Ralph started to follow them but he paused at the open cargo door of Sierra's vehicle.

He took a fist-sized object out of his jacket and tossed it into the rear of the vehicle. There was a muffled *whoomph*.

Sierra watched, stunned, as her precious SUV exploded in flames.

"But I was still making payments on it," she whispered.

North clamped a hand over her mouth to silence her.

Not that the Puppets would have heard her. They were all piling back into their own SUV. Ralph got behind the wheel, did a tight three-point turn and roared off back down the mountain road.

CHAPTER 30

North took his hand off Sierra's mouth. She looked a little annoyed but mostly she looked worried.

"They're gone," she said, "for now, at any rate. Do you think the fire will spread to the trees?"

North studied the burning SUV. The fire was already dying. Rain had fallen earlier in the day. The ground was damp and the trees on both sides of the road still dripped.

"I don't think there's any danger of a fire, not in these woods," he said. "Let's see if we can find somewhere out of the fog to spend the night."

"Remember what Olivia said—if we wander too far away from the road we're likely to get disoriented."

North opened his senses. Darkness was closing in fast, which made it easier to read the energy currents around them. One thin trickle of ice-bright light caught his attention.

"Maybe not," he said.

"What do you mean?"

"See those quicksilver currents in the fog? I think they are ema-nating from a nearby source. This mountain is riddled with caves and tunnels, some natural, some human-engineered. Don't know about you, but I'd rather spend the night inside a cavern than outdoors."

Sierra watched him with a cautious expression. "What quicksilver currents?" She glanced around at the fog-choked woods. "This mist is infused with enough paranormal heat to make it glow but I don't see any currents in it."

North contemplated the stream of energy pouring through the fog. "There are two possibilities here. Either I'm hallucinating again or my talent is back in good working condition."

"You're not sure?"

"My senses feel normal again, but there's one way to find out if that quicksilver energy stream is real. If I'm right, it's powerful. You'll probably be able to sense it if you get close to it. But we should maintain physical contact. Hold on to my belt."

"Okay." She reached under his leather jacket and took a grip on his belt. "For what it's worth, I don't think you're hallucinating," she said. "I took a look at your aura in the car mirror a couple of times on the way up here. You're stable."

Her faith in him fortified him as nothing else could have at that moment. He tightened his grip on the tuning machine and waded into the energy stream. The waves of quicksilver glowed like moon-light in the green fog. Sierra followed close behind.

She caught her breath. "I can't see them, but I can definitely feel the currents now."

"I've been told that the caverns and tunnels are the source of the paranormal energy in these mountains. Some of it is natural. Lucas Pine says that's probably the reason the site was chosen as a location for one of the labs. But the heavy stuff is most likely the result of all the experiments and research that were done inside the caves. I'm betting that a strong river of heat like this indicates a nearby lab tunnel."

"That sounds reasonable."

"I can't tell you how relieved I am to hear you say that."

"Because it means I don't think you're unstable?"

"It's the small things in a relationship."

"Absolutely."

The currents of the quicksilver energy got stronger and more intense. North discovered that it required an increasing amount of effort from all of his senses, normal and paranormal, to forge ahead.

"I feel like a salmon trying to swim upstream," Sierra said.

"Bad analogy. Salmon that swim upriver usually come to a bad end."

"Oh, right. The spawn-and-die thing."

"That's assuming they don't get caught in a fishing net or eaten by a bear along the way."

Night was coming on fast now. He knew that theoretically they could survive outside in the damp, disorienting fog, but it would be an ordeal. Olivia had warned them that people who got trapped in the mist tended to hallucinate. They got disoriented and they got lost, often permanently. North figured he'd had enough of ghostly visions.

And then he saw it—the narrow river of quicksilver was pouring out of a dark opening in the rocks.

"I see the entrance to a cave," he said.

"I'll take your word for it. I still can't make out anything except this damn green fog."

It dawned on him that she had been following him blindly for the past several minutes, trusting him to navigate the mist-clouded darkness. He was pretty sure the majority of people who knew about his shattered talent—and understood exactly what that meant—would have been terrified by now.

"Almost there," he said.

He steered her through the cave entrance. To his relief, the interior of the cavern was big and mercifully clear of the mist. It was obvious at once that they had entered a human-engineered tunnel, not a natural rock cave. The walls, ceiling and floor of the space were lined with what looked like black glass. The material radiated enough energy to illuminate the room in an icy blue glow.

"Can you see now?" North asked.

Sierra looked around, took a deep breath and released her grip on his belt. "No problem. The light in here is visible to me. There's some heat as well. We won't be cold tonight. Can you still make out the quicksilver river?"

"Yes. The currents are coming from that side tunnel." He indicated the entrance to a narrow passageway. "We should be able to use the energy river to navigate back to the road in the morning."

"Olivia said the first rule of survival in the Fogg Lake tunnel system is to find the strongest current and follow it in. Then use the same current to find your way back out."

"Got news for you—that rule applies to navigating any sort of paranormal energy," North said. "There's just one problem with the concept."

"What?"

"You may not like what you find when you reach the source of the energy stream you're following."

Sierra looked around. "I think we'll be okay in here tonight, but it's going to be a long hike into Fogg Lake tomorrow."

"When we fail to show up tonight, the Foundation team in Fogg Lake will assume we got stranded in the fog. They'll come looking for us in the morning. When they see the burned-out wreck of your SUV on the side of the road they'll know where to start the search."

"Assuming they realize we didn't die in that explosion," Sierra said.

"No bodies, remember? Trust me, they'll look for us. We'll go back to the road first thing in the morning. I'll bet we run straight into the search party."

"Or the Puppets," Sierra said.

"Right now those four are probably telling themselves that we'll be dead or hopelessly lost by morning. They aren't our main problem, anyway."

"Could have fooled me. In case you didn't notice they just tried to kill us and they destroyed my car," Sierra said.

"I know, but it's the man they're working for we have to worry about."

"Delbridge Loring. Yes, well, he must know that the Foundation is looking for him. If he's smart he'll disappear."

"He can't do that," North said.

Sierra slanted him a considering look. "Why not?"

North set the tuning machine down on the floor of the cavern and studied it for a moment. "Because he's obsessed with finding something. Maybe the tuning device that was designed for Crocker Rancourt."

"Or maybe he's looking for more paranormal weapons," Sierra suggested. "It's obvious he found a couple."

"They're no good to him unless he finds a tuning crystal he can use." North let his pack slide off his shoulder. "Somehow he ended up with the one that was made for Griffin Chastain."

"You're sure there would have been two tuning machines?"

"Rancourt and my grandfather were equal partners in their lab. I'm sure they would each have had a device they could use to work the weapons. But somehow Rancourt must have ended up with Griffin Chastain's machine."

"So Loring is looking for Rancourt's?"

North thought about it for a minute. Got the ping of knowing. "It fits. He's found a cache of powerful weapons but he doesn't dare use them for fear of destroying his own aura. He needs Rancourt's tuning crystal. I think he attacked my father because he thought Dad had found something important at Swan Antiques, maybe an artifact that could lead him to Rancourt's crystal. That broken radio could have been mistaken for some sort of tuning device."

Sierra lowered her pack to the floor and gave him an odd look. "You think you've found an angle you can work, don't you?"

"I know what Loring wants now. Yes, I can work with that."

"There's only one reason he would think the other tuning crystal will work on the weapons he found," Sierra said. "Loring must be convinced he inherited Crocker Rancourt's psychic signature."

"A man who is willing to take the risks that Loring is taking is in the grip of an obsession. That's his vulnerability."

"Okay, I'm not going to argue with your logic," Sierra said. She sat down on the floor next to her pack and braced her back against the black glass wall. "In my business I run into obsessive types a lot. They'll take big risks and spend a lot of money to get what they want. They can also be extremely dangerous."

North lowered himself to the floor beside her. "You don't really want to work with clients like that for the rest of your career."

"There must be a better way to make a living. But so far I haven't found it." Sierra looked around. "I wonder why they lined this tunnel with black glass."

"Glass has some interesting properties when it comes to conducting and controlling paranormal energy. It's not a liquid and it's not a true crystal. No telling what Bluestone used this tunnel for, but I wouldn't be surprised if it had something to do with channeling power, maybe from that quicksilver river."

"So where's the generator?"

"It was probably destroyed when the orders were given to close down the labs." North studied the quicksilver river. "I'd like to see where that energy stream is coming from."

"I don't know about you but I'm hungry." Sierra reached for her bulging pack. "I vote we eat."

"Good plan." North opened his own pack. He rummaged around for a moment before producing a bottle of vitamin water and a couple of energy bars. "Save some of your emergency rations for breakfast."

"Sure," Sierra said.

He watched her open her pack. The first item she removed was a neatly folded square of red-and-white checkered cloth. She spread the fabric out on the glass floor.

"What the hell?" he said. "You brought a tablecloth?"

"Don't be silly. It's just a big napkin."

She reached back into her pack and took out a plastic baggie. There was a large wedge of cheddar cheese inside. Next came a foot-long baguette. The bread was followed by a plastic container of mixed olives.

North stared at the food, stunned. "You were buying those things at the grocery store while I was stocking up on nutrition bars?"

She raised her brows. "Got a problem with my food?"

"You call those emergency rations? It looks like you packed for a picnic."

"Just because people are trying to kill us doesn't mean I have to eat boring food."

Annoyed for no discernible reason, North ripped off the wrapper of one of the nutrition bars and took a bite. It tasted like sawdust.

Sierra pulled off a chunk of the baguette and used a small knife to cut a slice of the cheddar cheese. She took a bite of each and then opened the container of olives.

"I don't believe this," North muttered. "Next thing I know you'll be taking out a bottle of wine."

"Of course not," she said. "Glass bottles are heavy, plus they break easily." She reached back into the pack and removed a carton. "Wine in a box is so much easier to transport. It's not the finest cabernet on the market, but it's a surprisingly drinkable red blend. They've made a lot of progress in the quality of boxed wines."

North gazed, floored, at the winery label on the box. "You brought wine."

She glanced at the plastic bottle that he had taken out of his own pack.

"Beats vitamin water," she said. "Besides, I need a drink. I deserve a drink. I lost my beautiful little SUV this afternoon. It was brand-new."

"Damn."

"I'm going to put it on the bill that I send to Victor Arganbright."

North felt the rush of laughter rise up from somewhere deep inside. It burst forth, echoing off the black glass walls of the cave. It was, he reflected, the first time he had laughed in a very long time.

"Here, help yourself," Sierra said. She thrust the box of wine into his hand. "Sorry, I forgot the cups. That's the problem with shopping in a hurry. I should have made a proper list."

He stopped laughing, took the box from her hand and swallowed some of the wine. It tasted good. A hell of a lot better than vitamin water.

"A very fine vintage," he declared.

"Goes better with cheese than with a nutrition bar."

Sierra offered him a chunk of cheese. He took it and ate it. She was right. It paired well with the wine.

"How about some bread?" she suggested.

He tore off a chunk of the baguette and ate it with some more cheese. Then he plucked a couple of olives out of the container.

"Next time I pack emergency rations I'm going to let you do the grocery shopping," he said.

"Okay." She retrieved the wine, took a sip and lowered the box. "Had any more thoughts about who might have poisoned you?"

"No, but given the timing, I'm sure the attempt to destroy my talent is linked to this case."

Sierra nodded. "Sounds reasonable. If we're right about Delbridge Loring—if he is a direct descendant of Crocker Rancourt—there's a personal connection. Dosing you with a slow-acting poison feels like an act of revenge."

North took the box of wine and drank some of it while he thought about that.

"You're right," he said. "This has to go back to my grandfather's generation."

"You said Griffin Chastain disappeared?"

"After being labeled a traitor. Dad and I don't believe that he was executed by a spymaster who recruited him to steal Bluestone secrets. But we do believe he was most likely murdered."

"By Crocker Rancourt."

"Right. Now we can assume that Rancourt murdered Griffin in order to get the weapons and the tuning device. But something went wrong. Rancourt wound up with the wrong tuner."

"Wonder how that happened," Sierra said.

North rested his head against the wall and smiled a little, thinking about the question. "My grandfather was a very, very fine magician. One of a magician's most basic skills is sleight of hand."

Sierra raised her brows. "You're thinking he somehow made sure Rancourt got the wrong tuner?"

"Yep." North hoisted the wine box. "Nice work, Granddad."

"Well, one way or another, it seems obvious now that Vortex was not the only lab working on weaponizing paranormal energy."

North looked around at the glowing black glass walls. "Bluestone was supposed to be a wide-ranging research project designed to explore the possibilities of paranormal power in a variety of fields—communications, medicine, transportation, energy. But given that it was a government project, a lot of the emphasis was on national security and weapons. At the time, everyone was afraid the Soviet Union was way ahead of us in paranormal research."

"But you said the lab code-named Vortex was the lab that was dedicated to weaponizing paranormal energy."

"Yes, but that doesn't mean there wasn't a lot of similar research going on in the other labs. What set Vortex apart and made it a legend was that it was the only lab believed to have succeeded in creating some genuine prototypes of paranormal weapons."

"Well, we now know some other psychic engineers also created some weapons," Sierra said

"Griffin Chastain and Crocker Rancourt, working in their lab at the Fogg Lake facility."

Sierra nodded and ate another chunk of the baguette. "I keep wondering where those weapons have been all this time."

"I'm guessing they were found quite recently. If the Rancourts had been hiding a cache of weapons all these years, I think Victor and Lucas would have figured it out."

They finished the meal in silence. When they were done, Sierra packed up the picnic things, secured them in a baggie and stowed them in her pack.

"I don't suppose you brought breakfast, too?" North asked.

"Sorry. I was assuming that the cheese and bread would last a couple of days if necessary."

"Instead you ended up sharing them with me." North smiled. "Don't worry, I'll be happy to give you a couple of nutrition bars and an energy drink in the morning."

"Yay." Sierra fastened the pack. "Got any idea what you'll do when this situation is finished?"

"Now that I've got my talent back, I'll probably continue working with my cleaner team."

Sierra gave him a shrewd look. "But that's not really what you want to do with the rest of your life, is it?"

"It's a job," North said. "You?"

"Working as a Vault agent is a job, but no, I don't want to do it much longer. I really want to find my calling, North. I feel I was meant to do something more meaningful than delivering hot artifacts."

"Maybe some of us don't have a calling."

"My dad says if you *want* a calling it means you have one."

"I thought I had one once," North said.

"Being a badass Foundation cleaner?" Sierra asked. "What made you think that was your calling?"

"I saw it as a way to clear the family name. There are a lot of people in the Foundation who believe my grandfather was a traitor. I thought working as a cleaner and taking down the bad guys might wipe away the stain on my family's name." North shrugged. "But it doesn't work that way, not when it comes to reputations. Nothing I've accomplished has changed the legend of my grandfather."

Sierra smiled and quoted softly.

"As if my sense of self," you claim,
"Has drifted into air,
And nothing that I try to do
Brings credit to my name."

North looked at her. "That pretty well says it all. What's it from?"

"'Hope and Love,' a poem my dad sent to me just before I met you."

"What's the rest of the poem?"

"There's some advice about attending and listening so that you can hear the voice calling to you. The poem is on my phone, but phones don't work in this atmosphere. I'll read the whole thing to you when we get a connection."

"Okay." North tried to figure out how to ease into the conversation he needed to have. "There's something else we should talk about," he said.

"If this is about what happened very early this morning—"

"Yeah." He exhaled slowly. "I noticed you haven't mentioned it."

"Were you waiting for me to bring up the subject?" Sierra said.

"I think so, yes. And the fact that you haven't mentioned it is making me nervous."

"Don't worry, it was just a kiss," Sierra said. "I have a strict rule when it comes to sleeping with clients. It's a definite no-no. Last night things got a little weird because people had tried to kill us and we had saved each other's lives and we had just realized you had been poisoned. All in all, a lot going on. You spent hours fighting to regain control of your talent. I was awake all night helping you. Our physical response to each other was a natural reaction to the stress."

He nodded. "Got it. Let me know when you run out of reasonable explanations for what was the most amazing kiss of my entire life."

Sierra's eyes widened. "Amazing?"

"I'm terrified to ask the obvious question but I can't resist. Was it good for you, too?"

She drew a deep breath as though she was preparing to jump out of an airplane and she wasn't sure the parachute would open.

"It was . . . amazing," she said. "Definitely the best kiss ever."

"Then why—?"

"I was afraid you were just feeling grateful because I helped you get over the effects of the poison."

"I *was* feeling grateful. But that was not a gratitude kiss. I don't do gratitude kisses."

"You're sure?"

"Positive. Gratitude hugs, maybe, but definitely not gratitude kisses."

"Okay," Sierra said. "That's good to know."

North told himself he was satisfied. For now.

"Let's get some sleep," he said. He unbuckled his holster and put it down on the floor within easy reach. Then he arranged his pack as a pillow. "We've got a long hike in the morning."

CHAPTER 31

Sierra awoke to find herself intimately tucked into the curve of North's lean, hard frame. They were both fully dressed, but his arm was draped around her midsection and her butt was nestled into his thighs.

For a moment she lay absolutely still, afraid to make a move. She had never awakened in a man's arms because she never did sleepovers. Waking up in North's arms was an interesting experience.

After a moment she opened her eyes to the light emanating from the black glass walls of the tunnel. At the mouth of the cavern the radiant green fog was dissipating. Dawn had arrived.

She was stiff and sore from sleeping on the hard floor but she was reluctant to move out from under the comforting weight of North's arm.

It was North who moved first. He released her and rolled to his feet in an easy, lithe movement. He went to the mouth of the cave.

"Fog's lifting," he announced. He turned around to face her. "Time to hit the road."

Sierra stretched cautiously, wincing a little at the stiffness in her shoulders, and climbed to her feet.

"If you'll excuse me, I'm going outside to pee," she announced.

"Good plan." North shoved his fingers through his hair and squinted a little.

"Still seeing and hearing things that aren't there?" Sierra asked.

"Yes, damn it. But the whispers are not nearly as loud as they were yesterday. I can suppress them now."

"Those poisoned crystals disrupted your talent for a few weeks. It's going to take some time to recover. You didn't sleep well last night, did you?"

"I spent a lot of time wondering exactly how this connects to the past."

"Isn't it obvious? Loring is after a dangerous and valuable artifact."

North shook his head. "I don't think this is just about a relic. There's something else going on here. Trying to murder my father and blind me feels like an act of revenge."

They used the woods for personal business and rinsed their hands in the nearby stream before munching on the nutrition bars. They each drank a bottle of vitamin water and slung their packs over their shoulders.

"With luck there will be coffee waiting for us in Fogg Lake," Sierra said.

"Let's just hope they send out a search party to look for us," North said. "Otherwise it's going to be a long day. Ten miles in these mountains is a serious walk."

"What if the Puppets decide to return this morning?"

North shook his head. "They won't come hunting on foot. They'll be driving that SUV we saw last night. Don't worry, we'll hear them long before they get anywhere near us."

"Can you still see the quicksilver energy you detected last night?" Sierra asked.

"Yes. Shouldn't be any problem following it back to the road."

"I can sense it but I still can't see it."

North started toward the entrance, but he stopped and turned around.

"What?" Sierra asked.

"Before we leave I want to take a quick look down that side tunnel to see if I can determine the source of the quicksilver energy."

"I'll come with you, but we shouldn't go too far. Olivia says people can get lost forever in these tunnels."

"Don't worry. This will just take a minute or two."

North led the way into the side tunnel. Sierra fell into step behind him. The energy stream got noticeably stronger, tugging at all of her senses.

"It's sort of exciting, isn't it?" she said. "Like walking through a thunderstorm."

North glanced back over his shoulder. He looked amused. "Exactly like that."

They rounded a bend in the tunnel. North stopped so suddenly that Sierra nearly collided with him.

"What is it?" she asked.

He gestured with one hand. "Take a look."

She moved a little to get a better view and caught her breath when she saw the tower of glowing, multicolored crystals. The stones were cut in hexagonal shapes and stacked in a way that reminded Sierra of a honeycomb.

"Someone turned that machine on back in the last century and left it running," she said, awed.

"The honeycomb is a highly efficient way to arrange paranormal crystals if you're trying to produce and generate energy," North said. He walked to the tower and touched a couple of the stones. "I've never seen anything like these before. I wonder what the researchers planned to do with the energy this thing is producing?"

"Just one more lost lab mystery," Sierra said. She studied the jeweled honeycomb. "With so much significant work going on, I wonder why the government shut down the Bluestone Project?"

"No one knows for sure, but there are several theories," North said. "One explanation is that paranormal research fell out of favor in the last quarter of the twentieth century. People who claimed to take it seriously were considered charlatans, con artists or delusional. There's no denying that was true about a lot of the so-called psychics of the era. Hell, it still is today. Politicians didn't want their names associated with paranormal research, so the funding dried up."

"What about the other theories?"

"A lot of people are convinced the reason the research was shut down is simply because it never yielded any useful technology, at least none that proved practical. The costs couldn't be justified."

"My parents and grandparents told me that everyone from Fogg Lake thinks the program was halted because of the explosion that took place there," Sierra said. "It became obvious to the people in charge they were dealing with forces they could not control."

"That may have been part of the explanation, but Victor Arganbright has another, slightly different theory."

"Would this be one of his conspiracy theories?"

"You could call it that. Victor doesn't think the government pulled the plug on Bluestone because of the failure of the weapons to work or because of the explosion at Fogg Lake. He thinks whoever was in charge panicked when it became evident the Bluestone Project was on the brink of creating something even more dangerous than paranormal guns."

Sierra considered that briefly. "Bombs that might be as devastating as nuclear bombs, maybe? Radiation that might have unpredictable effects on the population?"

"Maybe. No one knows. Like I said, it's just a theory of Victor's. He says he's come across hints of panic toward the end of the project. Something scared the hell out of whoever was in charge. But he's never found out what it was that caused the program to be shut down so abruptly." North paused. "There's a weird painting in his office. There are a *lot* of weird paintings in his office. But one in particular stands out."

"What's the subject of the painting?"

"It appears to show an oracle—not one from the days of Delphi, but from the era of the lost labs. In the painting a hooded figure is gesturing toward a crystal pyramid. A prophecy is written on the bottom of the picture. 'Here there be monsters.' Victor thinks the picture was intended to re-create a scene inside the Vortex lab. He believes it was done from a drawing or a photograph. There are a lot of details in the image that indicate the artist knew the setting."

A chill arced across the back of Sierra's neck, lifting the small hairs there.

"That does not sound encouraging," she said.

"No, it doesn't. The Foundation cleaners talk about hunting down the monsters, but what if we haven't seen the real thing yet?"

"A scary thought."

North headed back down the side tunnel. "Time to get to work. Let's see if my glasses survived the fire. With luck, the lockbox protected them."

Sierra hurried after him. "The Foundation team in Fogg Lake is bound to have heard the rumors of your loss of talent. What will you tell them when they ask why you're not wearing the glasses?"

"I've been thinking about that. If someone is targeting my family, I want whoever it is to think they've been successful in blinding me. For now I'm going to let everyone believe that I no longer need the glasses because my night vision talent has disappeared entirely. That I've still got my sensitivity to paranormal vibes and my intuition, but as far as my special ability goes, I'm a burnout."

"In other words, you no longer know who you can trust at the Foundation."

"Right."

The poisoned glasses had survived the fire. North decided to leave them in the charred lockbox. "They're as safe in there as anywhere," he said. "I'll pick them up later. The box is too heavy to carry and I sure as hell don't want those damned glasses anywhere near me."

"I agree," Sierra said.

They started hiking toward Fogg Lake.

They did not have to walk very far before a Foundation team in a big SUV found them. The driver introduced himself as Dexter Rose.

"Figured you'd have enough sense to pull over and stop once the fog closed in," he said. He eyed the charred hulk of metal sitting on the side of the road. "What the hell happened to your vehicle?"

"It was sabotaged by some Puppets," North said.

"Puppets, huh?" Dexter snorted in disgust. "Just what we need. We've got our hands full dealing with the raider crews who keep trying to sneak into the caves. Word of the discovery of the Fogg Lake lab is spreading fast in the underground market."

"Arganbright and the others back at headquarters knew they wouldn't be able to keep it a secret for long," North said.

"True." Dexter gave him a considering look. "Are you okay? I heard you had to wear some fancy sunglasses these days."

"Turns out I don't need them anymore," North said.

Dexter frowned in concern. "Is that good news or bad news?"

"Bad news," North said.

The members of Dexter's team shifted awkwardly and made sympathetic noises.

Dexter nodded, his eyes grim. "Shit. Sorry to hear that."

"You and me both," North said. "But hey, I'm still a pretty good investigator."

Dexter gave him a comradely slap on the back. "Never doubted it for a moment." He glanced at the black metal box. "That thing feels hot."

"Lost lab heat," North said.

"I've got a steel lockbox in the back of the car. We'll put it inside."

The tuner was stored in the lockbox and they all piled into the big SUV. Dexter got behind the wheel and drove toward town.

Squashed between North and a muscular cleaner named Ted, Sierra peered out the window, curious to see if anything had changed in Fogg Lake since her visit as a teen.

As far as she could tell, with the exception of a handful of trailers bearing the Foundation logo, the small mountain community looked exactly as she remembered it. Even the battered sign on the outskirts of town was the same.

WELCOME TO FOGG LAKE.
NOTHING TO SEE HERE.

CHAPTER 32

The door of one of the trailers flew open. An attractive brunette wearing a Foundation uniform dashed down the steps and ran toward North.

"You made it," she said. "We've all been so worried."

North hauled the lockbox out of the back of the SUV and turned to greet her.

"Hi, Larissa," he said.

She stopped directly in front of him, eyes widening in concern. "You're not wearing your glasses. Please tell me that means your talent has returned."

North gave her a wry smile. "Let's just say I'm no longer experiencing hallucinations."

"That is such good news." Larissa threw her arms around North and hugged him quickly before stepping back. Her eyes widened in alarm. "Or is it? Your talent?"

"Isn't what it used to be," North said.

She closed her eyes briefly. "Oh, North. I'm so sorry."

"But I'm still a pretty good investigator," North said. "How is the Fogg Lake project going?"

"Great," Larissa said. Her eyes widened with enthusiasm. "You wouldn't believe what we're finding inside the ruins. It's as if the whole place has been locked in a time warp since the night of the big explosion. A real treasure trove. But what on earth are you doing in Fogg Lake? Yesterday afternoon we got word from headquarters that you were on your way up here, but no one said why. Something to do with your father's situation?"

"Long story," North said. "Sierra, this is Larissa Whittier. She's on the museum staff. Larissa, Sierra Raines, a specialist in authenticating antiques and artifacts with a paranormal provenance in the private market."

Sierra gave Larissa a wry smile. "That's a fancy way of saying I'm a go-between."

Larissa chuckled. "Sounds like we're both in the same line of work, except that your job probably involves a lot more danger than mine does. I've met a few private collectors in my time. They can be downright dangerous. I swear, some of them belong at Halcyon Manor."

"I agree," Sierra said.

Larissa started to hold out her hand. She noticed Sierra's gloves and raised her eyebrows in a knowing manner.

"A bad burn from a very hot artifact," Sierra said. "I'm still sensitized."

"Been there." Larissa grimaced in sympathy and lowered her hand. "You think your senses will warn you if an artifact is on fire but there's always that one object that surprises the hell out of you."

"I try to take precautions," Sierra said. She shoved her gloved hands into the pockets of her leather jacket. "Doesn't always work."

Larissa turned back to North and gave him a searching look. "Any news on your dad's condition?"

"For the moment he's stable," North said.

"That's something, at least," Larissa said. "If the doctors have stabilized his condition there may be time to reverse the trauma." She glanced down at the lockbox North gripped in his left hand. "Find an interesting artifact?"

"Yes. One that might have something to do with my dad's situation. I want to show it to a witness."

"A witness?" Larissa looked startled. "Who in Fogg Lake would know anything about . . . ? Oh, you must mean Marge, the street lady they brought in from Seattle. There are rumors that the Foundation sent her here because she needs protection. How is she involved?"

"We don't know," North said. "Where is she?"

"In the library." Larissa waved a hand toward a two-story building in the small town square. "The Oracle is keeping an eye on her."

North raised his brows. "The Oracle?"

Larissa laughed. "Her name is Harmony. No last name as far as I know. You'll understand when you meet her."

"Right." North started across the square. "Let's go, Sierra."

Sierra smiled at Larissa. "Nice to meet you."

"Same here." Larissa lowered her voice. "Take good care of him, okay? He's been through a lot."

"I know," Sierra said.

Larissa raised a hand in farewell and hurried back to the trailer that evidently served as her office.

Sierra jogged a little to catch up with North.

"I heard that," he growled.

"That business about taking good care of you because you've been through a lot? She means well."

"I know. But here's the thing. You don't want gratitude. I don't want pity."

Sierra decided to shut up.

The door of the library opened just as North reached for the big brass handle. A dramatic figure loomed at the entrance. She was nearly six feet tall and was constructed along statuesque proportions.

A long mane of silver hair framed features that would have done justice to a warrior-saint. She wore knee-high leather boots and an ankle-length black cloak. She appeared to be in her sixties, but her eyes were a thousand years old. They were the eyes of a woman who saw more than she wanted to see, the eyes of a woman who lived with an unrelenting mission.

Sierra smiled. "Hi, Harmony. Nice to see you again. It's been a long time."

"*I've been expecting you,*" Harmony said, speaking in resonant, ringing tones that could have been used to announce the apocalypse. "*You are late. Time is running out. The ghosts of the Bluestone Project have been aroused. They seek vengeance and power. Just as one fights fire with fire, the dark forces of the past must be met with the light of the future.*"

"Thanks for the prophecy," Sierra said. "This is my client, North Chastain. But then, you probably know that already."

"Are you kidding?" Harmony's voice switched to a normal pitch. She held out a hand to North. "By now everyone in town knows who you are. We expected you late yesterday. Come on inside."

Sierra moved through the doorway. North followed.

The library was crammed with shelves filled with books, some old and bound in leather. Others were new. At the rear of the room there was a staircase. One set of steps led to the upper floor. The other went down into the basement.

Sierra remembered that the upstairs space was the apartment where Harmony lived. By tradition, the Oracle of Fogg Lake always lived in the library.

The basement was where the oldest and most valuable volumes were housed, as well as the Fogg Lake ancestry records and a few artifacts.

"We got caught in the fog," North said. "Had some car trouble." He gave Sierra an inquiring glance. "You two know each other?"

"I struggled when I first came into my talent," Sierra said. "Broke a lot of mirrors before I learned how to get some control. My parents brought me here so Harmony could assess my situation and do some research. She's the one who figured out that I needed the mirrored crystal to focus my psychic vibe."

"It's obviously a rare gift," Harmony said. "But I found some data in an old journal written back in the nineteenth century by a researcher who took the paranormal quite seriously. Turns out the ability to channel energy via mirrors and glass is not only unusual, it is a particularly difficult talent to handle."

North glanced at the locket Sierra wore. "Where did you find the right crystal?"

Harmony chuckled. "I didn't. It found her."

Sierra smiled. "Harmony was able to tell my parents what I needed. They took me around to every rock and crystal shop in the Pacific Northwest. We attended endless auctions that featured old jewelry. Eventually this locket turned up in an estate sale. I knew as soon as I saw it that I could use it. There were no other bidders."

"You two must have had a very uncomfortable night," Harmony said. "How about coffee?"

"Coffee sounds wonderful," North said.

"Yes, please," Sierra said.

"Follow me," Harmony said. She led the way toward the staircase.

North looked around. "How did you land this gig as the Oracle of Fogg Lake?"

"Believe me, I didn't set out to become an oracle," Harmony said. "It definitely wasn't on the list of career paths that my high school guidance counselor suggested."

"I don't think my high school guidance counselor mentioned a career as a go-between," Sierra said.

Harmony gave her a knowing look. "We all have to stumble around until we find our callings. It can be hard to hear the voice above all the noise in the world."

"So I'm told," Sierra said.

"I was trained as a librarian," Harmony continued. "But here in Fogg Lake the jobs of Oracle and librarian always seem to go together. No one knows why. The day I arrived in town the previous Oracle announced she had been waiting for me to show up. She said it was time for her to move on and that I was supposed to take her place here. She packed a bag and left. I was on my own. I've been figuring it out ever since. Learn something new every day in this job."

North looked at her. "Do you see visions? Hear prophecies?"

Harmony shrugged. "It's hard to describe how I work. Sometimes I just get this vibe and I feel compelled to speak up. But the process is like trying to explain a dream. You think you understand it but you don't, not really. Unfortunately, things are almost never crystal clear for me. Interpretation is always a bitch."

Sierra nodded. "Same with my father's psychic poems."

"I know." Harmony smiled a cryptic smile. "I consult with your father from time to time, remember?"

"Of course," Sierra said.

North looked at Harmony. "I don't suppose you have anything to add to that announcement about the ghosts of the Bluestone Project and the need to fight the dark forces with the light of the future?"

"Sorry," Harmony said. "That's all I have for now. I give you my word that if I get any more flashes of prophecy along those lines I'll let you know. Meanwhile, you're here to speak with Marge, and I know you're in a hurry. She's working down in the basement. The coffee is down there, too."

"Marge is working here in the library?" Sierra asked. "What in the world is she doing down there?"

Harmony winked. "Marge has the ability to see auras and a preternatural eye for detail. She's helping me fill in some of the missing data from the Fogg Lake ancestry logs. Turns out that while she was at that horrible Riverview hospital she met a lot of other inmates who had a psychic vibe. Some of them had parents or grandparents who were living here in Fogg Lake at the time of the Incident."

The basement was a concrete structure filled with more crammed shelves and the glass-and-steel cases that protected the artifacts. The currents of energy in the underground space were a lot hotter than they were upstairs.

"The Oracles of Fogg Lake have been collecting books, treatises and occasionally artifacts relating to the paranormal since the days of the Incident," Harmony explained.

North looked around. "I'm surprised Victor hasn't tried to convince you to give this collection to the Foundation library."

Harmony snorted. "Victor Arganbright and I have an understanding. He stays off my turf and I stay off his. However, we have agreed to consult with each other whenever one of us thinks it would be wise to share information. For example, we are both concerned about the new rumors of Vortex that have begun to circulate. Until now that old lab was treated as a myth or a legend. But something has changed."

"The chatter about Vortex is heating up in the hot artifacts market, too," Sierra said.

A middle-aged woman dressed in a long, flowing caftan patterned in an exotic print sat at a table in the middle of the room. She wore a pair of sneakers and a knit cap. A yellow notepad, a pen and a can of soda were in front of her.

She watched Harmony lead Sierra and North across the room.

"Took you two long enough to get here," she announced.

"This is Marge," Harmony said. "Marge, meet Sierra Raines and North Chastain."

"Nice to meet you, Marge," Sierra said.

Marge grunted.

"Thanks for agreeing to see us," North said.

"Not like I had a choice," Marge said. "Got to stop those ETs from Riverview before they launch their attack."

"ETs?" Sierra repeated.

"Extraterrestrials," Harmony explained. "Marge says Riverview is their secret laboratory. They use rogue human doctors to conduct experiments on people like her."

"Oh, right," Sierra said. "Olivia LeClair explained that."

North looked at Marge. "You'll be glad to know that the Foundation has taken charge of Riverview. Dr. Garraway is dead."

"No loss," Marge growled. "Who got to him?"

"We think it was one of the orderlies," Sierra said.

"The clones." Marge nodded sagely. "That figures. They did all the dirty work for Loring and Garraway. Probably got pissed off when they realized they'd been conned. Did you get the doc and the clones, too?"

"Not yet," North said. "But we're working on it. You think the clones were conned?"

Marge rolled her eyes. "The fools believed Loring when he said he could increase their talents and give them serious paranormal powers. But he was lying. He made them practice with something he called a night gun. He said once they mastered it there were more weapons where it came from. But that thing was scrambling the clones' energy fields. I could see that clear as day."

North set the lockbox on the table. "Tell me about the night gun," he said.

Marge drank some soda and put down the can. "That's what Loring called it. Don't know where it came from. Looked sort of like a flashlight. You could see clear through it. Made of glass or crystal or something."

"What did it fire?" North asked. "Bullets?"

"No, some kind of weird light. Hard to describe. Loring said it could destabilize a person's aura. Called it the perfect murder weapon on account of it wouldn't leave any evidence."

"I think someone used that gun on my father," North said.

Marge scowled. "What happened to him?"

"He's awake but unresponsive," North said. "The doctors think his aura has been badly traumatized."

Marge exhaled heavily. "Sorry to hear that. Loring talked a lot about how the damned thing had to be tuned. He was always telling the clones that he was aligning their aura currents to the wavelengths of the gun but I could see that every time they fired that thing their auras got wobbly."

North looked thoughtful. "The weapon was too powerful for the clones. They couldn't handle the psychic recoil."

Marge shrugged. "Whatever. Didn't look good for the clones, I can tell you that much. Made 'em real mean, too. They were never what you'd call nice, but after they started getting tuned up to use that gun they got real short-tempered. Violent."

"Did Loring try to tune the weapon to his own aura?" North said.

Marge took a swig from the can of soda and shook her head. "I think he was afraid to use the tuner thing on himself. The clones didn't know it, but he was experimenting on them."

"Were there any other weapons in the lab?" North asked.

"Loring had a couple of other gadgets around—a glass ball thing and a little metal box—but he said they didn't require tuning, not like the gun. He said they were more like grenades or small bombs. One-time use."

North opened the lockbox and took out the machine he had found in Loring's lab. He set it on the table. "Is this what Loring used to try to tune the clones to the vibe in the crystal gun?" he asked.

Marge eyed the machine and snorted in disgust. "Yep. That's it. How'd you get hold of it?"

"Found it in Loring's lab at Riverview."

Marge looked grim. "Too bad Loring and those clones got away."

"We'll get them," North said. "Just a matter of time."

Sierra looked at Marge. "Did the clones use the night gun on you and the other patients at Riverview?"

"Nah." Marge grunted. "Between you and me, I think Loring and Garraway were scared to let the clones use it on us. They would have had to deal with a lot of dead bodies, or maybe a lot of people in comas. Hard to explain that to the local cops. Anyway, that wasn't why me and the others were kidnapped. They needed us for something else."

"What?" North asked.

"Most of us could see the energy around people, y'know?" Marge said.

"Auras," Sierra said.

"Right. Auras. Loring shot us full of drugs that were supposed to jack up our senses. He wanted to see if he could make us do more stuff."

"Like what?" Sierra asked.

"He made us hold old objects and describe the places where they came from."

"Remote viewing," Harmony said quietly.

"What kind of objects?" North asked.

Marge shrugged. "One time it was a desk tray, the kind you keep pens and pencils in. Another time it was a busted coffeepot. A lot of the stuff looked like it came from an old office. I could tell it made him crazy when I said I couldn't feel a damn thing."

Sierra smiled. "You lied to him, didn't you?"

"Damn straight," Marge said. "None of us ever told Loring the truth if we could help it."

"Any idea why he wanted you to test the artifacts?" Sierra asked.

"The bastard never explained anything to us. He thought we were stupid, I guess. But some of us talked about it when he wasn't around. We figured out that Loring and Garraway were looking for something. Guess they thought one of us might be able to pick up a vibe in an object that would somehow tell him where it came from. Heard Loring talk about a paranormal GPS or something."

North whistled softly. "A dowsing stick."

Sierra got a ping. "The artifact we picked up at Swan's?"

"Maybe." North nodded. He reached back into his pack and took out the black metal rod that he had picked up at Swan Antiques. Energy whispered in the atmosphere. He smiled slowly. "I think Dad found Griffin Chastain's magic wand."

Harmony raised her brows. "Are you serious?"

"Better known as a dowsing stick or rod," North said. "A paranormal GPS and compass combined."

"Dowsing sticks were used in the old days to find a source of water underground," Sierra said. "People hired dowsers to tell them where to dig wells."

Harmony looked thoughtful. "Theoretically, in the hands of a true sensitive, dowsing sticks or rods could be used to find a lot of things. Gold. Lost valuables. Water. But they were almost always used by con men and fake psychics."

Sierra looked at Marge. "We were told that you escaped Riverview a couple of months ago. Any idea why Loring came looking for you in Seattle after all this time?"

Marge winked. "Expect he finally figured out I'm the one who took his precious notebook. He kept it in a vault, you see. Didn't look at it very often, so he might not have noticed it was gone until he decided to look up something. And even then I'll bet he had a hard time figuring out that I'm the one who swiped it. He thought I was just a crazy old lady. But I've got a good memory for numbers. I saw him punch in the code for that vault so often it was easy to memorize."

North watched her intently. "You took his research notebook?"

"Not his." Marge smirked. "Reckon it's yours."

"I'm getting a little confused here," North said.

Marge bent down and opened a big satchel that was sitting on the floor next to her chair. She pulled out a black leather logbook and put it on the table.

"The night I left I opened the vault and helped myself to this," she said. "I knew it was important to Loring. That was good enough for me."

North contemplated the logbook. "Mind if I have a look at it?"

"Nope." Marge waved a hand. "It belongs to you."

"Why do you say that?" North asked.

It was Harmony who responded. She picked up the logbook, opened it and glanced at the first page. With a smile she handed it to North.

"Take a look," she suggested.

North opened the logbook with exquisite care, as if he was afraid it would shatter in his hands. For a long moment he just stared at whatever was written on the first page.

"Well?" Sierra asked, unable to contain her curiosity.

He looked up, dazed. "This logbook belonged to Griffin Chastain. It's a record of research into the potential uses of energy from the dark end of the spectrum. There's a note that the work was done in a lab here at Fogg Lake."

"We knew your grandfather was on one of the research teams here," Sierra said.

North flipped rapidly through the pages. He paused when he got toward the end.

"Listen to this," he said.

He read aloud.

"I no longer trust my research partner. Crocker Rancourt is obsessed with weaponizing dark light energy. I am convinced he will attempt to steal the prototype devices and the tuning crystals. I do not know if he is working as a spy for a foreign power. I doubt it. I think he intends to use the machines to make himself the most powerful man in the country. He is borderline delusional. Drunk on his own visions.

"Until I can persuade my superiors that he should be removed from the project I must protect the devices. I will seal the laboratory and destroy all records linked to it. I will send a crystal and the locator to my wife. I have tuned the locator to my signature.

Only I or someone from my bloodline will be able to use it to open the lab."

North looked up. "My grandmother got a crystal like the one in this machine but she never got the dowsing rod."

"It must have been stolen at some point and wound up on the black market, where it landed in the hands of a collector," Sierra said. "Eventually it ended up in Gwendolyn Swan's shop, where your father found it."

"Loring was searching for the dowsing rod," North said. "He knew it existed, because he had Griffin Chastain's logbook, but evidently he had no idea what it looked like. He probably heard the rumor that it was at Swan's shop at the same time Dad did. My father got there first, but he suspected he was being followed, so he bought another object, the radio, and left the dowsing rod behind."

"That fits," Sierra said.

North looked at Marge. "Did you mean it when you said I could have the logbook?"

"It's all yours," Marge said.

"Thanks," North said.

Harmony looked at the locator. She smiled. "It does look like a magician's wand."

North tightened his grip on the dowsing rod. His eyes burned with midnight fire.

"Yes," he said. "It does."

CHAPTER 33

For the record," Dexter said, "I think this is one hell of a risk. If it weren't for the fact that you're sure you need to find some long-lost machine to save your dad, I would refuse to allow you to enter this sector. We haven't even begun to map it. The energy in most of those tunnels is too damn hot and disorienting."

They were standing at the entrance to the large cavern that marked the main entrance of the Fogg Lake cave system. Sierra sensed North's impatience but she did not blame Dexter for issuing yet another warning. Dexter was in charge, after all. If she and North did not return from their foray, he would be the one who would have to explain things to headquarters. And he would no doubt blame himself, because he was a good team leader, and that's what good team leaders did when things went wrong.

She and North and Dexter were not the only ones gathered at the cavern entrance. A worried-looking Larissa and most of the Foundation team stationed at the Fogg Lake site were there, too. In addition,

Harmony, Marge and several residents of the town, including the mayor, Euclid Oaks, were present.

A member of Dexter's team spoke up. According to the label on his shirt pocket his name was Jenkins. He was short and bald, and he looked worried.

"The only tunnel we've actually been able to map is the one that leads to what we think was the site of the explosion that took place here several decades ago," he said. "The chamber was blocked by an energy gate of some kind. We finally managed to disable it but it took a while. Even if that dowsing tool works and you find the right tunnel, the entrance might be blocked by a similar gate."

"Or a rockfall or an underground river," Larissa added.

"I understand," North said. "But I don't have a choice. I have to try to locate that old lab and open it."

"Are you sure you can work that locator device?" Dexter asked. "You've been through a lot lately."

No one else spoke up, but Sierra knew what they were all thinking. As far as they were aware, North was psi-blind.

"This rod has my grandfather's signature," North said. "Don't worry, I've got enough intuition left to handle it. I don't need my night vision for that."

Dexter drew a long breath and exhaled slowly. "Okay, then. Your call."

"Don't forget, I'll be with him," Sierra said. "I can identify hazards along the way and make sure we avoid them. I'm a go-between. I know what I'm doing when it comes to hot zones and artifacts."

North had tried to talk her out of accompanying him but she had refused to back down, pointing out the simple truth that they had no idea what they would encounter once they entered the tunnels. While it was true that he wasn't blind, it would take a lot of energy and concentration to work the dowsing stick. He needed someone to ride shotgun, and since she had a talent for identifying potentially dangerous relics, she was the obvious choice for the job.

Several members of the Foundation team had volunteered to accompany them, but Sierra had explained that it would be hard enough to guard North and herself. She did not want to be distracted by having to keep an eye on a large group of people while they tried to navigate the powerful, disorienting currents inside the caves.

"Got spare flashlights?" Dexter asked. "It's not dark inside. There's a lot of low-level radiation infused throughout the cave system, enough to see where you're going. But you never know what you'll run into. You're looking for Griffin Chastain's old lab. We know he had an amazing talent for magic. No telling how he protected his secrets."

"I've got a few ideas on the subject," North said. "And yes, we've got flashlights." He glanced at Sierra. "Let's go."

He took a firm grip on the dowsing rod and walked through the cavern entrance. Sierra followed close behind, heightening her talent in anticipation of what Dexter and the others had told her to expect.

The interior of the big cave made her think of the ruins of some ancient cathedral. A river of crystal-clear water flowed out of the rocks on one side, twisted its way through a deep channel and vanished into the mouth of a side tunnel. They had been warned not to get near the edge of the river. The currents were deceptive and powerful.

Once safely out of sight of the crowd at the entrance, North stopped and surveyed the interior of the cavern.

"Lot of energy in here," he said.

"You can say that again." Sierra looked around at the rocky walls and floor. Unlike the black glass tunnel where they had spent the night, this cave appeared natural. "According to the team, it's nothing compared to what we'll encounter when we go deeper inside the cave system."

Paranormal currents of energy issued from the side tunnels, creating a mildly disorienting but exciting sensation that aroused all of

Sierra's senses. Dexter had told them that when they entered one of the narrower passageways, the effects of the paranormal radiation would grow stronger. The deeper they went into the cave system, the more likely they were to encounter extremely disturbing hallucinations.

North moved to the center of the cavern, raised the dowsing rod and turned in a slow circle. Sierra was standing close enough to feel the raw power of his aura when he heightened his senses.

The metal rod began to glow, a deep, dark, paranormal blue.

"Got a fix," North said. "That tunnel over there."

Without any hesitation, he headed for a shadowed side cave. Sierra followed quickly, automatically sorting through the rippling crosscurrents of energy, watching for the heat that indicated the most dangerous riptides and storms. It was obvious that North was focusing exclusively on the sensations he was receiving via Griffin Chastain's locator device.

Once they were in the side tunnel the rod glowed more intensely. So did the walls of the cave. Dexter had been right about the paranormal radiance infused into the rocks. The flashlights were not needed.

The Foundation team leader had also been right about the power of the currents that pulsed and seethed in the tunnels. The deeper they went, the hotter the energy became. At every juncture North waited briefly for the locator to point to the right tunnel.

Twenty minutes later they found themselves in the ruins of what had clearly been an engineered corridor. Broken tiles of black glass still clung to the walls. The paranormal heat levels rose rapidly. The evidence of disaster was everywhere. They had to wade through the wreckage of vintage metal desks, old telephones, lamps, chairs and smashed glassware that littered the floor. It looked like the aftermath of a hurricane or a tornado.

"The explosion that took place here must have been very powerful," Sierra said.

"So powerful that it changed the lives of everyone in Fogg Lake," North said. "Not to mention their DNA."

"I wonder if the researchers who were working here at the time made it out alive or if one of these days the Foundation team is going to find a huge pile of bodies, like the archaeologists did when they excavated Herculaneum and Pompeii."

"The authorities at the Foundation think most of the staff survived," North said. "They got a warning before the explosion. But there was no time to warn the residents of Fogg Lake. The people in town didn't even know there was a secret government research lab hidden inside these caves until after the explosion. That's when the authorities arrived to assess the damage."

Sierra smiled. "And discovered a town full of people who claimed they were just fine, thank you very much."

"Fogg Lake is one tough little town," North said. "The residents had every right to be pissed off when they found out they had been the unwitting subjects in a government experiment that went bad."

The dowsing stick abruptly changed color. The paranormal blue radiance took on an ultraviolet heat.

"What does that mean?" Sierra asked.

North stopped and surveyed the rock walls around them. "I think it means we're right on top of the lab."

"But there's nothing here. We're standing in the middle of a tunnel."

North's aura got hotter. So did his gaze. Sierra realized he was looking at what appeared to be a solid wall of rock and shattered black glass. He smiled a slow, cold, knowing smile.

"Just a trick of the light," he said softly. "My grandfather was very, very good with light."

Sierra felt more heat rise in the narrow confines of the passageway. North was pulling on all of his powerful talent. A storm of energy swirled around them.

The seemingly solid wall shimmered and dissolved, leaving what appeared to be a view into the depths of a starless universe. The sense of eternal nothingness was terrifying.

All of Sierra's senses responded by slamming into panic mode. She felt the mirror crystal in her locket heat. *It's just an illusion,* she told herself. But instinctively, she took a step back.

"The abyss," North said. "Griffin Chastain's most spectacular trick."

Sierra's pulse skittered wildly. "Is it real?"

North's smile turned into a crack of appreciative laughter. "Real enough to do the job it was designed to do."

"Which is?"

"Conceal the lab."

"I see." Sierra took a deep breath to steady her nerves. "Well, I can certainly understand why your grandfather thought it would protect his secrets. No sensible person would walk into that weird energy. It feels as if it could stop your heart."

"It might just do that."

"Then how do we get into the chamber?"

"I've spent a year studying my grandfather's techniques, and I've got his talent." North's eyes burned with anticipation. "Stand back and let me show you how it's done."

"Go for it," Sierra said. But she took his advice and moved back another couple of steps. She opened her locket and glanced at the reflection of North's aura. It blazed dark, hot and icy cold. An aurora of paranormal light flooded the space.

When she looked up she saw that deep within the abyss, dangerous energy was stirring. Sierra's palms prickled. The fine hair on the back of her neck lifted.

North did not appear to be unnerved by what was happening inside the chamber. Just the opposite. She sensed he was riding a high like no other, glorying in the rush of controlling the powerful currents of paranormal energy.

The abyss was suddenly illuminated in a thousand bolts of paranormal lightning. A fiery aurora appeared.

"You said the night was filled with light," Sierra whispered. "You were right."

"No other magician was ever able to duplicate Chastain's abyss. No one could figure out how it was done."

"Because it wasn't really stage magic at all," Sierra said. "Your grandfather used his talent to manipulate energy from the dark end of the spectrum. But it's not just a trick of the light, is it? There's real danger in that energy. I can feel it."

"No one can enter this chamber without going mad or possibly dying—not until the abyss is gone."

"So, uh, how do you plan to do this?"

North raised both hands in a grand, theatrical gesture.

"*Shazam,*" he said.

Sierra felt a powerful wave of energy shift in the atmosphere. As she watched, enthralled, the endless well of night abruptly winked out of existence. The sense of dread and doom vanished at the same instant. She found herself looking at a vintage research laboratory. Over the years the walls, ceiling and floor had absorbed enough background paranormal radiation to illuminate a half dozen workbenches covered with old-fashioned, clunky-looking instruments and machines.

She smiled. "Show-off."

North flashed her a triumphant grin. "Not my first abyss."

She moved closer to the entrance and looked around. "This is incredible. There isn't even much dust. It's as if whoever was working in this lab just went down the hall for a meeting and never came back."

"Not everyone," North said. He moved through the entrance and walked toward what appeared to be a bundle of old clothes on the floor. "He never left."

Sierra followed North. When she got a little closer she could see what remained of a white lab coat and a green uniform. The front of the lab coat was stained with old blood.

The bones inside the clothes shifted and rattled when North gently turned the skeleton onto its back. The skull gazed sightlessly up at the ceiling.

North picked up the lanyard that had once hung around the dead man's neck and read the ID.

"Griffin Chastain," North said. He reached gently into the bone pile and picked up a couple of bullet cartridges. "He didn't sell Bluestone secrets to the Soviets and get executed behind the Iron Curtain. He died trying to protect whatever he and Rancourt invented in this lab.

"He was trying to keep it out of the hands of his research partner, Crocker Rancourt."

CHAPTER 34

North got to his feet and crossed to a wall where a badly yellowed lab coat dangled from a hook. He took down the coat and returned to the skeletal remains of his grandfather. He arranged the coat as a makeshift shroud to cover Griffin Chastain.

"I'll be back for you, Granddad," he vowed. "But first I have to save Dad and recover those weapons."

He rose again and surveyed the old lab, aware that Sierra was waiting for him to decide how to proceed. The rush he had experienced a short time ago when he defeated the abyss was fading fast. The overpowering need to keep moving was back in full force.

"We need to find the other tuning crystal, the one that was made for Crocker Rancourt," he said. "It's got to be here. It's the only explanation that fits. With luck it will still be live."

Sierra walked slowly down an aisle formed by two long stainless steel workbenches. She looked across the room and saw the door of a vault.

"Maybe it's in there," she suggested.

North went to the door of the vault, prepared to pull out his lock-pick. But when he tugged on the handle the heavy steel door swung open on rusty hinges.

The interior of the vault was lined with glass and steel shelving. There were no artifacts.

"Empty," he said. "Looks like Rancourt managed to grab all the prototype weapons. That's probably what triggered the final confrontation. Give me a minute to see if I can figure out exactly what went down in here."

Sierra stopped at the far end of the two workbenches and looked back at him. "You can work out what happened at the scene of the crime?"

"It's what I do as a cleaner. No one except you and me has been in here since my grandfather sealed the entrance. I should be able to read the psychic prints."

He went back to the door of the chamber and heightened his senses. Immediately old footprints began to glow on the floor of the chamber. He sorted through them, separating Griffin Chastain's tracks from those of the other person who had entered the room.

Even after so many years both sets of prints still seethed with violence, rage and panic.

"It went down hard and fast," North said. "The killer was standing where I am now when he fired the gun. I can see the heat of his excitement. He's about to get exactly what he wants but he's taking a terrible risk and he knows it. He's nervous. That energy changes at the entrance."

"Meaning?" Sierra asked.

North concentrated, trying to piece together the story told by the hot prints.

"The killer wasn't able to get more than a few steps into the chamber after pulling the trigger," North said. "He's shocked. There's a lot of rage and frustration out here in this hallway. He realizes he's not going to get what he wants after all. He panics and runs."

"Your grandfather must have generated the abyss and sealed the doorway even as he was dying."

"Yes."

"To protect the second tuning crystal?" Sierra asked.

"As far as I can tell, there is nothing else left in here to protect." North walked slowly through the laboratory, opening doors and closets. He stopped in front of the vault and contemplated the empty shelves inside. "Rancourt had already stolen the weapons and, probably, the tuning crystal he thought was his. Later he must have realized he had grabbed Griffin's crystal instead. He returned to get the one that was made for him. That's when Griffin confronted him. But this is your area of expertise. Picking up any artifact heat?"

Sierra moved slowly through the space and shook her head. "This whole place is infused with energy. Everything in this lab is an artifact."

"Keep looking. Griffin concealed this chamber for a reason."

Sierra stopped halfway along a workbench and studied what looked like a vintage radio.

"Hmm," she said.

North watched her strip off one leather glove and gingerly reach out to touch the radio.

"Damn." She gasped and jerked her fingers off the radio as if it were red-hot. "If this isn't your tuning crystal I'd be happy to take it off your hands. Whatever it is, it's worth a fortune on the underground market."

"Everything in here is technically the property of the Foundation, remember?"

"Yeah, right. It was just a thought." Sierra pulled on her glove. "I'm trying to run a business, you know."

"Don't worry, you'll be well paid for this job."

"Remind Victor Arganbright of that when he complains that I padded my invoice by adding the cost of a brand-new SUV."

"I will."

North went down the aisle and stopped at the radio. He could feel the power trapped inside before he touched it. It spoke to him in a thousand shades of darkness.

He took the screwdriver out of his small tool kit and went to work on the back plate of the radio.

A moment later he lifted it off and set it aside. A gray crystal the size of a fist occupied most of the interior space. But unlike the crystal in Loring's machine, this one was hot. Very, very hot.

"This is what my grandfather died trying to protect," North said. "The second tuning crystal."

Sierra shivered. "I can sense the energy in it. Is it tuned to your grandfather's signature?"

"No," North said. "This crystal was originally designed for someone else to use."

"Crocker Rancourt."

"Most likely." Gently, North inserted the crystal back into the radio. "It's obvious that when Griffin began to get suspicious of Rancourt he switched out the crystals. Rancourt ended up with the one that was engineered for Griffin to use."

"That's the one we found in Loring's lab. The crystal that was shattered."

"Because Loring tried to make it work on the Puppets," North said. "But that attempt was doomed to fail eventually. This is the crystal he needs, the one tuned to Rancourt's signature."

"Now what?"

"Now we do a deal."

Sierra eyed him warily. "What deal?"

North's eyes heated. "I've finally got something that Loring wants. I'm going to offer him this live crystal in exchange for the weapon that was used on my dad."

"And just how do you propose to do that?"

North smiled an ice-cold smile. "The usual way. I'll hire a go-between."

Sierra groaned. "I was afraid you were going to say that. Okay, I can try asking Mr. Jones to set up a deal, but there's no guarantee that Loring will go for it."

"He will. I told you, he's obsessed with this thing. Let's get out of here."

Sierra looked around. "What about your grandfather's body and the stuff in this chamber?"

"I'll reset the abyss gate on our way out."

"Wow. You can do that?"

"Sure. Griffin has waited this long for a proper burial. He can wait a little longer."

CHAPTER 35

Sierra made the phone call to Ambrose Jones using the landline phone in the library. She explained the deal she was trying to put together.

"All right," Jones said. "I'll get the word out. Can't guarantee that Loring will respond."

"My client is very certain Loring will jump at the chance to get his hands on this particular artifact," Sierra said. "There's just one problem."

"Only one?"

Sierra looked out the window of the library. The fog was already creeping through the trees and settling in the small town square.

"Mr. Chastain and I are stuck here in Fogg Lake until tomorrow morning," she said. "The night mist has made the road out of town impassable. We're told it will linger until daylight. That means the earliest we can get back to Seattle is tomorrow around noon."

"No rush," Jones said. "You know as well as I do deals like this always go down at night. That means if it happens, it will happen tomorrow night. I'll call you as soon as I hear from the buyer."

"My cell phone doesn't work here. You'll have to use the number I'm calling on—it's a landline. The local library."

"What time does the library open in the morning?" Jones asked.

"This particular library operates twenty-four hours a day," Sierra said. "Call as soon as you hear anything. We'll be here."

"You're spending the night in the library?"

"There's no motel in town," Sierra said. "Fogg Lake is filled with Foundation teams. Every trailer and every spare cabin is rented. Most of the locals are taking in Foundation staff as boarders to make a few extra bucks. Sleeping quarters are at a premium. Marge is bunking down in the back room of the general store. The Oracle graciously offered us the library basement."

"Hang on, you're losing me here. Who's Marge?"

"The street lady who turned out to be a key witness in this case."

"And the Oracle?"

"Town librarian," Sierra said. "It's complicated. Call as soon as you hear from the buyer."

"Will do," Jones said.

He ended the connection.

Sierra was seated at the librarian's desk. She put the phone down and looked at North, who was pacing through the stacks.

"Now we wait," she said.

North came to a halt at the desk. Before he could say anything Harmony appeared on the stairs. Energy shivered in the atmosphere.

"The fog grows stronger," she intoned in her prophecy voice. *"The danger is coming closer. This storm will end in madness and death."*

North looked at her. "Out of curiosity, do you ever do happy, cheerful, positive-thinking prophecies?"

"Sadly, not very often." Harmony fell back into her normal voice. "Certainly not lately. How about dinner and a drink over at the restaurant? It's lasagna night."

"Sounds good," North said.

CHAPTER 36

Harmony came down the basement stairs after dinner bearing twin piles of quilts, sheets and pillows. She gave one stack to Sierra and the other to North.

"There's a bathroom down here in the basement," she said. "It even has a shower. The library was originally built as a private house. Somewhere along the line it got donated to the town, and the local citizens voted to make it into a library. The heat's working, so you should be warm enough. Get some sleep. You both need it. See you in the morning."

She disappeared back up the stairs to the main floor and then continued on to the upper level, where her own quarters were located.

An odd silence gripped the basement. Sierra clutched her pile of bedding and reminded herself that she and North had spent two nights together. Granted, the first night had been dedicated to helping North overcome the effects of the poison infused into his special glasses. And sure, the second night had been spent on the hard floor of a cave, but still. Two nights together. To say nothing of the night when he had slept in her bed, which didn't count. Or maybe it did. Regardless, they were both professionals. They could do this.

Sierra took a deep breath and studied the labels on the end panels of each book shelf.

"I'll take 'Fogg Lake Ancestry Records A–Z,'" she said.

North wandered down one aisle, turned the corner at the end and reappeared in the neighboring aisle. "'Records of Nineteenth-Century Paranormal Organizations' looks like an interesting section." He pulled a volume off the shelves. "Ever hear of the Arcane Society?"

"I think my father may have mentioned it. Very secretive. Probably a legend. Why?"

North flipped through the old book. "Evidently a family named Jones was heavily involved in it."

"Hmm. You're wondering if Mr. Jones might be in some secret paranormal society? That wouldn't surprise me. He's been operating the Vault for a couple of years now, but no one knows much about him."

"Jones is a common name," North said. "Probably just a coincidence. Except—"

"There are no coincidences."

"Right." North put the book back on the shelf. "Okay, I'll bed down in this aisle."

Sierra went down the ancestry-records aisle and spread the thick quilt on the floor. She arranged a sheet on top and a pillow at one end. She was aware that North was doing the same thing two aisles over.

When she emerged from the small bathroom in the flannel pajamas she had manage to squeeze into her pack, she gave him a bright smile.

"Your turn," she said.

"Right. Thanks."

He vanished into the bathroom.

When he returned he flipped a light switch, plunging the basement into darkness. Sierra had been in the process of settling into her sheet and quilt. She jerked upright to a sitting position.

"No," she yelped. "Please. I know you can see just fine in the dark but I can't stand a totally dark room. We're in a basement, for heaven's sake. No windows."

"Sorry." North turned on the bathroom light and left the door open. "Does that work for you?"

"Yes. Thanks."

In the shadows she could see that he was wearing a T-shirt and his cargo pants. He had his holstered gun in one hand.

Sierra settled back down into the quilt and sheet. She listened to the small sounds North made as he removed the trousers. There was a muffled clunk when he put the gun on the floor.

There was a long silence. Sierra gazed up at the shelves of books towering above her.

"It occurs to me," she said, "that this is not a good idea."

"What's not a good idea?"

"You and me, sleeping between rows of library shelves."

"I know I'm going to regret asking this, but what could possibly go wrong?"

"If there was an earthquake we would be buried under a pile of heavy books. Maybe killed."

"Thanks for pointing that out," North said. "Now I won't be able to sleep a wink."

"We could move under the big table," Sierra said. "That would be much safer."

"In the event of an earthquake, you mean."

"Right."

There was another short silence.

"All right," North said. "Let's move."

Sierra scrambled to her feet, gathered up the quilt, sheet and pillow, and walked, barefoot, out of the ancestry-records aisle. North was already at the long table, moving the chairs out of the way. She noticed he had taken the time to pull on his trousers and collect the gun.

They arranged the quilts, sheets and pillows side by side. When they were finished North looked at her across the table.

"There's just one thing I would like to clarify," he said.

She summoned up her breeziest smile. "Don't worry, I'm a professional."

"In Vegas, that could be interpreted a couple of different ways."

She felt the heat rise in her face and then worried that with his special night vision he might be able to tell that she was embarrassed. Annoyed, she glared at him.

"You know what I mean," she said.

"Sure. And I respect your professionalism. Last night in the cave I told you that I didn't kiss you the other morning because I was feeling grateful."

"Right."

"I also want to make it clear that I didn't kiss you because I was overcome with a rush of post-adrenaline energy due to the fact that we nearly got killed that night."

"Oh." She paused. "You're sure?"

"Positive."

"Because we were both riding an emotional roller coaster after all the excitement," she said. "Everyone knows that kind of experience can induce a temporary sense of physical attraction."

"Turns out that in my case, it doesn't seem to be temporary."

She took another deep breath. "It doesn't seem to be temporary for me, either."

"Want to run an experiment? Try another kiss?"

A thrill of anticipation zapped across her senses.

"Yes," she said. "Yes, I would like that. A lot."

North moved to the far end of the table. She went to meet him.

For a few seconds they just stood there, looking at each other. She reached up and traced the line of his jaw with one finger.

"Sierra," he rasped.

He covered her mouth with his own.

The kiss exploded like a light grenade.

Sierra told herself the raw energy that charged the atmosphere around them was probably generated by another adrenaline overload— it had been a busy day—but in that moment she did not give a damn. The heat filled her with a glorious sense of being alive. The fierce hunger in North's kiss told her that he was caught up in the same crashing wave of desire.

She wrapped her arms around his neck, inviting him to deepen the kiss. He uttered a muffled groan and started to unfasten the front of her pajamas. The garment fell away. North's palms closed over her breasts.

"You feel so damn good," he said.

She inhaled his scent and got a little giddy.

"You smell good," she said.

He gave a hoarse chuckle and went to work on the pajama bottoms.

She got his T-shirt off and flattened her hands against his chest, savoring the sleek, hard feel of his body.

"It's been a while for me," he said. "I want to take the time to do this right but I'm not sure—"

"This is the no-waiting line," she said. "It's been a while for me, too."

She unfastened the front of his trousers and pushed them down over his lean hips. There were a couple of clinks and some small muffled thuds when the cargo pants hit the floor.

"So many tools," she whispered.

He kissed her throat. "It's important to use the right tool for the job."

She moved her hand down to the hard, fierce erection pushing against the fabric of his briefs.

"Very true," she said.

He wanted her. The knowledge sent shivers of intense excitement across all of her senses.

When she started to stroke him, he caught her hand.

"I need a minute here," he said. "Don't go anywhere, okay?"

"Okay," she said.

He took off the briefs, unzipped his pack and reached into an inside pocket. He produced a small foil packet, tore it open and sheathed himself in one smooth motion.

"Do all badass Foundation cleaners carry condoms in their packs?" she asked.

"Can't speak for the others but this particular cleaner bought some while you were shopping for cheese, wine and olives."

"Good to know you weren't wasting all your time over in the nutrition-bar-and-vitamin-water aisle."

He came back to her, caught her face between his hands and gave her another heavy, drugging, senses-dazzling kiss. She was suddenly damp and consumed with an unfamiliar sense of urgency.

North leaned down to haul the quilts and sheets out from under the table. He rearranged the bedding on the floor again, went down on one knee and drew her down in front of him.

The next thing she knew he was flat on his back and she was sprawled on top of him. He was fever-hot and everything about him was rock-hard. When he reached down between her thighs she realized that she was soaking wet. He stroked her gently and she nearly screamed.

He froze.

"Damn," he said. "Did I hurt you?"

"No, no, it's fine." She dropped wild little kisses all over his chest. "Really. I just wasn't expecting it to feel so . . . so . . ."

"What?"

"Good," she gasped. "I wasn't expecting it to feel so good."

"So much for your intuition. Clearly I'm the psychic here. I knew you were going to feel good. Fantastic. Incredible."

She laughed with the sheer wonder of it all.

He touched her intimately again, searching out the secret places, thrilling her senses. She moved one hand down to his erection and lower, cupping him.

He grunted. "If you don't stop I'm not going to last another two minutes."

"Of course you can last more than two minutes. You're a tough, badass Foundation cleaner. You've got stamina. You've got talent. You've even got a magic wand. I know this because I am currently holding it in my hand."

"Of all the go-betweens working out of the Vault, I had to get the one with a locker-room sense of humor."

She laughed and squeezed him gently.

"That does it," he said.

He used his hand on her again and she suddenly stopped laughing. She could not breathe. The tension that had clenched her lower body was released in a series of deep, rolling waves that rocked all of her senses.

Before it was over—before she could catch her breath—he was easing her onto her back and coming down on top of her. He braced himself on his elbows and thrust into her in one slow, relentless move, filling her, stretching her. Tight. Tighter. She found herself hovering on the edge of another climax.

"About the magic wand," he said against her throat.

She finally managed to take a full breath. "Impressive."

She gripped his shoulders with such force she knew she would probably leave marks from her nails on his skin. She wanted to scream with the sheer glory of it all. It was as if they were both drawing on the power of each other's auras, channeling it into a force that was stronger and wilder than anything either of them could generate individually.

And then, just when Sierra did not think she could handle any more stimulation, she came undone in a wildfire of sensual energy. She did scream then, but North covered her mouth with his own, swallowing the primal shriek. She wrapped her legs around him, trapping him.

His climax pounded through both of them.

Sierra opened her eyes. The basement was illuminated in a thousand colors that had no names.

CHAPTER 37

The phone on the librarian's desk rang shortly after two o'clock in the morning, bringing Sierra out of a deep sleep. It took her a few seconds to orient herself.

"That will be Mr. Jones," she said, struggling to untangle herself from North's arms and the bedding.

North got to his feet first and tossed her the shirt she had been wearing earlier. She pulled it on and reached for her trousers. North yanked on his pants. He zipped the fly as he went up the steps. She bounded after him.

"I'll get it," she said. "My job, remember?"

She grabbed the receiver of the old landline phone. "This is Sierra."

"The deal is on," Ambrose Jones said. "Tomorrow night. Make that tonight, given that it's after two. You'll have plenty of time to drive back to Seattle during the daytime tomorrow. Exchange will take place using the enhanced security services you and the buyer both requested. It will be handled by me personally. There's just one catch."

Sierra clutched the phone very tightly to her ear. "What?"

"The buyer insists on testing the artifact," Jones said. "Says he'll know if it's the right one. He made it clear that if he thinks he's been cheated he will destroy the artifact that your client wants."

Sierra looked at North, who was leaning over the librarian's desk, hands planted on the surface while he listened to the one-sided conversation.

"The buyer insists on testing the artifact," she said.

North smiled his ice-cold smile. His eyes got a little hot.

"No problem," he said.

CHAPTER 38

The last of the disorienting fog evaporated half an hour after sunrise. Sierra tossed her pack into the back of the big Foundation SUV that Dexter had provided and hopped up onto the passenger's seat. North took the wheel and they got on the road, stopping briefly at the remains of the burned-out vehicle to retrieve the poisoned glasses. North tossed them into the lockbox in the rear of the Foundation SUV and got back behind the wheel. Sierra didn't need any psychic talent to sense the prowling anticipation that electrified the atmosphere around him.

It was clear they were not going to talk about the adrenaline-fueled passion that had overwhelmed both of them a few hours earlier. Probably just as well, she decided. What could you say about that kind of elemental desire aside from the fact that it had been the most exciting sex she had ever had?

She reminded herself no promises had been exchanged. There had been no talk of commitment. No discussion of the future of their relationship. When it was over they had both fallen into an exhausted sleep.

This morning North was focused on his mission. She understood. They had a job to do before they could figure out their personal situation. She took comfort from a couple of the lines of the psychic poem her father had sent to her:

Hope and Love are better paths
For what ahead may lay.

It dawned on her that this was the first time she had been able to conjure some serious hope for a relationship. In the past she had tried to think positively at the start of each new affair, but deep down she had always known things would end badly. This time, however, she was not hearing the annoying little ping that whispered, *Enjoy the moment. It won't last.*

She warned herself to keep the situation in perspective. She and North had shared a lot of tense, dangerous experiences lately. That kind of thing created a bond of sorts but not necessarily a permanent one. Nevertheless, this morning she had hope.

Unfortunately, hope was a fragile thing, a mirror easily shattered.

"You do realize that, in spite of the precautions and security Mr. Jones will provide, we have to assume Loring will try to cheat tonight," she said when the silence in the front of the SUV became oppressive.

"Sure," North said. "Just business as usual when you're dealing with the bad guys."

CHAPTER 39

I don't like this," North said.

"Believe it or not, I know what I'm doing," Sierra said. "And so does Mr. Jones. Under other circumstances I wouldn't be using his special services. But given those crazy Puppets that Loring is running, it makes sense to purchase the security upgrade. Besides, Las Vegas is paying for it. Arganbright can afford it."

"I understand. But when I gave that crystal tuner to Jones this evening I lost control of it. It's my only leverage."

"Don't worry, Mr. Jones is handling this exchange personally," Sierra said. "He knows an artifact when he sees one. He won't hand over your tuner unless he's sure he's got the night gun."

"He's never even seen a night gun."

"Neither have we. But you gave him a description, and if it's the real deal it will be very hot," Sierra said. "It's not as if you can fake that kind of heat."

"I know."

"But you're not happy about losing control of the tuner. I get that."

They were sitting in her booth in the basement level of the Vault. There were two glasses of sparkling water on the table. The music from the club on the upper level reverberated through the floorboards that formed the ceiling. It was twelve thirty. Most of the tables and booths were occupied. This was the busy time of night for those who dealt in the paranormal. In the shadowed corners of the club, deals were going down. Buyers and sellers were scheduling deliveries with go-betweens.

Two hours ago she had delivered the tuner to Jones. He had disappeared with it and several members of his security team.

Sierra's phone pinged. Even though she had been expecting the message, she was startled. She glanced down. Exchange completed. Private quarters.

"Here we go," she said.

She slid out of the booth. North joined her. They went toward an unmarked door. It opened just as Sierra raised her hand to knock. A woman in her twenties who was dressed as a Vault security guard smiled.

"Hi, Sierra," she said. "Mr. Jones is expecting you. Downstairs in the showroom. You know the drill."

"I do," Sierra said. "Thanks, Ally."

"Congratulations on a major deal, by the way." Ally surveyed North. "A Foundation client, no less. Sweet. That outfit has money, and they always pay their bills."

It occurred to Sierra that her reputation as a go-between was going to go up several notches if all went well tonight.

"Thanks," she said again.

She walked through the door with North at her heels. They descended another set of steps into a sleek, contemporary office. The door above closed, cutting off the last of the throbbing music.

"Sierra." Ambrose rose from behind a glass-and-steel desk. He was dressed, as usual, in a black pullover and black trousers and a black linen jacket. He nodded at North. "Welcome to the Vault, Chastain. Always a pleasure doing business with the Foundation."

"Just to be clear, this is a personal matter for me," North said.

"I understand." Ambrose came out from behind the desk. "I never did believe those stories about your grandfather, by the way. Always figured Rancourt got to him."

"You were right," North said. "Sierra and I found Griffin Chastain's body yesterday. He was shot twice at close range and left in a lab at the Fogg Lake facility."

Ambrose nodded. "I'm sorry your family didn't get the satisfaction of seeing Crocker Rancourt brought to justice. Heard he died of a heart attack years ago."

"All I care about at the moment is the weapon that was used on my father," North said. "Did you get it?"

"I got a crystal artifact shaped rather like a flashlight, just as you described. No question but that it's hot, and the heat definitely has the vibe of vintage lab energy. I hope it's what you need."

"Let's see it," North said.

"Follow me," Ambrose said. "Your artifact is in my private vault."

He crossed the room and pressed a concealed lever. A section of wooden paneling slid aside, revealing a steel door. A security panel glowed a faint yellow. Sierra sensed paranormal heat in the mechanism.

North smiled for the first time, a faint, appreciative smile. "Crystal tech?"

"In my spare time I fancy myself something of an inventor," Jones said. "I specialize in security technology. This lock responds only to my paranormal signature."

"I've got a similar setup at home," North said. "My grandfather installed it."

"According to the legends, Griffin Chastain was a brilliant engineer."

When Ambrose touched the panel the color changed from a pale yellow to bright green. There was a series of muffled clicks before the thick steel door opened.

Heavy currents of energy wafted out of the vault. Sierra's senses rose in response. Artifacts of all kinds lined the shelves. Many of them glittered and glowed with the unmistakable radiance of the paranormal.

"This is an amazing collection," North said.

"Thank you," Ambrose said. "Not all of these items belong to me. In addition to my other services, I offer to store and secure artifacts that are especially valuable or dangerous until a go-between can put a buyer and a seller together."

North studied the array of relics. "Not just lost lab artifacts. Some of these relics are very old."

"Humans have been messing around with the paranormal since they discovered fire," Ambrose said. "My own family has a long history linked to the study of psychic phenomena."

Sierra remembered the old book North had pulled off a shelf in the Fogg Lake library.

"Are you by any chance talking about the Arcane Society?" she asked.

For the first time since she had met him, Ambrose Jones appeared to have been taken by surprise.

"You know about the Society?" he asked.

"North found a reference to it in the library at Fogg Lake," she said.

"A family named Jones was evidently at the heart of the Society," North said. "We wondered if it was just a coincidence that you're also a Jones."

Ambrose gave him a cryptic look. "You know what they say—there's no such thing as coincidence."

And that, Sierra knew, was all they were going to get out of Ambrose Jones on the subject of the Arcane Society. North apparently came to the same conclusion.

"If you ever get tired of trying to protect these artifacts from the raiders, the Foundation would be happy to take them off your hands," he said.

Ambrose chuckled. "Victor Arganbright has already made that clear. But at the moment I'm quite capable of protecting my little trinkets. The weapon you want is in that glass case, by the way."

The object in the case looked exactly like the night gun that Marge and Matt Harper had described—a clear crystal artifact shaped like a flashlight.

North went swiftly across the room and started to open the case.

"Hang on," Sierra said. "It's my job to authenticate the artifact, remember?"

Reluctantly, North stepped back

Sierra opened the lid of the glass case, stripped off one leather glove and reached inside to pick up the crystal device. The instant she touched it she sensed the energy in it.

"It's definitely hot," she said. "And definitely dates from the era of the lost labs." She handed it to North. "Also, the last person to handle this gun was very unstable."

"Probably one of the Puppets," North said. He took the weapon from her. Energy shifted in the atmosphere. "It's been damaged but it definitely has Griffin's signature."

Ambrose watched him with an interested expression.

"Can I ask what you plan to do with that artifact?" he asked.

North glanced up. "Reverse engineer it to figure out how it works and then retune it."

"You sound like an engineer."

"Probably because I was trained as one."

Ambrose nodded. "I see. A family talent. But you became a cleaner instead."

"I had my reasons," North said. "Turns out criminal investigations require a similar skill set." He slipped the night gun inside his jacket. "There's no way to know yet if I can use this to save my dad, but it's the artifact I've been chasing. Thanks, Jones. I owe you."

"You'll get my bill," Ambrose said. "And Sierra's as well."

North looked at him. "Loring was satisfied with the crystal in that radio you traded for this?"

"Yes." Ambrose raised his brows. "Any reason why he might not have been satisfied?"

"No, the crystal was originally tuned for Crocker Rancourt. I'm sure it has his psychic signature."

"I see. Well, I can tell you that all Loring seemed to care about was that the crystal was live. Not shattered."

"He would also have known that the provenance was clean," Sierra said. "After all, the crystal has been sealed up inside the old Fogg Lake lab since the day Griffin Chastain was murdered."

Ambrose studied North. "What do you know about Loring?"

"We have reason to believe he's the grandson of Crocker Rancourt," North said. "Stenson Rancourt's son. If we're right, Loring is Harlan Rancourt."

"Interesting." Ambrose looked intrigued. "I'm aware of the explosion that was said to have killed Stenson Rancourt and his son. I don't believe they ever found Harlan Rancourt's body."

"No," North said, "they didn't."

Ambrose looked at North. "I assume the crystal is dangerous?"

"It was originally tuned for Crocker Rancourt," North said. He paused. "But the last person to have access to it was my grandfather. By that time he was well aware that he could not trust his research partner."

Ambrose got a knowing look. "Your grandfather was a magician, wasn't he?"

"And an engineer."

Ambrose nodded. "So that crystal is very dangerous. It will be interesting to see if Loring can handle it. If you're right about his identity, he probably has his grandfather's psychic signature."

North smiled a grim smile. "I'm counting on it."

CHAPTER 40

Sierra vaulted up into the passenger's seat of the SUV and closed the door. She thought about the vibe she had picked up when she authenticated the crystal gun.

"Whatever you do, don't try to fire that weapon," she warned, "at least not without taking precautions. It's genuine, but there's something really off about it."

"I know." North cranked up the engine and pulled away from the curb. "The currents are out of sync. Whoever has been using it couldn't resonate with the vibe of the weapon. Every time it was fired the crystal was damaged."

"That explains why Loring was so eager to agree to the exchange." Sierra put on her seat belt. "He realized the gun is no longer usable."

"Yes, but he must have other weapons he thinks he can tune to the Rancourt vibe using that crystal I gave him tonight."

"Are you certain you'll be able to retune that night gun so you can use it?"

"Shortly before he was murdered, Griffin Chastain gave his wife, my grandmother, a package containing a crystal. It looks exactly like the two we've encountered in this case. He told her to keep it safe and above all to make sure it stayed within the family. She never knew what it was for but she understood it was valuable. She gave it to me when I moved into the Abyss. I knew it was important but I didn't know why. Now I do."

"There was a third tuning crystal?"

"Yes," North said. "I'm pretty sure it's the rock sitting on the mantel of my fireplace back in Vegas. If I'm right, I'll be able to use it to retune the night gun."

"Even if you're successful, what makes you think you can use it to reverse your father's condition?"

"As I keep reminding everyone, Griffin Chastain was a magician. He performed spectacular, death-defying stunts. He was also an engineer. He always built in an escape mechanism of some kind; a way to reverse the trick in the event that something went wrong. I'm hoping he did the same thing when he invented the night gun."

"But it's a weapon. It's designed to cause harm or even kill. What makes you think he would have wanted to add a way to reverse the effects?"

"Two reasons," North said. "The first is that building in a safety feature fits with his style of magic and engineering. He had to know there was a possibility the weapon might fall into the wrong hands."

"And the second reason?"

"I'm not sure the gun is actually a weapon."

Sierra looked at him, startled. "What else could it be?"

"I don't know. Yet. But from what I have been able to learn about my grandfather, he was never interested in creating weapons."

"Well, we know one thing for sure. Delbridge Loring now has a crystal tuned to Crocker Rancourt's vibe. If he does have access to all the prototype weapons that disappeared from that lab at Fogg Lake, he's going to try to use the crystal to tune them."

"Loring got what he demanded—the crystal that was sealed inside the Fogg Lake lab. And yes, that crystal was originally tuned to Rancourt's signature. But it doesn't take much to tweak the tuning of a crystal that is designed to resonate with an individual's aura. The smallest adjustment, done with finesse and skill by someone who knows a lot about engineering and magic, can render it useless."

Sierra smiled. "You're saying your grandfather tweaked Rancourt's crystal?"

"Griffin Chastain was a master of the subtle magic arts. If I'm right, Loring won't discover that the crystal is useless until he tries to use it to tune a weapon."

"And when he does?"

"The crystal will shatter. In the process it will probably do some serious damage to the aura of whoever is in physical contact with it at the time."

"In other words, Griffin Chastain made certain that Crocker Rancourt and his descendants would never be able to use those weapons. Your grandfather may have saved a lot of lives. He may even have saved the country. The Rancourts were powerful but their history with the Foundation is nothing compared to what would have happened if they had been able to access true paranormal weapons."

Sierra sat back in the seat and watched the city streets. It was late. There was very little traffic. Next stop was the airport, where the Foundation jet was waiting. In a few minutes she would be waving goodbye to North, maybe for good.

"Hard to believe it's over," she said. "It seems like we've been on the move ever since you landed in Seattle."

Except for those few thrilling hours in the basement of the Fogg Lake library, she thought. She would treasure that time—that night—for the rest of her life.

"It's not over until I find out if I can unfreeze the paralyzed bands of my father's aura with that crystal gun," North said.

"Of course. Promise me you'll let me know as soon as you find out if the gun works on your dad."

"Don't worry, you'll be one of the first to know."

"You have my phone number."

"Yes, but I won't be needing it. You're going with me to Vegas."

"I am?" She straightened in her seat. Then she caught sight of a familiar sign. "Wait, you missed the on-ramp."

"We've got time to stop at your place first so that you can pack a bag. Don't worry about bringing a lot of stuff. You can buy anything you need in Vegas."

Sierra tried—and failed—to suppress a little thrill of delight. "Don't get me wrong. I'm anxious to see if the gun works on your dad, so I'm okay with a side trip to Las Vegas. Besides, my parents are still there. But technically speaking, you don't need me anymore."

"I know," North said. "But you need the protection of the Foundation a little while longer. Security will be easier to handle in Vegas than it is here."

She winced. So much for hoping that he wasn't ready to end their very short relationship. Then again, one night of hot sex in a library basement didn't actually amount to a relationship. She forced herself to consider the logic of the situation.

"You think Loring might send his Puppets after me?" she asked. "But I'm just the go-between." She groaned. "Not that it seems to matter to some people."

"Sooner or later the Foundation cleaners will pick up Loring and the Puppets and recover the cache of weapons, but until they get this thing wrapped up, you're vulnerable."

"Because I know too much?"

"Yes. And because when Loring finds out he can't use that tuning crystal to activate the rest of the weapons, he's going to be pissed. Enraged. And probably a little crazy. He'll be out for revenge. It will be hard to get to me, but you're an easy target."

"I can take care of myself," she muttered.

"You'll be outgunned and outnumbered."

She folded her arms. "Okay."

North glanced at her. "I was sort of hoping you would want to come with me to Las Vegas."

"Oh," Sierra said. "Yeah. Well, I do."

"We're a team, right?"

"Uh-huh."

"The lack of enthusiasm is hard on my ego."

"You want enthusiasm?"

North flexed his hands on the steering wheel. "Well, shit, I thought we were at the start of an affair. Was I wrong? Was last night just adrenaline sex?"

She went very still in her seat. "No. No, last night was not just adrenaline sex. I never sleep with clients."

"But you slept with me."

"Yes." She took a deep breath. "Yes, I did."

"Do you regret it?"

"Nope. Not one bit. But I should warn you that I've never actually had a successful long-term affair. My relationships tend to end quickly and badly."

"So do mine. But the way I look at it, there's always a first time for everything, including a successful relationship."

Her spirits skyrocketed. "You're right. Always a first time."

"Good," he said. "That settles it, then."

She looked at him. "It does?"

"For now."

So much for an intimate conversation. Well, this was hardly the time for one of those anyway. They had other priorities.

North drove down the alley behind her apartment tower and stopped in front of the heavy garage gate.

"Damn." Sierra unbuckled her seat belt. "I just remembered I lost the remote opener when those Puppets firebombed my SUV. There's a security box beside that door over there to the right of the gate. I'll use my fob to open the door. Once I'm inside I can open the garage gate."

She got the SUV door open, jumped down to the pavement and hurried toward the door. A swipe of her fob and she was inside. She went to the security panel next to the gate and punched in the code.

The big steel gate rumbled as it rolled up into the ceiling. North drove into the garage and stopped. She opened the passenger-side door and used a handhold to hoist herself onto the seat.

"My parking spot is number one-oh-three," she said. "Second level."

North waited until the gate closed before driving up the ramp. He turned the corner and cruised down an aisle created by two rows of vehicles.

A screech of tires on cement shattered the gloom-filled silence of the garage. The vehicle appeared at the far end of the aisle. It stopped, blocking the exit.

"We have a problem," North said.

He threw the SUV into reverse and started to retreat swiftly back toward the opposite end of the aisle. He slammed to a halt when another set of headlights appeared, blocking that route.

"Out," he said.

He unclipped his seat belt and leaped from behind the wheel. Sierra scrambled out of the passenger's side.

"The elevator lobby and the emergency stairs are that way," she said, pointing toward the center of the garage. "The lobby is locked. If we get inside we'll be safe."

"We don't have enough time," North said.

The doors of the cars blocking them slammed open. Two of Loring's men charged out of one of the vehicles. The other two emerged from the second car. They raced toward the Foundation SUV. Sierra saw that three of them were clutching conventional handguns, not paranormal weapons. The fourth, Ralph, had a glass globe in one hand.

"They'll head for the elevators," Ralph shouted.

"They'll never make it inside," Joe said. "I disabled the security panel." He raised his voice. "Hear that, Chastain? You and the bitch are trapped."

North pushed Sierra down behind the protection of a car and crouched beside her. He slipped his gun out from under his leather jacket. She sensed energy rise in the atmosphere. They were both running hot now.

"Loring got the damn crystal," North said, raising his voice to be heard in the echoing garage. "What do you want from us?"

"The boss says he wants to talk to you," Ralph said. "He wants to do a deal with the Foundation."

"What kind of a deal?"

"He'll turn over the entire cache of weapons if Arganbright agrees to let him and the four of us leave the country," Ralph said.

"I'll deliver the message to Victor Arganbright," North said. "You can go now."

"Not quite that simple," Ralph said. "We need a little leverage to make sure Arganbright doesn't send his cleaners after us."

"You mean you want us for hostages."

"Just until we're in the clear," Ralph said.

"You really expect me to believe that story?" North said. "Loring sent you here to get rid of us. You might as well get on with the job."

"Whatever," Ralph said.

He lobbed the glass globe across a row of parked cars. The device shattered on the concrete floor.

In the next instant a dazzling light exploded. Currents of energy flooded the atmosphere. They struck Sierra like a giant ocean wave, making it impossible to breathe. A heavy weight settled on all of her senses, dragging her under.

She realized she was losing consciousness. Frantically she tried to fight her way back to the surface.

She felt North wrap one hand around her upper arm, pulling her into the protection of his aura. He hauled her upright and gripped her fingers.

"Whatever you do, don't let go," he said.

She felt his energy field flare, swallowing up all the light. The garage was plunged into an impossibly deep darkness. Bottom-of-the-ocean darkness. Monsters-under-the-bed darkness. Mind-shattering darkness.

And then she felt North's energy resonating with her own aura. Suddenly she could see the night as she had never known it. Auroras shimmered and glowed. She realized that because of the physical contact, she was seeing the world as North saw it in that moment, his senses revved to the max.

That was when the screaming began.

"Welcome to the abyss," North said.

CHAPTER 41

The problem with using the abyss trick was that while it was visually impressive, it did not effectively blind anyone beyond a radius of about twenty to thirty feet. Human-generated paranormal energy had its limits.

But at least two of the Puppets were close enough to be hit with the lightning shock produced by the paranormal forces involved. North studied the footsteps that seethed on the concrete floor of the garage. They glowed with a twisted energy that indicated a deeply disturbed aura. He followed them, careful to keep his grip on Sierra's hand. He knew from the way she moved that she could see their surroundings almost as clearly as he did.

The footsteps led to the orderly who had confronted them with a gun the night they had taken the crystal tuner from the locked ward. He was cowering between two cars, sobbing in panic. When North touched him he flinched violently and screamed.

"I can take care of him," Sierra said.

She palmed her locket. Energy sparked. The Puppet crumpled, unconscious, to the cold floor.

The next set of footsteps radiated equally erratic currents. They led to a second man, who was clearly in the grip of a panic attack. Sierra did her thing with the locket. He collapsed.

"Two down," North said. "That leaves us with Ralph and Joe."

He turned, searching for more footprints. A car engine roared. Tires screeched.

"They're getting away," Sierra said.

North lowered his senses. The abyss evaporated. The dazzling light of the glass bomb had dissipated. In its place was the cold, dull glow of the garage fixtures.

One of the two vehicles the Puppets had used was rapidly speeding down the ramp toward the exit.

"Gone," Sierra said. "What do we do now?"

North took out his phone. "Now we call Olivia LeClair and ask her to arrange for a local Foundation team to pick up the two Puppets we took down. With luck they will be able to give the cleaners a lead on Loring and the others."

"And we head for Vegas."

"Right. Forget packing a bag. We can't waste any more time. We're going straight to the airport."

CHAPTER 42

"Are you sure you know what you're doing, North?" Lucas Pine asked.

North got another cold chill of near-panic. If he screwed up he was probably going to kill his father. But his intuition was riding high. The tuning crystal on the mantel at Griffin Chastain's big house had come to life when he poured energy through it. He had used it to reignite and retune the currents of power that had devolved into chaos in the night gun. The device would function as it had been designed to do, he was certain of it. He was also sure he could control it. The real question was whether it could actually reverse the damage it had done when it had been used on Chandler.

North looked at Lucas, who was standing on the opposite side of Chandler's hospital bed.

"No," he said. "What I'm sure of is that this is the only chance we've got to reverse what's happening to Dad's aura."

The hospital room was crowded. Victor and Lucas were present.

Lily gripped Chandler's hand. Sierra and her parents were watching from a few steps away.

The medical team had been ordered out of the room. If the project went bad, North did not want to be responsible for any more collateral damage than was necessary. Half of the staff of Halcyon Manor appeared to be gathered at the observation window. Someone had asked him how he could operate the light gun now that he was psiblind. He had explained that he still had the Chastain psychic signature, and that was all that was required to activate the device.

Sierra flashed him a reassuring smile. "Hey, no pressure. You've got this."

"Right," he said.

For some reason the exchange broke some of the tension. North took a firm grip on the crystal gun.

Lily looked at him. "Go ahead, North. We know it's a risk, but I promise you your father wants you to try."

"Of course he does," Victor said. "The bottom line here is we don't have any other options." He glanced at Sierra's mother. "Agreed?"

"Agreed," Allegra said. "I might be able to keep him stable for a while longer, but that's not a cure. I know he doesn't want to be trapped in that dream state for the rest of his life."

There was no point dragging it out, North thought. His father had suffered enough. Either the gun would work or it wouldn't. The waiting wasn't helping anyone.

He eased energy into the crystal weapon. It responded just as it had when he had retuned it an hour ago, as if it had been made for him. He could control it the same way he did the crystal tech gadgets in his grandfather's mansion—intuitively.

The colors of midnight began to glow, illuminating the hospital room in the strange light of dreams. The auras of everyone gathered around the bed flared, bright and strong, a distraction he did not want.

"Step back," he ordered quietly. "I need to focus on Dad's energy field."

Sierra and her parents retreated a few more steps. Victor and Lucas also moved away. Lily hesitated.

"Please, Mom," North said. "I have to isolate Dad's aura."

Lily squeezed Chandler's hand one last time and stepped back.

In the light of the night gun, Chandler's aura was revealed in brilliant detail. North wielded the gun gently, raising the energy level bit by bit.

And suddenly he could see the power lines that affected every part of Chandler's body. It was like looking at a human version of the grid of the legendary ley lines said to connect the sacred places on Earth; like viewing a chart of the meridians and qi in the human body described in ancient medical treatises; like a detailed illustration of the delicately balanced humors medieval doctors had used to diagnose their patients.

In the light of the night gun it was clear which wavelengths in Chandler's aura had been disrupted.

Relying on his intuition, North concentrated on resetting the distortions in his father's energy grid. He worked carefully, delicately, aware that if he made a mistake he could easily stop Chandler's heart.

Gradually the disrupted currents began to oscillate in a regular, healthy pattern.

Chandler blinked a couple of times, sucked in a deep breath and lurched upright to a sitting position. For a moment he just stared at the room, as if he had found himself in another dimension.

Then he looked at North.

"Thanks, son," he said. He managed a shaky grin. "I needed that."

North shut down the artifact. He realized he was shivering a little—adrenaline and relief.

Lily flew into Chandler's arms. "I've been so scared."

Chandler hugged her close. "You and me both." He looked at North. "I take it you found the dowsing rod?"

"Gwendolyn Swan gave it to me when Sierra and I interviewed her," North said. "Took me a while to figure out what it was good for, though."

Chandler nodded. "I got a message from someone claiming to be a go-between informing me a crate of artifacts that had been picked up at auction by Swan contained some items that might be of interest to me. At first I figured it was just one of the freelancers trying to put together a deal. But I suspected I was being followed. When Swan showed me the items in the crate I recognized the vibe in the dowsing rod immediately."

"That's when you got suspicious?" North said.

"I knew a find like that wasn't a matter of luck. I realized I was probably being watched. I bought the rod and another artifact."

"The old radio," North said. "We found it in Loring's lab. He had smashed it. Guess he was pissed."

"It was definitely vintage and definitely had some heat, but it was nothing special. I told Swan I would be back for the rod but that if you showed up instead she was to give it to you."

"Do you remember anything about the person or persons who attacked you?" Sierra asked.

Chandler rubbed his temples. "Not much. A couple of men dressed as hotel maintenance staff were waiting for me in the hallway outside my room. One of them had that crystal gun you're holding."

"Not a gun," North said. He hefted the crystal artifact, aware of the energy locked inside. And suddenly he understood. He smiled. "An aura-balancing device."

Chandler winced. "Call it what you want. One of the men pointed it at me and that's the last I remember."

Victor and Lucas looked at North.

"Nice work," Lucas said.

Victor regarded the artifact with a thoughtful expression. "Interesting. You're sure it's not a weapon of some kind?"

"Positive," North said. "Although it can kill."

A euphoric sense of discovery slammed through him. The experience of manipulating the artifact had charged him, energized him, in a thousand different ways. A whole new world had just opened up for him. He knew what the night gun really was, what it had been intended to do.

He now knew who and what he was; what he was meant to do.

He wanted to roar his discovery from the top of the tallest hotel casino in Vegas. He was intoxicated with the knowledge that the crystal device had worked.

Sierra went to him and wrapped her arms around him.

"You did it," she whispered into his shirt. "I knew you would."

And this, he realized, was exactly what he needed to make his new world absolutely perfect—Sierra in his arms.

"I found it," he said.

Everyone in the room was looking at him, wondering what he meant. But Sierra understood. She smiled and stepped back to look at him.

"Your calling?" she said.

"I know this is going to sound a little over the top, but yes, I know what I need to do. I'm going to carry on Griffin Chastain's research."

Lily frowned. "You want to become a magician?"

North laughed. "That was just a day job for Griffin Chastain. I think he found his true passion when he designed and created the crystal devices that Rancourt eventually stole from the laboratory at Fogg Lake."

Chandler eyed the crystal gun. "You want to design paranormal weapons?"

Lucas groaned. "We've got enough trouble as it is dealing with the fallout of the old lost labs research."

Victor grunted. "The very last thing we need is to have more unpredictable weapons floating around."

North shook his head. "You don't understand. Griffin Chastain wasn't inventing weapons. He was designing paranormal medical devices. His research was all about using dark light to help balance and heal the human aura, specifically the auras of people who have some extra senses. People like us."

Victor looked dubious. "That may have been his intention, but it's obvious the technology he created can be used to injure or kill."

Byron Raines spoke up. "Hasn't that always been true of the healing arts? Any medicine or medical device that is powerful enough to save a life is usually powerful enough to injure or even kill. From potent medications to a surgeon's knife, it's always about balance and intent."

"Byron is right," Lucas said. "In any event, we don't have a lot of options here. We now know for certain the technology exists. It's out there. No putting that toothpaste back in the tube. Who knows what dangerous devices will turn up from the era of the lost labs? There will be other people like Loring who will try to weaponize artifacts. We're going to need defenses, including technology that can heal the damage done to auras. Our best bet is to take control of that research. It fits into our core mission."

Chandler looked at Lucas and Victor. "There's no one better qualified to take charge of the R and D of my father's work than his grandson."

Victor exhaled heavily and then nodded. "You're right. The Foundation will provide you with a lab, North."

"Thank you," North said. "The first step is to find the rest of the devices Rancourt stole from the Fogg Lake lab."

"Got a plan?" Sierra asked.

"Same plan I had back at the start of this thing," North said. "Just haven't had time to follow through on it."

"What's that?"

"Follow the money."

Victor raised his brows. "The forensics accounting department may be able to help you out with that project."

CHAPTER 43

Lily followed Sierra out into the hall.

"I don't know how to thank you," she said. "You saved my son and my husband. I am so grateful I'm afraid I'm going to burst into tears any second now."

"North is the one who saved Mr. Chastain," Sierra said. "I'm just the go-between. I was hired to help track down the artifact and arrange for North to acquire it. I did my job, that's all."

Her parents were standing nearby, sipping coffee. She was aware that Byron was studying her with an assessing gaze, as if he were analyzing her words the way he intuitively analyzed a poem. Her mother had a knowing look.

Lily smiled a misty smile and shook her head. She looked through the observation window of the hospital room. Inside, North and Chandler were talking with Victor and Lucas. It was obvious the conversation was serious in nature.

"North told me you discovered that someone deliberately sabotaged those damned glasses he'd worn for the past few weeks," Lily said. "There's no telling what might have happened if you hadn't come into his life when you did."

"There's a lot of talent at Foundation headquarters," Sierra said. "I'm sure eventually someone would have figured out what was going on."

"Maybe, but probably not in time to save his night vision. What matters to me is that you were the one who was there when he needed you." Lily turned away from the window. "There's something else I want to thank you for as well. All these years Chandler and North have lived with the knowledge that Griffin Chastain might have been a traitor. I know the sins of the fathers are not supposed to be handed down to the sons, but that is exactly what happens in real life. Chandler and North have both tried to overcome Griffin's reputation as a traitor, but they couldn't, not entirely."

"'. . . And nothing that I try to do brings credit to my name,'" Sierra quoted softly.

Lily gave her a searching look. "I don't understand."

"It's a line from a poem Dad sent to me a few days ago," Sierra explained. She glanced at Byron. "I read the whole thing to North on the plane. He told me 'Hope and Love' could have been written for him. He said he felt as if he was always dealing dust. That his cards crumbled in his hands."

"Evidently North was also searching for his calling," Byron said. He glanced through the observation window. "Looks like he found it."

Lily smiled at Sierra. "I'm not sure about the calling business, but I do know you helped North restore the family honor. That means more than you can possibly imagine to both him and his father. And because it matters so much to them, it matters to me, too."

"Thank you," Sierra said. "But until the cleaners find Loring and those last two Puppets, I'm afraid your family is still in danger. It's obvious that Loring has a personal vendetta going against the Chastains."

Byron nodded in a somber manner. "The desire for revenge can be handed down through a family as surely as the sins of the fathers. And it is equally destructive."

The door of the hospital room opened just as he finished speaking. Victor emerged.

"Unfortunately, you're right, Byron," he said. "We've got all the cleaners looking for Loring and his thugs. It's just a matter of time before we track them down. By now the two Puppets who got away are probably highly unstable, but that will only make them more dangerous."

North came out of the room, followed by Chandler and Lucas.

North focused on Victor. "You've had time to look into the background of Garraway, the director at Riverview. Find anything useful?"

Victor frowned. "As far as we can tell, Garraway was, as your intuition indicated, just the money guy. He was a skilled con man who made a fortune with a sophisticated pyramid scheme. Indications are he had some talent. Loring evidently convinced him to back the Riverview project."

"Takes a psychic con man to con another psychic con man," Lucas observed. "Loring must have promised to tune some of the weapons to Garraway's signature. Either that or he promised Garraway a cut of the action. Whatever the case, Garraway went for it."

"Everything relating to Riverview was in the name of a shell corporation," Victor added. "But we haven't found anything that directly connects to Loring. No bank accounts. No credit cards. No cell phone. He was living as far off the grid as it was possible to get."

"What about his car?" North asked.

"That was in the name of the Riverview corporation," Victor said. "Just like everything else."

North got a thoughtful expression. "He'll have a safe house, not just for himself but for the devices that Rancourt stole. They're all red-hot."

"But somehow they've remained concealed all these years," Sierra said. "There haven't even been any rumors about them. Trust me—Mr. Jones, the serious dealers and the go-betweens who work the underground market would have heard about such a valuable cache of crystal tech. You just can't keep something like that quiet, not for decades."

"Unless," North said, "the artifacts have been stored in a collector's vault all this time."

Lucas got a speculative look. "If you're right, we're talking about a collector who stole the cache before the lost labs were shut down."

"Crocker Rancourt," North said. "He took them from the lab vault shortly before he murdered my grandfather and evidently died without revealing where he hid them. Somehow Loring discovered the artifacts. They must have been stashed in a very secure vault, one that hasn't been opened since Crocker Rancourt locked the relics inside."

"We tore the Riverview hospital apart as soon as we moved the patients out," Victor said. "We've still got a team there to secure Loring's lab, but so far they haven't found anything except the artifacts that were stored in the lab vault there."

"I need to take a look at what the forensic accountants found," North said. "Everything."

CHAPTER 44

North walked into the crimson-and-gold living room of the Abyss. He had a sheaf of printouts in his hand.

"I've got it," he said.

The satisfaction of the hunter who has picked up the trail resonated in his voice.

Sierra had been dozing on a red velvet sofa, a cashmere throw tucked around her. She sat up slowly, yawning, and glanced at the big clock above the fireplace. It was two in the morning.

"What, exactly, have you got?" she asked.

"I found Loring's bolt-hole. With luck, he'll still be there, because he has no reason to think we've located his hideout. If I'm right, the cache of weapons will also be in the house."

"What house?"

"An old one on a private estate on Bainbridge Island."

"Lots of old estates tucked away on Bainbridge," Sierra said. "You never really notice them, because the island is still surprisingly rural."

"An entity called the Riverview Trust has owned this particular estate since the days of the lost labs. The trust fund has paid the taxes on it every year since the purchase. Here's the kicker—Victor's forensic accounting people were able to discover that the trust was originally established by Crocker Rancourt. The property has never been sold."

"If Loring really is Harlan Rancourt, that means the house stayed in the family all these years," Sierra said. "If that's true, why didn't Stenson Rancourt go after Crocker Rancourt's tuning device years ago, when he was running the Foundation?"

"Maybe," North said softly, "Stenson never knew about the artifacts. Maybe Crocker Rancourt died with his secret."

"There's another possibility," Sierra said. "Talent does go down through the bloodline, but it never shows up in exactly the same way in each generation. Maybe Stenson didn't get a full dose of Crocker Rancourt's ability or maybe his psychic talent took a different twist."

North sat down beside her. "So Stenson either didn't know about the relics or else he couldn't find them. Yet somehow the man who calls himself Delbridge Loring managed to locate them. He probably found the tuning device at the same time. He must have been thrilled at first."

"Until he discovered that the tuning device did not respond to his psychic signature. That was when he realized that it had probably been engineered for Griffin Chastain. It was the most likely explanation because your grandfather and Crocker Rancourt were the only two people involved in the creation of the night gun. They would not have tuned it to anyone else. It was too dangerous."

"With his knowledge of the paranormal he would have understood that using the improperly tuned devices was extremely dangerous," North said. "But he could not abandon such a valuable cache of paranormal tech. Whatever else he is, Loring is clearly a scientist who has studied the paranormal. He knows his way around a laboratory. He was desperate. He opened the Riverview Psychiatric Hospital with financial backing from Garraway, recruited the Puppets and started conducting experiments on street people who had some talent."

"He must have heard the rumors about Griffin Chastain's dowsing rod coming onto the market," Sierra said. "He knew he might be able to use it to find the old lab. But he didn't know what the locator device looked like. Only a Chastain could recognize the psychic signature of the artifact."

"So Loring made sure my father heard the rumor that a Chastain artifact had been picked up by Swan Antiques. Then he had Chandler followed. After Dad emerged from Swan's with the radio, Loring figured he had it made."

"He ordered his Puppets to murder your father and grab the artifact. He told them to use the crystal weapon because he did not want to leave any evidence at the scene that the Foundation investigators could follow."

"But the device failed to kill Dad," North said.

"And suddenly you were on the scene, asking questions."

North leaned over and gave her a quick kiss. "I wasn't alone. I had the best go-between in Seattle working with me."

"A Vault go-between strives to uphold the highest professional standards."

"Spoken like a pro." North looked down at the financial papers he was holding. "This whole damned business is about to come to an end. But we have to move fast. I talked to Victor a few minutes ago. He's giving orders to get the Foundation jet fueled and ready. I'm leaving for Seattle with a team of cleaners in about forty minutes."

"I'm coming with you," Sierra said. She stood and tossed the cashmere throw over the back of the sofa. "This is my contract. I deserve to be in on the ending."

"Yes," North said. "You do."

CHAPTER 45

The big house was Victorian in style—architecturally speaking, you couldn't call it a Gothic nightmare, North thought, but with its darkened windows, wildly overgrown gardens and big iron gates, it certainly qualified as ominous. It looked as if it had been abandoned decades earlier.

There was no sign of a vehicle, but the doors of the three-car garage were all closed.

He looked at his team—his old team, the one he had worked with for the past couple of years. Jake Martindale, Zeke, Dallas and Brianna had volunteered to accompany him on this operation. Everyone at the Foundation knew he had regained his vision, but the fact that the special glasses had been poisoned was a closely kept secret.

"All right," he said, "stick to the plan. Jake, take Zeke and go in from the back when I give the word. First priority is to secure the basement. If I'm right and there is a vault, it will most likely be underground. The objective is to make sure Loring doesn't get into it. If he does, he will probably escape through a tunnel. Every serious collector has a safe room and an exit strategy."

"And if we do run into Loring or one of his Puppets?" Jake asked.

"If Loring is armed, it will be with a standard-issue firearm, not one of the artifacts. He knows better than to take the risk. That's why we're all wearing vests. The Puppets, however, may still be armed with artifacts. Both the relics and the Puppets are highly unstable and unpredictable. Use the tranquilizer guns on anything that moves."

They were working with limited information about the layout of the house. North had found some aerial views but no floor plans. The mansion had never been on the market, so there were no photographs of the interior.

Sierra waited quietly on the side. She had declined the offer of a tranquilizer gun on the grounds that she had no experience with one. Instead she had her locket out from under her leather jacket, within easy reach, and she had removed one glove.

"You'll follow Dallas, Brianna and me in," North said to her.

"Got it," she said. She looked at the mansion. "Lots of bad energy in that house."

There were murmurs of agreement from the team.

North took the lockpick out of the pocket of his trousers and went toward the gate. But at the last second he stopped and simply gave the gate a shove. It swung open on squeaking hinges.

"Unlocked," Jake said. "That could be good news or bad news."

"Pretty sure it's bad news," North said. "Loring is running."

It only went to prove the age-old wisdom that held that every good battle plan fell apart the minute you launched it.

They all moved through the gate into the heavily overgrown gardens.

"Same plan," North said. "Jake and Zeke, go in the back door. The rest of us will go in through the front door. Sierra, stay at the rear. If things get noisy, get out."

"Understood," Sierra said.

The front door was unlocked. North led the way into the hall. There was no indication that anyone was in the house.

"Back door was locked," Jake announced through the communicator, "but we're in. No sign of anyone around."

"Loring must have been in a hell of a hurry," Brianna said. "Didn't even bother to lock his front door. Think he was tipped off?"

"I doubt it," North said. "Victor and I kept this operation very tight. I think it's more likely Loring got scared and ran."

The inside of the mansion looked as if it had been locked in a time warp since the early 1960s.

"Wow," Sierra said. "The original version of mid-century modern. My grandmother says she never did understand why the style came back into fashion. She said the only reason people bought those plastic chairs and shag rugs the first time around was because they were cheap."

Jake and Zeke appeared from a hallway. "Place feels empty. But there's some heat."

"Take the upstairs," North said. "We'll go down."

"Right."

Jake and Zeke went up the stairs and disappeared onto the upper floor. They reappeared almost immediately.

"Nothing but a lot of dust," Jake reported. "No footprints. He wasn't spending time there."

North found the door to the basement in the big kitchen. When he opened it the unmistakable odor of death wafted up from the darkness. He flipped on the light switch.

Loring's lifeless body was sprawled at the foot of the steps. A large pool of dried blood stained the concrete floor.

"Looks like one or more of the Puppets got tired of waiting to become a super psychic," Sierra said quietly.

North led the way down the stairs. The rest of the team followed. Sierra paused in the doorway.

"Just a minute," she said.

North and the others looked at her. Cautiously she put her un-gloved hand on the knob of the basement door.

"Shit," she said.

She yanked her fingers off the knob and hastily pulled on the glove.

"What?" North asked.

She met his eyes. "Rage. A lot of it. And frustration."

"Loring would have been pissed as hell when he opened that door and came down here," North said. "His entire project was in ruins. His grand plan to control the technology Crocker Rancourt stole all those decades ago had fallen apart."

Jake slipped past Sierra and went down the basement steps.

"Whoever killed Loring would have been in a similar mood," he pointed out. "A Puppet who has figured out that he was conned would lay down a lot of rage, too."

"You're right," Sierra said. She started slowly down the steps.

North watched her closely. "Same vibe you picked up on the doorknob at the scene of the Garraway murder?"

"No. This is different. But also very unstable."

"It all fits," North said. "If Loring really was Rancourt's grand-son, he probably considered the cache of artifacts his inheritance. He must have blamed the entire Chastain line for depriving him of what he believed was rightfully his."

"Sins of the fathers and all that garbage," Jake said quietly.

"Whoever shot Loring went old-school with a pistol," Brianna observed. "Either the killer ran out of paranormal weapons—"

"Aura-balancing devices," North corrected absently.

Brianna shrugged. "Sure. Whatever. Either the Puppet didn't have any more lethal tech or else he couldn't make it function."

"There's another possibility," North said. "Maybe the two re-maining Puppets still believe in the con. If they think they can use the para tech without Loring's help, they may have decided they didn't need him anymore."

"You think they came here to kill Loring and steal the cache of devices?" Jake asked.

"It's a possible scenario." North surveyed the empty basement. "But I doubt if they found the artifacts. The devices have been concealed for decades. What are the odds that a couple of unbalanced Puppets would be able to find Rancourt's vault?"

"Not very good," Sierra said. "In my experience collectors usually go extremely high-tech when it comes to protecting their artifacts. Crocker Rancourt would have had good reason to take a lot of precautions. After all, he had committed murder to get his hands on the devices."

North began a slow prowl of the basement, his senses heightened. There was no sign of a vault or a gallery but he could see the psychic energy of footprints—a lot of them. They burned on the floor. Some were faint with age. Some were fresh. He followed the hottest prints, old and new, to a blank concrete wall.

"Here we go," he said. "There's a door here somewhere."

The concrete was a solid barrier that effectively blocked paranormal radiation, but there were always tiny cracks between even the most carefully concealed door and its frame.

He could sense small threads of energy leaking out from whatever was behind the wall. He recognized his grandfather's psychic signature and smiled a little.

"Whatever is behind that wall was designed and built by Griffin Chastain," he said.

He traced the faint threads of leaking energy with his fingertips, drawing an imaginary line straight down to the floor.

There was a small crack in the concrete that was too straight to be the result of the natural settling of an old house.

"Stand back," he said. "There's always a possibility that Loring left a trap behind."

Sierra and the others retreated a few steps. North studied the hot energy around the crack.

He pushed gently. A small section of the floor slid aside, revealing a traditional bank vault–style lock.

"We're in luck," he announced. "Crocker Rancourt used standard technology for his vault. It was probably state of the art at the time, but it's old and outdated now."

He dropped his pack on the floor and took out the electronic lockpick. He moved quickly, very sure of what he was doing. It didn't take long to break the old lock. Gears rumbled inside the wall. A large section of concrete slid aside, exposing the interior of a steel-lined vault. Energy poured out of the opening. An array of artifacts glowed hot on the shelves.

"The weapons," Jake said. "So they weren't just a legend after all."

"Medical devices," North said.

"Right," Jake said quickly. "Medical devices."

"I thought there would be more of them," Brianna said. "I count five artifacts."

"Keep in mind that Loring removed at least three that we know of," North said. "The crystal device that was used to try to murder my dad, the light grenade that Sierra and I encountered back at the start of this case, and another artifact that the Puppets used when they attacked us in the garage. All of the relics probably came from this vault."

"There wouldn't have been a lot of devices to begin with," Zeke pointed out. "The Bluestone Project was shut down while the engineers were still trying to figure out how to overcome the tuning problems. Everything we're looking at here is probably a one-of-a-kind prototype."

"And they are all apparently tuned to your vibe, North," Jake said. He got a speculative expression. "That's why Loring was never able to use any of them. Why he was desperate to get his hands on the tuning crystal that was intended to be used by Crocker Rancourt. The way things stand now, you're the only one who can activate any of these machines."

North looked at him. "Which means I'm the one with the best chance of figuring out exactly what they were designed to do. Let's get them packed up. The sooner they're safe in a Foundation vault, the sooner we can all relax."

"We've still got a couple of Puppets to pick up," Brianna said.

"Ralph and Joe," Sierra said.

"After we remove the artifacts we'll report Loring's murder to the local police and the Foundation cleaners stationed in Seattle," North said. "By now the Puppets will be disorganized and highly unstable. If they do still have some of the artifacts, they won't be able to use them, at least not effectively. It shouldn't take long to find them."

He waited until he and Sierra were done before he asked the question that he'd been wanting to ask.

"Well?" he said.

"The answer is yes," she said. "The energy on the basement door is the same that is on your glasses. Whoever poisoned the crystals murdered Loring."

CHAPTER 46

Three days later . . .

Sierra stopped just inside the heavily shadowed entrance of the Fogg Club. She gripped the balcony railing and surveyed the strobe-lit crowd. Fierce rock music reverberated across the room, adding energy to the already hot atmosphere.

She smiled. "Reminds me of the Vault. Is everyone in here connected to the Foundation?"

"Not everyone," North said. He did a quick scan of the room. "Even though the owner doesn't advertise, a few tourists and locals occasionally manage to stumble into this place or the Area Fifty-One club a couple of blocks away. It's another bar and casino that caters to the Foundation crowd."

The bartender looked up and saw Sierra and North. He raised a hand in a friendly greeting and went back to pouring drinks.

North wrapped his fingers around one of Sierra's gloved hands. "Come on, I'll introduce you to some friends."

He steered her through the crowded mezzanine. Several people greeted North and immediately turned to Sierra, varying degrees of interest and curiosity in their expressions. She recognized the heat in the eyes of a couple of the men and one of the women as polite sexual interest, but most were clearly intrigued by whatever they had heard about her. She realized she had become the subject of a great deal of rumor and speculation. She suspected her parents were at least partially to blame. Allegra's ability to stabilize Chandler Chastain's aura until North arrived with the balancing device had made the Raines family famous within the Foundation. The fascination had rubbed off on her father. Byron's inbox was piled high with requests for psychic poems.

The discovery that Griffin Chastain had died a hero and that the machines he had helped invent had been intended as medical devices had produced an instant Foundation legend. As Byron had pointed out, it didn't make the artifacts any less dangerous, but people were accustomed to the idea that a lot of medical instruments could kill as well as heal. The Halcyon doctors were eager to work with North in hopes of creating some therapies for the poorly understood disorders of the paranormal senses.

Perception was everything, Sierra thought.

She knew that tonight was North's first visit to the club since his vision had returned to normal. It was his way of making it clear he was back and in full command of his talent. Given the significance of the occasion for him, she had spent the afternoon shopping at the pricey boutiques that were tucked away in all the big hotel casinos on the Strip. She had taken her mother with her for a second opinion. In Vegas there was a fine line between fabulous and over the top.

Allegra had declared the black slip of a dress to be safely in the fabulous category. It was discreetly studded with black sequins that caught the light in an elegant but understated way. Her black locket, black jet earrings and stiletto heels were the perfect accessories. The slim black leather gloves added an edge to the look.

The outfit had cost a small fortune, but thanks to the generous bonus the Foundation had tacked on to her normal commission, she could afford it. Earlier that evening she had concluded the dress was worth it when she descended the grand staircase at the Abyss and saw North waiting for her at the bottom. There was so much hot energy in the atmosphere and so much heat in his eyes that she was amazed they hadn't started a fire right there in the foyer of the big house.

They made their way through the crowd to a booth on the mezzanine, greeting more of North's friends and associates along the way. When they were finally seated at the table a waiter took their orders for drinks. Sierra asked for a glass of wine. North went with whiskey. More people dropped by the table to congratulate North and ask him when he would be rejoining his team.

"I'm moving into engineering," he said. "Paranormal light R and D."

Several people turned to Sierra and asked her if she would be going to work at the Foundation.

"I've got a job back in Seattle," she said.

North gave her a brooding look each time she said it but he made no comment.

Jake arrived at the table, a beer in one hand. "About time you two showed up. The Loring case is the main topic of conversation here tonight."

"Any update on the two Puppets?" North asked.

"Not yet, but like you said, it's just a matter of time before they get picked up."

"What if they've left the country?" Sierra said.

Jake shrugged. "I doubt if they have the kind of cash it takes to just disappear. If we're right about their unstable conditions, they won't be capable of carrying out a complicated escape plan."

Another couple arrived at the table. An attractive woman with serious-looking glasses smiled at North. Her companion was a handsome man whose excellent profile and toned body were ruined by his arrogant vibe.

"Congratulations," the woman said. She gave Jake a quick, shy glance and then turned back to North. "I hear your father has recovered and that you and your team closed a major case."

"Nice work, Chastain," the man said.

His attention was on something else on the far side of the room. He hooked his hand around the woman's arm and started to urge her away.

His companion, however, stood her ground, pretending to ignore the tug on her arm.

"It was the team that closed the case," North said. "Jake was there, too."

The woman smiled tentatively at Jake. "I'm so glad everyone is safe. It sounds like you were dealing with some very dangerous relics."

"It's been interesting," Jake said.

Sierra got a ping. Jake's tone of voice was a little too neutral. The woman seemed to sense it, too. She turned quickly back to North.

"Aren't you going to introduce us to your friend?" she said.

"Sorry," North said. "This is Sierra Raines, the go-between who handled the case. Sierra, meet Kimberly Tolland and Grant Wallbrook. They are both researchers in one of the Foundation labs."

"How do you do?" Sierra said.

Wallbrook nodded once in a curt, barely polite greeting. "Sierra."

"Welcome to Las Vegas," Kimberly said. She started to offer her hand but she glanced at Sierra's black leather gloves and stopped. She smiled sympathetically. "I heard you got burned by an artifact."

"A job hazard for a go-between," Sierra said.

Out of the corner of her eye she noticed that Jake had gone uncharacteristically quiet. He looked as if he wanted to escape.

Grant pulled more forcefully on Kimberly's arm. "Let's get a drink, Kim. We have things to talk about."

Kimberly looked as if she wanted to protest but she managed a smile and acquiesced.

"Sure," she said.

She allowed Wallbrook to steer her away from the booth. The action took them directly past Jake. Sierra opened her locket as if to check her makeup in the mirror. She heightened her senses and turned her head just enough to catch a glimpse of the reflections of the auras of Jake, Wallbrook and Kimberly.

The couple disappeared into the crowd. Jake watched them go.

"Wallbrook just landed a big promotion," he said. "Head of a research lab."

"Is that right?" North said.

Jake downed some beer and lowered the bottle. "Came with a big raise, too. Earns a hell of a lot more than a cleaner does now. It's that damn PhD after his name. Kimberly thinks he's Mr. Right."

"He's not," Sierra said. She snapped her locket shut. "At least, not for her."

Jake scowled. "What makes you say that?"

"Intuition. I'm pretty good at figuring out that kind of thing."

North raised his brows.

"Except when it's personal," she added quickly. "Jake, if you want my opinion, you should ask Kimberly out on a date."

Jake looked dumbfounded.

"She'd never go out with a guy like me," he finally managed. "I dropped out of college in my junior year to go into security work at the Foundation. She's a scientist with a hell of a lot of fancy degrees."

"You never know," Sierra said. "Worth a try. I think you two would be an excellent match."

Jake looked as if he was about to argue the point. Instead he turned thoughtful. "I'll let you guys have some time together. Your first real date, right?"

"Right," North said, putting some emphasis on the word. "We've been a little busy lately. Haven't had time to get to know each other."

Jake chuckled. "Hint taken. Consider me gone."

He headed off into the crowd. A silence fell on the booth. Sierra cast about for a safe topic.

"How does it feel to finally know what you want to do with the rest of your life?" she asked.

North leaned back and looked at her over the rim of his whiskey glass. The energy in his eyes and in the atmosphere around him sent a zingy little thrill through all of her senses.

"Feels good," he said. "I think."

"You aren't sure?"

"Let's just say I'm still working on the logistics of the situation."

"What logistics?" she asked.

"Me working here in Las Vegas. You in Seattle, working at the Vault. That puts us about a thousand miles apart."

"Yes, it does," she agreed. "Where are you going with this?"

"It occurs to me," he said, speaking in a very careful, even manner, as if each word was potentially risky, "that you could work as a go-between for the Foundation museum. They collect artifacts from all over the world. They are always in need of people who have the kind of talent it takes to authenticate the objects. I'm not saying the museum would pay better than the Vault, but there is a nice benefits package and the working conditions would be safer."

"Is that right?"

"You wouldn't have to operate on your own," North said, warming to his argument now. "You'd have the backing of other members of the staff and even a team of cleaners on jobs that might be dangerous. No more midnight runs to deliver hot artifacts to crazy collectors on your own."

"Sounds interesting, but I wasn't cut out for the corporate world," Sierra said. "I learned that lesson when I worked for Ecclestone's Auction House."

Damned if she was going to make this easy for him, she thought.

"Ecclestone's was an entirely different situation," North said, very earnest now. "You were set up to take the fall for a scam the company was running."

"You're sure of that?"

"I never believed you were guilty. Not for long, at any rate."

"But for a little while?"

"The file Lucas gave me indicated that you had a somewhat unconventional background, so yes, I had a few questions at first," North said.

"Because my father sells psychic poems online and my mother does song therapy and I was raised in an intentional community populated by a lot of people who prefer to live off the grid."

"Like I said, your background looks a little unusual when it's detailed in a Foundation file. But as soon as I got to know you, I realized you weren't a fraud or a con artist."

She gave him a bright little smile. "Thanks for that."

"I'm not saying there might not be a few issues with management at the Foundation—office politics is a universal phenomenon—but it sure as hell isn't a corrupt auction house."

"I agree," she said. "Nevertheless, I don't think I would do well in any setting where I have to report to a boss or carry out corporate goals. I've got more of an entrepreneurial vibe. You've found your calling and that's a wonderful thing. I'm still searching for mine."

North looked wary. "Couldn't you search for it here in Vegas?"

"Possibly. But somehow this town doesn't strike me as the sort of place where I can hear the voice I'm trying to hear."

"You're talking about the voice in that poem?"

"Right," she said. "There's a lot of background noise in Vegas."

"It's quiet out in the desert where my house is located," North said.

"That's true," she said. "Are you inviting me to move in with you?"

North hesitated and then exhaled slowly. "I have it on good authority that no woman would ever want to live in the Abyss."

"Who is your authority?"

"My mother."

"I see," Sierra said. "Have you conducted any serious research to determine if she's right?"

"What do you mean by 'research'?"

"How many women have you invited to live at the Abyss?"

"None."

"Why don't you try asking one if she would be happy to move into the mansion?"

North went very still. "Where do you suggest I start this research?"

"How about with the woman who is closest at hand? Me."

"Are you saying you wouldn't mind living in the Abyss?"

"I find it rather . . . stimulating."

"Really? Because of the mirrors? *Shit*." North broke off and pulled his buzzing phone out of his pocket. He grimaced when he saw the screen. "It's Victor. I'd better take the call."

"Go ahead. Knowing Arganbright, it will either be very good news or very bad news. He doesn't seem to have any in-between mode." Sierra got to her feet. "I'm going to the women's room while you two chat."

North nodded and put the phone to his ear. "This better be important, Victor. I'm on a date tonight. My first in a very long time."

Sierra slipped away from the table and threaded a path toward the discreet sign at the far end of the mezzanine.

She ended up in a long, shadowed hallway. At the end of it she opened a door and found herself in a gaudily decorated lounge lined with mirrors and dressing tables. Through an arched doorway she saw four gleaming white stalls and a couple of sinks. More mirrors were positioned behind the sinks.

The door of the stall at the far end opened. Kimberly Tolland emerged. She looked as if she was trying to conceal some strong emotions. She managed a polite smile as she walked across the space to one of the sinks.

"Hello again," she said. "Enjoying the evening?"

"It's been interesting," Sierra said.

"I've heard some talk that you might be invited to join the museum staff."

"Funny you should mention my career prospects," Sierra said. "I was just telling North that I don't do well in a corporate setting. How do you like working in a Foundation lab?"

Kimberly turned on the faucet and studied her own reflection in the mirror as she washed her hands. "I loved it, at least until tonight."

"I don't understand," Sierra said.

"I just found out that bastard brought me here to dump me. I guess he thought it would be easier if he did it in a place where I was less likely to make a scene."

"Are we talking about Grant Wallbrook?"

"We are talking about that lying, cheating creep, yes." Kimberly turned off the faucet and yanked a paper towel out of the dispenser. She dried her hands and then she dabbed at her eyes. Her mouth trembled. "He used my research to get the promotion and now he no longer needs me. Oh, he didn't phrase it that way tonight when he told me we had to stop seeing each other. He said it wouldn't look right if we continued to date, but that was just an excuse. He used me, damn it."

"I know this isn't going to be much consolation, but I'm pretty good when it comes to assessing aura compatibility. Yours and Grant's definitely did not sing."

Kimberly crumpled the paper towel. "What?"

"It's just a knack I have. If you want to know how it feels when two auras sing together, I suggest you ask Jake out on a date."

"Jake?" Kimberly looked genuinely startled. "But he's a cleaner.

Everyone knows they go for flash and glamour. He wouldn't be interested in someone like me."

"Why not?"

Kimberly took a gold lipstick out of her purse and concentrated very hard on applying the color to her mouth.

"I'm sure that to him I'm just a boring nerd," she said.

"You're wrong. Take a risk. Ask him to dance and see what happens."

"What if he turns me down? I'd be totally humiliated."

"What are you now?"

"Totally humiliated."

"Right," Sierra said. "So you've got nothing to lose."

She went into the nearest stall and locked the door.

"I hope things go well with you and North," Kimberly called.

"We're working on it."

Kimberly walked past the row of stalls and moved into the carpeted lounge area. The outer door opened and closed.

Sierra stripped off her gloves and tucked them into her little evening bag. There were some things a woman could not do while wearing leather gloves. She was happy to see that the commode was a self-flushing model. No need to touch the handle.

The outer door opened again. A moment later stiletto heels tapped briskly on the white tiled floor and paused in front of a washbasin. Water splashed in the sink and then stopped. The towel dispenser rumbled.

The heels tapped back through the arched doorway into the lounge area.

Silence. The newcomer did not leave.

Probably freshening up her makeup, Sierra thought.

But a shiver of awareness iced her senses.

The outer door opened again. Another woman had arrived. Sierra relaxed. She was no longer alone with the stranger in the lounge. For some reason that was reassuring.

She used some tissues to open the stall door and crossed to the sink the newcomer had just used. Bracing herself for the inevitable jolt, she turned on the gleaming faucet.

Rage slammed across her senses.

It was a startlingly familiar fury. Frustration and psychic instability shivered through it. She recognized it because she had encountered it on two previous occasions. The first time was when she had touched the crystals in North's poisoned sunglasses. She had sensed the same white-hot heat on the handle of the basement door in the house on Bainbridge Island.

The person who had murdered Loring and tried to blind North was a woman.

Out of the corner of her eye she saw something sparkle on the narrow steel shelf above the neighboring sink. Kimberly had left her lipstick.

Tentatively Sierra touched the gold lipstick case with her bare fingers. She got a little sizzle but nothing like the energy that had been left by the woman who had used the first sink.

Sierra took a deep breath and turned off the faucet. Another shock jolted her but this time she was prepared. She tried to come up with a strategy. There were two women in the outer lounge. One of them was a killer.

Or were they working together?

Kimberly appeared in the arched doorway that separated the stalls-and-sinks room from the makeup lounge. Behind the lenses of her glasses her eyes were wide with horror.

There was a good reason for the expression. Larissa Whittier was directly behind her, a small pistol pointed at Kimberly's head.

"Hello, Larissa," Sierra said.

"Get rid of the locket," Larissa said. "I don't know how it works but back in Fogg Lake I overheard Marge and the town librarian discussing it. They said you could use it to make a person faint. Take it off now or Kimberly dies."

Sierra slipped the locket off over her head and set it down on the counter positioned above the two sinks.

"You can't risk shooting Kimberly," she said. "Someone will hear the shot."

"Not with the music going full blast. It's Kimberly's bad luck that she came back."

"My lipstick," Kimberly said weakly. "Look, no one is dead yet. This can end here and now."

"No," Larissa said. "It's not going to end until I get my inheritance. Those weapons that my grandfather invented belong to me."

Sierra didn't have to look at the reflection of Larissa's aura to pick up the instability in her energy field. The signs were evident in the unsteady pitch of her voice and her feverish eyes. Her fury was so great it dominated common sense, reason, perhaps even the instinct for self-preservation. In that moment the only thing that mattered to her was revenge.

"Griffin Chastain and Crocker Rancourt invented those devices together," Sierra said. "Chastain intended them to be used to heal."

"Rancourt understood the true potential of the light machines," Larissa said. "It's all there in his logbook. It was my grandfather who comprehended the real power of those artifacts. When Rancourt realized Chastain would never agree to weaponize the devices, he did what he had to do."

"Congratulations," Sierra said. "You did a nice job of hiding in plain sight while you let Delbridge Loring take all the risks. He wasn't running the Puppets—he was one of them. So was Garraway. You were the one pulling the strings."

"Loring and Garraway were both obsessed with the paranormal. I offered them what they could not resist—the promise of serious psychic power. They recruited the orderlies because they needed some muscle to pick up the research subjects and keep them under control at Riverview."

"You covered your tracks well," Sierra said. "You even left a few clues indicating that Loring was Crocker Rancourt's long-lost grandson, the one who supposedly died in an explosion."

"The file of obituary notices?" Larissa smiled a chilling smile. "I knew it would send North and Victor Arganbright off in the wrong direction. It's no secret that Arganbright never believed Harlan Rancourt died in that fire."

"The master stroke was letting Loring hide in your grandfather's old estate on Bainbridge Island," Sierra said. "How did you get hold of it?"

"An heir hunter found me after Stenson Rancourt and his son died in the explosion that Arganbright and Lucas Pine caused. I was Stenson's biological daughter, but he never acknowledged me. He never paid any attention to me at all. I was the product of a one-night stand. I doubt if he even remembered my mother's name. I'm sure he never realized that I was the one who got the full measure of Crocker Rancourt's talent."

"Did Harlan die in that blaze?"

Larissa shrugged. "I assume so. If he didn't, he has certainly managed to keep a low profile all these years. It was obvious he never went after the cache of weapons my grandfather hid at the estate."

"Maybe he never knew about them," Sierra said.

"It's possible. Who cares? What matters is that I'm the one who found them."

"You found your inheritance, but the devices were of no use to you because they were all tuned to Griffin Chastain's signature, and the tuning crystal that your grandfather stole was engineered to respond only to that signature."

"At first I thought it might be possible to retune the crystal. I couldn't risk it myself, but I knew someone in one of the Foundation labs who was an expert on crystals."

"Delbridge Loring."

"He had a different name when he was employed here," Larissa said. "I invented the Loring identity for him. He was good, I'll give him that much. He's the one who created the crystals the doctors insisted North wear after he began to go psi-blind."

"But you are the one who infused them with the poison you hoped would make North psi-blind. That's why your energy is all over these lenses."

"I found the formula in my grandfather's logbook. He had planned to use it on Griffin Chastain but he never got the opportunity."

"Because Griffin confronted him about the theft of the artifacts. Your grandfather ended up shooting Griffin instead of poisoning him."

"Initially I put the poison into North's drink here at the Fogg Club. Like the radiation in the crystals, it has hypnotic properties. All I had to do was provide the right suggestion. Sure enough, he started losing control of his talent within hours. The doctors at Halcyon had no explanation."

"You had proof of concept," Sierra said. "The poison worked. The problem was that you had to keep dosing North with the stuff until it had completely destroyed his talent. It wasn't practical to keep poisoning his drinks, so you infused the radiation into the crystals Loring made for North's glasses."

"It was easy enough to slip into the crystal lab and take the special eyeglasses out for a couple of hours one night. That's all the time I needed to irradiate the lenses. The techs never missed them. I put them back before the lab opened that morning. Every time North wore those sunglasses he was exposed to a small but steady dose of radiation."

"Were you going to try to poison his father next?"

"Yes, but suddenly Loring sent word about the rumors of a collection of artifacts that had been sold at auction in the Seattle area," Larissa said. "According to the chatter, a device that belonged to Griffin Chastain was among the relics. We knew it had to be important. Swan Antiques had bought the entire collection, but it was a large number of objects. Unfortunately, there was no description of the Chastain relic. It could have been any one of a hundred objects."

"You realized you needed a Chastain to identify the artifact," Sierra said. "You made sure Chandler got the rumor. But he knew he was being followed that day. He tricked Loring and the Puppets. They were left with a useless vintage radio."

"The next thing I knew, North Chastain was in Seattle." Larissa's voice rose to an even higher, edgier pitch. "He hired you and everything started to fall apart. *All because of you.*"

She aimed the gun at Sierra.

"Why kill me?" Sierra said. "I'm just the go-between."

"You destroyed everything I worked for years to achieve. That tuning crystal Loring traded for the night gun was *sabotaged*. I almost died trying to use it."

"The sabotage was carried out decades ago by Griffin Chastain. He knew that as long as that crystal existed there was a chance Rancourt or one of his descendants would get hold of it."

"You cheated me."

"You're losing it, Larissa," Sierra said. "Don't do this."

"It's all your fault, you stupid, interfering bitch." Larissa's hand tightened on the pistol.

"You have to know you can't get away with murdering us," Kimberly said. Her voice was astonishingly calm and controlled. The voice of reason.

"Oh, yes I can," Larissa said.

"Nope," Sierra said. "You can't."

She flattened her palm against the mirror over the sink and slammed energy into the sparkling glass.

The move had the intended effect of shocking the already unstable Larissa. She tried to regain her balance and aim the gun at Sierra again.

But the mirror was exploding. A storm of dazzling paranormal fire blazed in the room, igniting the other mirrors. The currents of energy became a wildfire that flowed into the lounge. Dressing table mirrors cracked and shattered. Some of the light fixtures popped.

"Kimberly, down!" Sierra shouted.

Kimberly dove to the floor.

Larissa screamed and pulled the trigger but she was blinded and disoriented by the violent, chaotic energy. The gun roared. Somewhere tiles cracked. Sierra grabbed her locket, got it open and sent a fierce pulse of heat through it.

The mirror crystal sent the currents of Larissa's aura rebounding back into her energy field, briefly destabilizing them. She jerked violently, froze for an instant and then collapsed on the white tile floor, unconscious.

Kimberly got to her feet and surveyed the destruction. "That was . . . amazing."

The restroom door crashed open. North was suddenly in the room, gun in hand, his hot aura blazing in the shards of broken mirrors. Jake was right behind him.

They both stopped when they saw Larissa on the floor.

North moved toward Sierra.

"Are you all right?" he said.

"Yes," she said. "Yes, I'm all right. How did you know?"

"Victor called to tell me the DNA tests showed that Loring had no biological connection to Rancourt. But I was sure that only someone with Rancourt's signature would have been so determined to find the tuning crystal that had been engineered for Crocker Rancourt. I knew there had to be someone else involved. When I realized Larissa had followed you into the restroom, I got what we in the psychic business like to call a real bad feeling. She wasn't supposed to be here in Vegas. She had told me her assignment at Fogg Lake would last two months."

Jake moved to Kimberly. "Are you hurt?"

"No." She gave him a shaky smile and used a forefinger to push her glasses higher on her nose. "I'm okay. Thanks."

Jake relaxed. "That's good. Great." He looked around at the shards of shattered mirrors. "What the hell just happened in here?"

"I've always had a little trouble controlling my talent without my mirror crystal," Sierra said. She picked up her locket and put it around her neck. "Turns out Larissa is the true descendant of Crocker Rancourt. She was born to a woman who had a one-night hookup with Stenson Rancourt. He never acknowledged her, but after his death an heir hunter found her. She inherited the Riverview Trust and eventually found her grandfather's vault. But the artifacts inside were useless to her."

North looked down at Larissa. "So she joined the Foundation to look for what she considered the rest of her inheritance—the other tuning crystal."

"That wasn't all she wanted," Sierra said. "She wanted revenge, too. She blamed the Chastain family for making her inheritance useless. And in the end she blamed me for ruining her grand plans. She's the one who poisoned you, North. Loring was just following her orders when he infused the radiation into the lenses of your glasses."

Jake took out his phone. "I'll call Arganbright and tell him what's going on."

North surveyed the wreckage in the women's room. "After you talk to Victor you'd better tell Hank that he's going to need to get some cleaners in here."

Jake grinned. "Oh, you mean the professional kind, the sort that actually know what they're doing when it comes to cleaning."

"Right."

"I'll take care of it."

Jake took Kimberly's arm and escorted her tenderly into the lounge. Sierra watched him seat her on a velvet stool. He hovered protectively over her as he made the phone call. Kimberly adjusted her glasses again and regarded him with a mix of admiration and fascination.

Sierra got a ping. It was accompanied by a deep sense of certainty. She smiled.

"What?" North asked.

"Who would have thought I'd hear the voice calling out to me in a Las Vegas nightclub restroom?" she said.

"You're losing me here."

She patted his arm. "I'll explain later. Right now all you need to know is that I finally found my calling."

CHAPTER 47

North touched the locket at Sierra's throat. "You didn't have a chance to use it when you confronted Larissa Whittier."

They were back at the Abyss. It was four in the morning. North had poured a glass of brandy for Sierra and one for himself. They were relaxing on the crimson velvet sofa, their feet propped on a couple of gold-tasseled hassocks. Victor Arganbright and Lucas Pine had taken charge of Larissa Whittier, who had yet to awaken.

"She made me take it off," Sierra said. "She threatened to shoot Kimberly if I didn't. Larissa assumed I needed the crystal to access my talent. But the truth is I can work with any kind of reflective surface. There are always plenty of mirrors in a women's room."

North smiled a little. "I get it. You just use the crystal to help you focus your talent."

"Right. Otherwise things tend to get out of hand very quickly."

North thought about the cracked and shattered mirrors in the restroom at the Fogg. When he had gone through the door he had been hit with a wave of wild storm energy—and that was just the aftermath of the forces that Sierra had unleashed.

"I noticed," he said.

"When I first came into my talent, my parents realized things were going to get complicated. But Harmony helped me get control."

"I think Victor Arganbright and Lucas Pine would like very much to recruit the Oracle of Fogg Lake. The Foundation could use her talent."

"I doubt if they'll be successful." Sierra smiled a knowing smile. "You saw her. It's obvious she has found her true calling. For now, at least, she needs to be in Fogg Lake."

"Speaking of callings, did you mean it when you said you found yours in the women's room at the Fogg Club tonight?"

"Yes." Sierra glowed. "It was watching Kimberly and Jake that finally made me realize what I want to do with my life."

"What's that?"

"Matchmaking. *Psychic* matchmaking."

That stopped him cold. Whatever he had been expecting her to say, that wasn't it.

"Matchmaking?" he repeated cautiously.

"Right. I've got a gift for it. I always have. But I never paid much attention to that aspect of my talent. I thought of it as just a parlor trick."

"How does it work?"

"If I see the reflections of two people together I can usually tell immediately if their auras are harmonious. I can also tell if it's a hopelessly bad match. I can tell you if two people will be friends or if they will always be in conflict. I can tell if the relationship will be great for a short-term fling but toxic over time, and vice versa."

"And you know if those two people could be a happy couple?"

"Right. When Kimberly and Grant Tolland stopped at our table I caught their reflections, along with Jake's, in my mirror locket. I knew Kimberly and Grant were headed for disaster. But I could tell that Jake and Kimberly would be perfect together."

North cleared his throat. "And now you think you've found your calling as a matchmaker."

"Yep."

"I hate to break this to you, but I'm not sure how much demand there is for a psychic matchmaker. Most people are doing the online dating thing these days or stumbling into affairs at the office."

"I'll go after a niche market—psychic dating for people who have a paranormal vibe. We all know it's really hard to meet other people who can accept the reality of the paranormal. I'll build a registry of people of talent. I bet I'll be booked solid as soon as the word gets out."

"Sounds like you've targeted your demographic."

Sierra spread her hands wide. It was clear she was energized and excited. North realized how much he liked seeing her happy and determined.

"Normal people spend fortunes on fake psychics and palm readers," she said. "Why wouldn't smart people of talent pay for the real deal? I bet all of the singles who work for the Foundation will want to sign up, to say nothing of people who have grown up and moved away from Fogg Lake. Then there are the residents of my hometown, Quest. There's also the underground market of people who are in the hot artifacts trade. The go-betweens. Collectors. Dealers. The world is waiting for my unique services."

North smiled. "Spoken like a true entrepreneur."

"If I don't have faith in my own ability, no one else will."

"True. Where do you propose to open your matchmaking business?"

"I can run it from anywhere, but every applicant will have to pass a background check. I'll hire Lark and LeClair to do that for me. Then I'll have to have a personal consultation in order to assess the stability of the candidate's aura and figure out what kind of aura would pair well with it. I'll need to develop a large but select roster of clients. The more people who sign up, the greater the odds of finding good matches."

"You'll need an office for that. You can't invite strangers into your home."

"Good point," Sierra said. "I'll discuss it with Victor Arganbright. I bet I can convince him to give me space at Foundation headquarters. Clients who don't live in the area will have to fly to Las Vegas for an appointment, but I don't think that will stop most people who are serious about finding the right mate."

"If anyone can talk Victor Arganbright into setting up a psychic matchmaking service, it's you." North pulled her into his arms. "Now let's get back to us."

"Okay." Sierra put her hands on his shoulders and gave him an expectant smile. "What specifically did you want to talk about?"

"I never got an answer to my question this evening. Do you think you could be happy here in the Abyss?"

Her eyes got deeper and more mysterious. She wrapped her arms around his neck.

"Yes," she said. "I could be very happy here."

"Be honest." He glanced around. "It's the mirrors, isn't it?"

"They are a very nice feature," she admitted.

He took a deep breath. "I love you, Sierra Raines. I fell in love with you that first night when we met at the Vault. I know you're afraid that my feelings might be based on gratitude, but I am very sure that isn't the case. I do know the difference between gratitude and love. I realize it's too soon to ask you to marry me, but will you move in here with me? Get to know me? Give me a chance to prove that my feelings for you are real?"

"I love you, North. And no, it's not too soon to ask me to marry you."

A rush of euphoria flashed through him. He pulled her back into his arms.

"Will you marry me?" he said.

Sierra opened her mouth to respond. Before she could say a word, a strobe light concealed in the recessed ceiling began flashing.

She glanced up and then hastily looked away from the senses-dazzling strobe.

"What in the world?" she said. "Is that an alarm?"

"Well, damn," North said. "If it isn't one thing tonight, it's another."

He released Sierra, took out his phone and hit the app that controlled the security camera screens. One of the mirrors on the wall slid aside, revealing a series of video screens. The views covered every part of the gardens inside the walls. There was movement in sector two, the pool and fountain area.

Sierra gazed at the screen, startled. "There's someone out there."

North glanced at the information that was coming in on the app. "Two people, to be precise."

Two men wearing baseball caps were prowling around the edge of the fountain pool, pistols in hand. North zoomed in on one of the faces.

"That's Ralph," Sierra said. "One of the orderlies from Riverview."

North got a close-up of the second man. "Joe. So much for hoping the cops back on Bainbridge or the cleaner team in Seattle would pick up the Puppets."

"Ralph and Joe are probably out for revenge. In their minds we ruined their chances of becoming super psychics armed with untraceable weapons. I doubt if they had to go to a lot of trouble to find us. By now everyone involved in this thing knows you're Griffin Chastain's grandson, and this house isn't exactly hard to identify."

"True. Luckily, the house can take care of itself."

He put the phone down and reached for her again. "Now, about my proposal. Will you—?"

"Wait," Sierra yelped. "You need to call the police. There are two armed intruders out there in the backyard."

"Don't worry about them," North said.

"I'm not worried about them; I'm worried about us. We're alone out here in the desert and those two creeps probably intend to murder us. Call nine-one-one."

"That won't be necessary," North said. "At least, not immediately. The house can take care of itself. About my question—"

"We can't discuss marriage while we're under attack."

The two men circling the fountain pool abruptly stiffened as if they had touched a live electrical wire. Their mouths opened in soundless horror. Joe collapsed on the concrete pool surround. Ralph, however, managed to fall facedown into the long, shallow fountain pool.

"Damn," North said. "You can drown in a few inches of water just as easily as you can if you go into the deep end of a pool." He got to his feet. "Why can't anything go right tonight?"

"Where are you going?"

"To haul Ralph out of the fountain. If he drowns there will be paperwork. My insurance company will probably have a fit. Go ahead, call nine-one-one. Those two Puppets have managed to kill the mood."

Sierra yanked out her phone. "Out of curiosity, what just happened to Ralph and Joe?"

"They tripped one of Griffin Chastain's little home security devices. They walked into the abyss trap that guards the backyard. You can't see it on the video monitors because they can't display paranormal energy. The shock temporarily stunned Ralph and Joe. They'll be out for a while."

He started down the hallway that led to the back gardens.

"Be careful," Sierra called after him.

"Will you marry me?" he yelled back.

"Yes."

"Okay, then." He smiled. "Okay."

He opened his senses and went outside to collect the unconscious

Puppets. He pulled Ralph out of the shallow pool, made sure he was breathing and then paused for a moment to savor the night.

He jacked up his senses and watched the paranormal auroras shimmer and flow across the vast desert sky.

Sierra was in his house. She loved the Abyss and she loved him. She had just agreed to marry him. He didn't have to be psychic to know the future looked terrific.

CHAPTER 48

The bell over the door of Swan Antiques chimed. Gwendolyn Swan paused in her dusting and watched a stylishly dressed woman with auburn hair walk into the shop.

"I got your message," Olivia LeClair said. "I'll be happy to discuss your problem."

Luring Olivia into the shop was incredibly risky, Gwendolyn thought, but time was running out. The underworld chatter about Vortex and paranormal weapons was getting louder. The myths and legends of the Bluestone Project were surfacing and starting to look very, very real.

She put down the duster and went behind the counter.

"Thank you for dropping by," she said. "As I told you on the phone, I'm a little concerned about some jewelry I picked up at an estate sale. I would like to hire Lark and LeClair to check the provenance. The paperwork from the auction house looks good but I can tell that the items have a strong vibe. I'm concerned some of the pieces may have been stolen. They came from the collection of a particularly reclusive collector. You know how it is with that sort. They rarely tell the truth about how they obtained their acquisitions."

"I can do some research for you," Olivia said. She looked around the room. "I'll need photographs of the pieces that you're concerned about."

"Certainly. The jewelry is downstairs." Gwendolyn waved a hand at the array of reproductions that cluttered the sales floor. "The items up here are for tourists and decorators who are looking for an interesting garden statue, or perhaps a vase for the hall. I keep the real collectibles, the items with a true paranormal provenance, in the basement. Easier to maintain security down there."

"I understand."

Olivia started through the maze of fake statuary, tables, vases and other assorted items. Halfway across the room she halted abruptly. She gazed down at the vintage camera, riveted.

Gwendolyn opened her senses. She wasn't an especially sharp aura reader—her talents were connected to artifacts. She was, after all, an archaeologist by training. But it wasn't difficult to tell that Olivia was responding to the old camera.

Tentatively Olivia touched the artifact. A visible shiver of energy went through her.

"This isn't a reproduction," she said, speaking very quietly. She did not take her eyes off the camera.

"Hmm?" Gwendolyn tried to sound only vaguely interested. "Oh, no. It's definitely got a little heat in it, but it's not the type of energy that appeals to true collectors. It's just a vintage camera. It probably picked up a bit of a vibe because it was sitting on a shelf with a lot of relatively hot artifacts."

Olivia used both hands to carefully lift the camera off the display stand.

"I'll take it," she said.

Excitement flashed through Gwendolyn.

"Are you sure?" she said. "I've got more interesting objects downstairs. I doubt if they even make film for that old camera anymore."

"I don't think it was intended to take traditional pictures," Olivia said. "How much?"

Gwendolyn took a deep breath. "Ninety-five dollars."

A reasonable price for a relic that wasn't supposed to have much value, she thought, but high enough to sound realistic.

"Fine." Olivia smiled and clutched the camera very firmly, possessively. "Now, let's go see the hot jewelry you've got downstairs."

———

Half an hour later Olivia left with the vintage camera and a promise to research the suspicious jewelry. Gwendolyn wasn't worried about the status of the bracelet, necklace and ring she had just hired Lark & LeClair to check out. The provenance on them was clean. But allowing the precious camera to be taken off the premises was unnerving. Still, it wasn't as if she'd had much choice.

She locked the front door, turned the sign over in the window and pulled down the shades. She hurried to the counter and picked up the landline phone. Eloisa answered immediately.

"The princess just left with our pea," Gwendolyn said. "She's obsessed with it."

"Olivia LeClair?"

"Yes. She practically jumped on the camera. I just hope we haven't made a terrible mistake."

"We both know she's our best bet," Eloisa said. "If we're right, she can lead us to the original Vortex lab."

"Yes. But Lark and LeClair are closely affiliated with the Foundation. If Victor Arganbright's people get into Aurora Winston's old lab first—"

"We don't have a choice. The rumors about Vortex are getting stronger. It's no longer just a legend or a myth. Other people are looking for it seriously now. We've got a head start but we could easily lose our edge if we don't move fast."

"If LeClair realizes what she's got, she may take the information straight to Victor Arganbright. If he gets involved—"

"Trust me," Eloisa said, "once LeClair figures out that the camera might be able to lead her to her mother's killer, she won't let anyone get in her way, not even Arganbright and his Foundation."

"I hope you're right. There may be one other possible complication, though."

"What?"

Gwendolyn thought about Olivia's reaction to the camera. "LeClair clearly picked up the vibe of the artifact. Her response was very intense. She did not put it down the entire time she was in my shop."

Eloisa went silent for a moment while she considered that information.

"I thought LeClair was just a strong aura reader," she said eventually.

"You didn't see her resonate with the artifact. I'm telling you, she's more than an aura reader."

"Think she's got her grandmother's talent?"

"I wouldn't be surprised."

"Do you think she knows that?"

"No," Gwendolyn said. "Not yet, at any rate. But now that she's got the camera—"

"Are you saying Olivia might be able to activate the camera?"

"I have no idea," Gwendolyn said. "All I know is that the camera is our only solid link to Vortex, and Olivia LeClair is the only one who has a chance of using it to find that old lab."

CHAPTER 49

Victor stood with Lucas at the edge of the grand ballroom. They sipped champagne and watched the happy crowd celebrate.

"To be honest," Lucas said, "I was afraid this would be one boring wedding. I didn't expect a bunch of people living in an intentional community on a rural island to know how to throw a party. Happy to say I was wrong."

"I wasn't too hopeful myself," Victor admitted. "It's a damn good thing everyone is staying overnight. The way the champagne and booze are flowing, no one should be driving."

"Couldn't get off the island tonight anyway," Lucas pointed out cheerfully. "Not without a boat or a plane. The ferry doesn't arrive until tomorrow morning."

"There is that," Victor said. "We're definitely not in Las Vegas anymore."

The bride's family had decided to combine the wedding with what the locals called a Moontide celebration. As far as Victor could tell, that aspect of the event had involved walking an elaborate labyrinth as a form of meditation, followed by music and the drinking of some special herbal tea. He had worried a little about what, exactly, was in the tea but Sierra had assured him that no hallucinogens were involved. *We only break out the good stuff for the winter and summer solstices,* she had said. He could not tell if she was teasing him. Lucas informed him the comment had, indeed, been intended as a joke. Victor was not so sure.

The ceremony had been an equally solemn affair. The bride's father had written a poem for the occasion, something about sticking to one's path once it has been illuminated. The bride's mother had sung an aria that bathed the crowd in the invisible energy of hope and optimism. Victor hadn't picked up on that right away. Lucas had been obliged to explain the nuances of the music.

The entire Quest community had turned out for the marriage of Sierra and North. The festivities took place in the elegant old hotel that was normally marketed by the locals as a corporate retreat. There were plenty of rooms for the guests, which was a good thing, because there were a lot of them. They came from Fogg Lake, Seattle and Las Vegas.

After the ceremony was concluded the bar had opened and the party had finally gotten started.

Lucas surveyed the crowd with a benevolent smile. "I love weddings. They're all about moving forward into the future. It's a transcendent experience, if you ask me. There's so much optimism. So much anticipation. So much sense of community."

"So much possibility of disaster," Victor muttered. He drank some of his champagne and lowered the glass. He studied the bridal couple, who were chatting with a circle of friends. "But I've got to admit Sierra and North do look right together. Some good energy in the atmosphere around them."

"This is the second couple you've managed to put together," Lucas said. "You hit a home run with Slater Arganbright and Catalina Lark and now you've pulled off another successful match with Sierra and North. If this director-of-the-Foundation gig doesn't work out for you, maybe you could get a job working for Sierra's new matchmaking business."

Victor looked at him.

Lucas chuckled. "That was another joke."

Before Victor could respond to that, he saw a familiar figure making her way through the crowd. It was hard to miss the Oracle of Fogg Lake. She was dressed, as usual, in knee-high leather boots and a long sweep of a black cloak. The only thing different about her this evening was that there was a garland of flowers crowning her long silver hair. The purposeful way she strode across the old ballroom, cutting a path through the crowd, was a warning in itself.

Victor tensed. Beside him, he felt Lucas go very still.

"Something tells me this is not good news coming our way," Victor said.

Lucas said nothing until Harmony halted in front of them, her eyes hot with energy.

"Please don't tell us you've got a feeling things are going to go badly for North and Sierra," Lucas said. "This is a wedding. We're supposed to think positive."

"What?" Harmony blinked, momentarily distracted. "Oh. Right. North and Sierra. They'll be fine. Excellent. Sierra's new business plans are going to go brilliantly. People will love the idea of a matchmaking psychic."

Victor allowed himself to relax just a little. "Good to know. So what's the problem?"

"Sorry to ruin your evening," Harmony said, "but I thought I'd better tell you about what just came to me."

Victor braced himself. He knew Lucas was doing the same thing.

Harmony began to speak, her voice resonating with power and certainty.

"Only the Oracle of Vortex can stop the forces that have been unleashed," she intoned.

Victor absorbed that. The image that came to mind was the painting in his office that showed the Oracle in flowing robes surrounded by people dressed in Bluestone Project uniforms. He remembered the prophecy: *Here there be monsters.*

"If there was an Oracle associated with the old Vortex lab," he said, "he or she must be dead. As far as we know, everyone associated with Vortex died a long time ago."

"Never forget the power of DNA," Harmony said, falling back into her normal voice. "Talent goes down through the bloodline."

Lucas frowned. "We're talking about a modern-day descendant of the original Oracle of Vortex?"

"I think so," Harmony said. "Based on my own experience and the research I've been able to do, I can tell you that realizing you got stuck with the curse of being an oracle usually comes after you're an adult. It's not a talent you discover in your teens."

"When did you realize you were an oracle?" Victor asked.

"When someone tried to murder me," Harmony said. "You'd be surprised how that kind of trauma can awaken a talent you never knew you had."

"Obviously the killer failed," Lucas said. "What happened to him? Or was it a woman?"

"It was a man," Harmony said. "He's dead. And now I need a drink."

She turned around, black cloak swirling out around her leather boots, and strode off into the crowd.

Victor watched her go. "Did you ever find out if Harmony has a last name?"

"Yes, as a matter of fact, I did," Lucas said. He drank some champagne and lowered the glass. "Her last name is Jones."

CHAPTER 50

That night they made love in the room that had once served as the bridal suite of the hotel. The drapes were left open, allowing the glow of a full moon to pour through the window. It transformed the big four-poster bed into a place of silver mysteries and secret shadows.

Each caress elicited a sense of wonder. Each softly spoken word was a vow. They wrapped themselves around each other, using the physical connection to seal the promises they had made at the altar earlier that day. *I love you. I will always love you.*

When they finally fell into a damp tangle of arms and legs, North pulled her snugly against him. He folded one arm behind his head. His eyes were half-closed. A small smile edged his mouth.

"What?" Sierra asked, stroking his chest with her fingertips.

He caught her left hand and touched the gold band on her finger. "I was just thinking about the last lines of that poem your father sent to you. Something about a ring."

She smiled and quoted the lines.

"The voice is patient, and will sing
The notes that help you close the ring."

"I've never paid much attention to poetry, but when you think about it, that whole poem was pointing the way, not just for you but for me as well," North said. "We closed a lot of rings. We discovered the truth about my grandfather. We solved some murders. We found our callings. And best of all, we found each other."

"My father will tell you all poetry has a psychic vibe."

North ran his fingers through her hair and pulled her closer. "Don't know much about poetry, but I do know I love you, Sierra."

"I love you, North."

The bridal suite was illuminated in all the colors of night.

AUTHOR'S NOTE

Somewhere in the middle of writing the first chapter of *All the Colors of Night* I knew the plot needed a psychic poet and a poem that would capture the soul of the story. As fate, luck or coincidence would have it—and we all know there are no coincidences—I happen to have a friend who is a poet: Jared Curtis, professor emeritus of English at Simon Fraser University. In the world of scholars he is known for his work editing the works and manuscript materials of William Words-worth and W. B. Yeats. I asked Jared to write a poem for the book. At that point the only thing I could tell him about the story—the only thing I knew for sure—was that I was working with a hero and heroine who were at turning points in their lives, characters search-ing for the path forward.

Equipped with only those vague details, Jared wrote "Hope and Love." It is the poem Sierra's father sends to her at the beginning of the book, the poem Sierra later shares with North Chastain. It touches on all the themes that matter in the story and includes several elements I didn't know were going to be important until I got there.

One of the things I learned while writing this book—and I always learn something along the way—is that poems have a seriously paranormal vibe, and apparently, so do the people who create them.

I want to take this opportunity to thank Jared Curtis for creating "Hope and Love" for *All the Colors of Night*. Turns out he's a genuine psychic poet.